LITTLE WITCH

Kevin Pufall

NORTH 83

ISBN 978-0-9714486-8-1

CHAPTER 1

Friday, April 21, 1995
4:08 a.m.

He jerked awake with a throaty gasp, bolting upright, his eyes bulging open in the dark. Sweat soaked his hair and coursed down his face and neck. A sickening sensation of incomprehension yawned wide inside him as he stared, panic-stricken, at the alien shapes in the shadows. His body was rigid; his mind flailed about, frantically grasping for some familiar form.

. . . fear fear fear fear . . .

The darkness was full of slithering menace. He was knotted with a panicky urge to escape but had no idea how to do so.

. . . fear fear fear fear . . .

An agonizing moment later, the shadow moving on his right resolved into his wife, Tricia.

"Wesley?" she said, sleepy and irritated.

He put his hand to his chest, feeling himself begin to relax almost immediately. *Omigod . . . I'm okay . . . I'm in bed . . .*

He remained still, letting the bedroom be the bedroom for a moment. Tricia's head was barely off her pillow, peering his way, waiting for some kind of response.

"Sorry," he breathed. "Bad dream."

"That's twice this week. What's going on?"

He heaved his legs off the bed and rose. "Dunno. Sorry."

She rolled over and squinted at her clock as he trundled toward the bathroom. "Uhh . . ." she moaned, rolling back.

Her head dropped heavily to her pillow as he closed the door. *Jeez, I do enough to irritate her without ruining her sleep. Maybe I should use the couch for a few days.*

He sighed heavily in the darkness, then felt around and flipped the switch to the night light plugged into the outlet near the sink. The tiny bulb was shrouded in a translucent cover sporting a miniature garden scene, a memento of a long-ago vacation trip. He looked into the medicine cabinet mirror. As expected, an aged monster stared back at him. Wes knew that the fleshy, jowly, bristly hulk now glowering at him would be transformed, in a couple of hours (by a shower, a shave, and one-and-a-half cups of coffee with sugar), into a reasonably attractive, reasonably healthy, large-featured thirty-nine-year-old. But mirrors are strictly pay-as-you-go, and he saw no reason to continue eye contact with his brutish image.

He shuffled sideways to the toilet, dropped the gym shorts he habitually wore to bed and began to urinate. *4 a.m. is the worst time to be awake* he thought, as he did every time he was awake at that hour. His lips felt dry and pasty as he ran his tongue back and forth across them. His head hung heavily as he stared at the urine stream splooshing into the center of the toilet. The panic of his nightmare still resonated in him; an image of grasping, pale hands reaching for his throat arose in his mind and momentarily tightened his breathing.

I was in a bad place for a long time . . . feverish . . . time went on and on. An old, dark neighborhood . . . towering trees, cold moon . . . familiar, kind of like the neighborhood where I grew up. I was trying to get away from something, or trying to find something, or both . . . sweaty and desperate. Then inside a big, empty house . . . abandoned and unsettling. Rising panic . . . someone was in there, looking for me, feeding on my fear, floating through the darkness. I was moving as fast as I could but not fast enough. Gray, confusing, threatening rooms. Running, searching for a way out, desperate to escape. Down the stairs to the basement, a worn concrete floor. Out of the shadows came the hands . . . thin fingers, ripped, as though they'd been dragged through a thorn bush. I was trapped and paralyzed as the hands reached for my throat. Just before they touched, just before the face came out of the blackness, I bolted awake . . .

The shakiness of the nightmare began to ease as he relieved himself. *Urination: one of the simple pleasures of life.* As the last few squirts plopped into the bowl, he sighed and relaxed. He pushed the flush lever, then bent stiffly and pulled up his shorts.

He squinted into the mirror again as he gave his hands a cursory pass under the faucet. *I always look like I've been drinking whether I've been drinking or not.* He shook his hands into the sink, wiped them on the sides of his shorts, and combed his fingers through his medium-brown, sleep-wild hair. *At least I still have hair. Dad was down to a fringe before he was forty.* Wes had followed the various hairstyling trends of his adolescence and young adulthood, but not long after becoming a father he had adopted what might be called the Men's Hairstyle, a standard cut that would not have looked all that out of place (with the application of an appropriate styling product) during the preceding century.

Shutting the light, he crept out of the bathroom, pausing to listen to Tricia's breathing. *Already back in Snoozeville. That gal can turn off like a switch.* He proceeded through the bedroom and down the hall toward the stairs, stopping to peek into Posie's room.

Posie, his thirteen-year-old daughter, had been saddled with the given name of Petunia in a delirious moment late in Tricia's pregnancy, in honor a great aunt she'd spent one summer with in her youth. The nickname "Posie" arrived and stuck almost immediately, courtesy of a young cousin. Posie was an only child. Everything about her conception and Tricia's pregnancy had been some combination of difficult, tiring, painful, and worrisome. At the moment of birth, Tricia was through. Fortunately, everything after that had gone well. Posie was intelligent, energetic, and cheerful, and had begun to show amazingly adult levels of observation and insight starting around age seven.

Visible in the greenish light from her clock-radio, she was in her usual coma-like slumber, sprawled on her back, medium-length black hair strewn about. Nestled into the top of her head was the curled form of Turnip, a stray male cat that had shown up a couple of years ago and become the family pet. *Every night I look at her and see a beautiful girl that I love dearly. Every day I lose sight of that and fritter away my time with her. When will I learn to really appreciate this gift I've been given? . . . well, nothing I can do about it now.* He moved on, down the stairs and into the kitchen.

The house, and the kitchen in particular, was still suffering the ill effects of the Seventies: dark woodwork and cabinets, faux-tile vinyl flooring, and wall treatments that included pressboard paneling, cork sheeting, and flocked wallpaper. As much as Tricia tried to keep Wes busy around the house, she still hadn't come close to transforming the place into the kind of home she wanted them to live in.

Wes slitted his eyes, opened the refrigerator and pulled out a two-liter bottle of cola. He listened for the carbonated hiss as he unscrewed the cap. *Ahh . . . plenty of punch left.* Lifting it high, he chugged deeply and felt the cold burn of the carbonation and phosphoric acid wash through his mouth, down his throat and into his stomach. *Nothing like it to clear out nightmouth.* The sides of the bottle blurped in and out as he drank, adding to his enjoyment. Finishing his last swallow, he sighed contentedly, screwed the cap back on and replaced the bottle in the refrigerator door. He glanced over the rest of the contents, illuminated by the light of the single bulb. *"Will you be dining tonight, sir?" Hmmm . . . no, thank you, Raoul, I'm just in for a drink. Have to watch the old waistline, you know, so I don't end up getting ticketed for carrying a concealed dick. Besides, the pizza's all gone. "Very good, sir. We'll expect you for breakfast."* He thumped the door shut.

Standing motionless in the dark, he took a deep breath and sighed.

"Fuck," he muttered. He scratched absently at the top of his head. *An inch taller. An inch taller and I'd be satisfied.* He'd always been disappointed that he had topped out at five-eleven. *Sure, it's plenty tall for a guy . . .* but his father had been two inches taller and his younger brother an inch beyond that, not to mention their baby sister, who had reached five-ten.

He slipped his hand down into his gym shorts and scratched the area between his testicles and his right leg. *And another inch on my dick. Just one inch. A day late, an inch short . . .* He was tired of thinking these thoughts, but his mind was weak when he got up like this, and he couldn't help it. Still, he felt better now that he'd emptied his bladder and refreshed his mouth. The effects of the nightmare had finally unknotted in his stomach.

He wandered into the living room, which was dimly lit by streetlight filtering in through the drapes, and dropped down on one end of the couch. He sunk his elbow into the padded armrest and supported his chin with his hand. His face felt flaccid and was rough with a night's growth of whiskers. *The thing is, even when I feel good I don't feel all that great. It's like having a low-grade fever all the time, but with anxiety instead of fever. There's always something wrong at work and at home. I don't know how it would feel, not being apprehensive all the time.* He rubbed his hand over his face a couple of times. "Shit."

He thought of Melanie, a young co-worker who had become an object of ongoing and increasing desire. *Now, there's one advantage to being awake in the wee hours: uninterrupted fantasy time.* His eyes closed slightly as he sat back in the couch. In his mind, he was transported to a generic bedroom in which he and his little Mel could safely play. Too sleep-saturated for the niceties of romance and foreplay, his imagination cut right to the chase.

We're naked on the bed. I'm up on my knees and she's crouched, facing me, somehow taking me all the way in with her small mouth, sucking like a cum-junkie. An erection uncoiled in his shorts as he pictured her glistening saliva lubricating his penis. *Now she turns around on hands and knees, her little round ass high in the air, spread wide open for me.* He pictured his hands sliding forward and under to cup her small, perfect breasts as he entered her from behind. *She's incredibly aroused, almost in agony; I'm riding a huge wave of mounting pressure.* His penis hardened to fully erect as this dream couple humped away in his mind. Melanie, Melanie. Melanie the young, Melanie the sexy, Melanie the unhave-able.

He slipped his hand under his waistband and lightly grasped his penis. Down inside the base, he could feel three days' worth of semen pushing to be released. *No more sleep 'til it's out.*

He crept down to the utility room and spread out an old bath towel he kept there for just such occasions. He knelt and began to masturbate, using saliva as a lubricant. His private porno movie, starring Melanie and himself, returned. His mind was the camera as he zoomed in on his penis, bigger and harder than it had ever been in reality, sliding tightly in and out of Melanie's engorged, deep-red vagina. *I'm so big she can hardly stand it, but she needs it bad.* He built toward climax rapidly and ran his fantasy accordingly. *She needs it, pushing back toward me, opening wide to get all of me.* He looked down through his dream eyes at his hands on her round little hips, at the cleft in her upturned bottom where he thrust and withdrew. *What a body . . . it's built for sex.* He felt semen flow into the final staging area. *Tubes flooded. Prepare to fire.*

At critical mass, fantasy and reality fused and focused into the singularity of ejaculation. His body became arched and rigid as he pumped the globules of fluid out onto the towel and deep into his dream-mistress. Relief washed through him as the contractions subsided. He worked the last drops up and out with his fingertips, cleaned himself with a dry portion of the towel, and stood up, slowly stretching his legs. *Once a guy gets married, he should automatically lose all interest in other women. Such frustration. Of course, he should also get plenty of good sex from his wife.*

He went back to bed and fell asleep immediately and the alarm clock went off and it was time to go to work.

CHAPTER 2

HiTek, Inc.: a medium-sized supplier of commercial computer hardware in a midwestern city that was just becoming a "metropolitan area." Wes's workdays as the manager of the shipping department inevitably became rolling crises, which he occasionally abandoned to attend tedious meetings, eat vending-machine food, and bullshit with the crew.

His office was a glassy cubicle that jutted out into the work area, which was visible on three sides. *I feel like a prison guard* he thought, when he first got the position. He should have had a quiet, carpeted, private office like those of the other managers, but the remodeling going on at the time necessitated flexibility, and this had been his lot. Over time, he realized that his exposed location in the middle of an active workspace served to shield him from the intrusive drop-ins his boss seemed to enjoy, so he never brought up the issue of moving. He tended to keep the blinds down, with the slats angled enough to provide some privacy but open enough to keep a glancing eye on the events outside.

His stint in shipping had started four years ago, a lateral move out of sales. That had been the point at which both he and Tricia had finally accepted, on some level, that he wasn't going to accomplish much of anything in this life.

They'd met in school, both enrolled in the teaching program. He spotted her in the bookstore at the beginning of their first year, and it was, well, avid interest at first sight.

Tricia was the fortunate recipient of an artful gene mix. She had her father's deep, dark eyes and ink-black hair, which she wore short even by the standards of the era because it suited her features so well. She had experimented with eye makeup in high school but abandoned most of it as unnecessary. She had her mother's warm, open smile and perfect teeth, and her finely sculpted chin. No one was quite sure where her nose came from, but it was an unobtrusive feature with just a little button on the tip for character. She had the medium-dark family complexion, which meant that even in winter she never looked as sallow as the rest of the population. Like Wes, her family tended toward tallness – she was 5'8" and had an athletic build. She had been on the softball team in high school and made regular use of the college's workout facilities.

Wes came from a town small enough that everyone kind of knew everyone and there were only a certain number of places to go and things to do, so there wasn't a need for advanced dating techniques. The best he could manage, on first meeting her, was eye contact and a smile, which she returned noncommittally. *I have no pickup lines. I have no social skills. How the hell am I going to get her to go out with me?* It was only the repeated contact of shared classes during that first year that gave the relationship a chance. She had a number of suitors and would occasionally consent to a very casual date with one, much to Wes's dismay, but she gradually became fond of his intelligence, calm nature, and self-deprecating humor.

"How did you do on the test?" she would ask.

"I, uh, did better than the polls indicated I would. It was a moral victory for the campaign. Thank you, no more questions, please . . ."

He also gave off the subtle scent, compelling to so many women, of being a fixer-upper, a project. She saw untapped potential, buried perhaps deeper than she realized.

They began to spend time together and date informally during the spring semester, but when they parted ways for the summer (she went home, he did groundskeeping at the school), they misunderstood each other's view of the relationship. Tricia had the sense that Wes saw them as a couple, but he still felt like just one pursuer among many, and nearly wrecked the whole thing by sleeping with Tricia's roommate, who had stayed on to attend the summer session.

This led to a rather rocky beginning to their sophomore year, but Wes was so impressed by Tricia's jealous reaction that he kept after her in a dogged, inept, charming sort of way that finally led her to forgive him and instruct him in the proper ways of wooing a woman.

"Wesley, ask me out. Pick a time, a date, and a place, and ask me to go out with you. When I say, 'yes,' come by and pick me up. Then, all you need to do is be polite and act interested all evening. It's easy."

Tricia came tremblingly close to an affair with a married instructor during their junior year, an emotional transgression that she tearfully confessed to Wes, thereby cementing their relationship. They were in a pre-marriage configuration from then on, although even then she had to tell him to propose to her during the Christmas break before graduation.

Tricia had signed a high school teaching contract that spring and would go on to earn her Masters – always striving to increase her value – but Wes had no real job when they got married in June. They both taught summer school classes and Wes found some substitute work starting that autumn, but his inability to find a permanent position, brought about by a combination of his mediocre level of drive and moderately high level of bad luck, continued. To supplement his meager subbing wages, he worked a series of part-time jobs: clothing salesman, waiter, temp work on a production line. He started with HiTek's marketing department five years after graduation, and, basically by not quitting, floated up through the organization as the company grew, taking positions he didn't want and wasn't all that good at because the money helped to compensate for the fact that he wasn't doing something at which he thought he could excel.

This meandering took a slow toll on the marriage, and although he and Tricia established a typical life together – house, child, trips, holiday traditions – they gradually became little more than tolerant roommates. Tricia's vision of their future, and in particular what kind of husband he would be, was too different from the reality for her to avoid disillusionment and emotional withering. What had impressed her as his inner calm had turned out to be more like inertia, his self-deprecation a cover for failure.

After eight years with the company, and less than a year as manager of marketing, he was offered the position in shipping . . . *they're "offering" me a chance to not get fired . . .* and he let what little was left of his ambition, his pride, and his hope slowly burn away in the fluorescent glare of his office. (In her only visit to the place, Tricia half-jokingly called it his "gerbil cage.") He got by in the position, but continued growth and change in the company were increasingly highlighting his inadequacies, and he suspected that he was still employed only because his current boss enjoyed criticizing him so much.

Of the very few things he enjoyed about his workday, his favorite was the ten-minute period around three o'clock when Melanie often made an appearance. She worked a phone in customer service, but – workload permitting – would extend her afternoon bathroom break to meander through areas with higher concentrations of male employees, like shipping. She had joined the company five years ago, not long out of high school, and had immediately become an object of intense masculine interest and conversation.

To Wes, Melanie was a Nordic nymph . . . *small and fine, her hair a field of wavy white gold, her eyes the color of an ocean wave backlit by the sun, with a thin band of dark blue circling the iris, accentuating the sea-blue within. Around her, I'm a damn poet.* She had a thin nose, just a trifle long for her face, below which was a small, pillowy mouth. Her body was little changed from adolescence, slender, with the narrow hips of a woman who hasn't given birth. *Her breasts are small, but they're perfectly shaped. What I wouldn't give to see them . . .* Her skin alternated seasonally from ivory to gingerbread and back again as tanning opportunities came and went.

An observer with some degree of objectivity might note that a healthy portion of her physical allure was due to three things: youth, careful attention to the condition of her hair and makeup (which she tended to use a little excessively) and what was referred to in times past as "inappropriate dress." Wes, who had given the matter considerable thought, had decided that her wardrobe was *well above "biker chick," classier than "trailer park bimbo," racier than "teen tease" – right around "high school slut."* Not surprisingly, she was extremely popular with the men at work and had dated more than one.

Melanie's real asset was invisible and therefore difficult to quantify: she had true charisma. Her attractiveness exceeded the sum of her not-unpleasant parts; she was the type who would rate as mildly attractive if a stranger viewed her yearbook photo, but in person she was hard to resist.

She always had a smile and a good word for Wes, teasing as often as not, more so lately. On this particular spring day she showed up in typical finery: a washed-out denim skirt that was notably shorter than what the other female employees were wearing, short black leather boots ornamented with silver, pantyhose of a shade she hoped her tan would soon match, and a long-sleeve shirt with the sleeves partly rolled up. It was unbuttoned and tied at the waist, layered over a black lacy thing that might as well have been underwear.

As usual, Wes had found a reason to be out on the floor when she arrived. She weaved her way through a gauntlet of interested males like a hostess at a dinner party, doling out suggestive compliments and humorous insults as she went. There had been one occasion a year or so ago when a dating relationship had gone bad and she and the fellow had gotten into it on the floor, but out of pique or wisdom she stayed away for a week and upon return they simply avoided each other.

Today she wasted little time in strutting over to him, smiling a knockout smile and filling his nostrils with a shot of the perfumed cloud that followed her everywhere. Her favorite cologne had a sharp edge in a rich, musky base. It worked well with her body chemistry, but on other women it could be unpleasant, sometimes smelling of dirt.

"Hey, Wes," she said, speaking up over the hubbub of the bustling workspace. "What's shakin', big guy? How's it hangin'?" She stood a step too close to him and gave him a couple of gentle punches to the arm.

She smells so good, she looks so good . . . "Goin' great, young lady. What's up with you?"

"I am just fine, sir," she replied merrily, tilting her head slightly. "Heard you guys were behind again, so I thought I'd better crack the whip." She tapped his chest with an open hand. "Crack, crack . . . work faster!"

"Ah, yes, I am now amazingly motivated. Thank you so much." *I really do feel motivated, just not to get work done.*

She signaled that he should bend down to listen, and as he did so she put her mouth close to his ear. "This'll motivate you . . . if you ever do get caught up, I'll let you spank *me* instead!" *Oh, my* . . . She pulled away, waggling her eyebrows in an exaggerated expression of complicity, her eyes sparkling.

Say something encouraging but not inappropriate. "Now, how am I supposed to concentrate on work when you say things like that?"

She giggled. "Y'know, Wes, we really need to get you out to the farm this summer. You kept saying you'd come last year and you never did. You missed a lot of fun." Her uncle had a large farm north of town and she had stayed there a couple of summers as a child. A new house had been built a mile or so from the original farmstead but the old house was kept up enough for occasional family use. Melanie usually had three or four parties there during the warm season and always invited Wes, but he had found it impossible to come up with an excuse that would get him out of the house alone on a Friday or Saturday night. Tricia would likely have consented to him attending a work party but might also have assumed that she would go with him, negating any chances for a drunken flirtation, or – dare he even imagine it? – a thrilling indiscretion in an upstairs room.

"Well, don't give up on me. I'll get out there yet." *I wish Trish had more things she liked to do on her own. There's no time when I'm free outside of work.*

"I sure wish you would. I bet you were a big party stud in your day." *"In your day?" Gee, don't make me feel too old!* He chuckled noncommittally. "So," she continued, her face and voice taking on a shade of seriousness, "how are things at home?"

"Uh," he grunted, scowling a little. "Same old thing." The condition of his marriage had become a topic of conversation during the last year, and the more he exaggerated its state of disrepair, the friendlier and more sympathetic Melanie had become.

She leaned close again and smiled a warm little smile. "Maybe you need a new, young thing." A wave of heat rushed through him, and his stomach jumped. His barely-restrained desire wriggled uncomfortably close to the surface. *Oh, man, that's far enough for now.*

He smiled and arched an eyebrow, tilting his head in a mildly rebuking motion, then attempted to turn the conversation. "And how are *you* these days? You weren't feeling too well earlier this week."

"Oh, you know me, I don't let anything get me down for long," she said, smiling brightly.

"I don't suppose you've been out sunning much, as cool as it was. I know you usually get to it as soon as possible."

"Oh, yeah, I've been out. My little deck gets the afternoon sun, and the side of the building heats up. I've been getting out on the weekends and a little after work and it's nice. But it has been kind of cloudy, maybe I need to go to a tanning salon. But it feels great just to lie out."

"It's been nice to finally . . ."

At that moment, Mark, the supervisor, oozed over for a leer and an ogle. "Mel, babe, what's new?" he said, addressing her breasts. Mark was married, with two young children, but acted like a perpetual – and irritating – adolescent.

Shit. What a moron. Wes tried to head him off. "Mark, weren't you scheduled to be crushed by a forklift this morning? I'm sure you . . ."

"Oh, Wes, don't be so hard on the boy," Melanie giggled. "He can't help it if he's a sleazeball."

"I'm *your* sleazeball, babe," breathed Mark, fondling four days' growth of whiskers on his chin. "Slow and sleazy, that's me-zy."

"Mark . . ." began Wes. Mark ignored him and continued.

"Hey, Mel, I was thinking about putting together a Girls of HiTek calendar for next year . . . we could sell it and use the money to fly me and all the girls to Jamaica for a week. Interested?"

"Let me guess . . . *you'd* be the photographer."

"Well, yes, of course . . . but *you'd* get to pick the outfit that you'd slowly take off during the photo session. Very discreet." *This guy is going to get nailed for harassment some day and take me down with him.*

"Well, boys," chirped Melanie, "I really hate to eat and run, but . . ." *Shit! He's chasing her off!*

Mark grinned. "You sure you're full, little girl? I could just . . ."

Wes interrupted him. "Shut up, Mark. Go shrink-wrap

15

yourself." *She must get a lot of this crap.* Mark was, as usual, pleased with the insults he was receiving.

Melanie waved an index-finger goodbye, winked at Wes, stuck out the tip of her tongue at Mark and strutted off, awash in a sea of lustful gazes.

"Mark, I'm surprised you ever got more than thirty seconds into a date."

Mark was mesmerized by Melanie's receding buttocks. "I'll tell you what, Wes, I may not know what love is, but I do know the definition of a relationship. A relationship is when you're with a babe, and she's got her tongue up your ass, really in there getting a good taste. That's when you know you've got a good relationship going."

"Uh, sure . . . they say that in all the advice columns."

"I'm tellin' you, man, a babe who'll do that is so hot for you that she'll do *anything* for you. And that is my definition of a good relationship."

"You know, it's always right into the toilet when we talk. We could start out talking about Easter services at the Vatican and in three minutes we'd be on how big an elephant's dick is."

"No more elephant dicks. I'm tired of elephant dicks. Now, *whale* dicks . . ."

"Alright, alright. How are we doing right now?"

"Why do you punish yourself with questions like that? If things are ever going well, you'll be the first to know. I'll send you a strip-o-gram."

"Did you find those monitors for First National?"

"Yeah, they were lost in the warehouse, as usual. I think they were stored in the can, or something stupid like that. They are such idiots."

"So, they went out."

"No, I thought we'd hold them in quarantine for a couple of days . . . yeah, of *course* they went out, what do you think?"

"Wesley Sargent, call the operator," crackled a nasal

voice over the speakers. "Wesley Sargent, call the operator, please." *Shit. Time for another reaming.*

"Well, Big W, looks like it's back to work. Let me know when you fuck Melanie."

"Sure. If you need anything, don't hesitate to ask someone else." *I suppose my interest is pretty obvious . . . but every guy is interested, and . . . oh, screw it. I'm not going to give up what little fun I have in this stinking hole.*

As Wes headed toward his office, he semiconsciously took in the people and activities on the way: *Brian, the newest temp . . . not too bright, he won't last long . . . all the temps seem to be named Brian . . . Steve, maintenance . . . he could stretch out any job to fill a day . . . Rick still thinks I don't know how much he slows down when I'm off the floor . . . shit, that super-rush order still hasn't make it out . . . Danny, Mr. Reliable . . . wish there were more like him . . .* Then he was in his office and on the phone to the operator. "Hey, Susie, I'm guessing it's Benjy?"

"Yeah. Sorry."

"Swell." *Now off to the office of Mr. Benjamin "Ben" Albertson, Vice-President in Charge of an Absurd Salary. Prick-on-a-stick. Dope-on-a-rope.* Wes trudged out of his office.

The route to Ben's lair seemed to be permanently paved with quicksand. Every trip was unpleasant and it took some willpower to push forward through the apprehension. *I feel like I did when I got called to the principal's office. I didn't think, back then, that adults could feel the same way . . .*

"Hello, Judy," he said, to the dour woman who served as the gatekeeper to the executive offices. *Hey kids, welcome to the Bad Perm Museum! It looks like she's wearing a poodle on speed with a stick up its ass. You couldn't get tighter curls if you used a power drill.*

"Hello," she said flatly, with only a perfunctory glance in his direction. *She seems to have a hard time looking up. Must be all those layers of makeup.*

"Here to see Ben," he said. *Of course, she already knows. She wouldn't allow anything to not be known by her.* He stood there, waiting for permission to go in. *She has to show everyone, every time, that she has "the power."*

She glanced up at him sideways. "You may go in."

Ben, whose flat features, wooden facial expressions, and overly-tended pompadour combined to give him a look of practiced artificiality, was tapping away at his keyboard, his monitor positioned so that Wes couldn't see the screen. *As usual, pretending to work to make me wait.*

Ben glanced at him, barely smiling. "Have a seat, Wesley. I'll be with you in a moment." Wes sat.

I hate this. He looks like a televangelist and acts like a junior high assistant principal. Ben ended his keyboarding with a flourish and squared himself off to face Wes. A lone folder was in front of him on the desk. *Gee, what could that be?*

Ben cleared his throat reflexively. "Wesley, I know we usually discuss these figures at our regular meetings, but . . ." he glanced down at the folder and touched it with his fingertips. *You discuss numbers any time you can ream someone out, you micromanaging little bastard. All you do all day is run reports and chew people's asses.* Ben carefully opened the folder. ". . . I was quite concerned when I saw the numbers for the past few days. I was under the impression that you had identified and were going to take care of the little bottlenecks that have caused us to fall so far short of our standards during recent weeks. You gave me the impression that you had things well in hand." *I tried to give you the impression that I wanted you off my back!* "How close are you to being fully staffed?"

"Well, I'm doing a lot of interviewing," Wes lied.

"How difficult can it be to find qualified applicants for those positions?" *Pretty hard, with the scurvy options Kim sends to me.*

"It's not all that easy. With what we can pay them . . ."

"What about those increases in productivity we were discussing? Have you come up with a plan for increasing individual output?"

"I've come up with a pretty complete list of ideas, and I'm in the process of cost-justifying them." *More lies.*

"Yes, well, I'd like to have that as soon as possible. In any event, why do we have this rather substantial dip in the last few days?"

"Well, for one thing, Mark was directed . . ." *by you* ". . . to move all the Milland orders ahead of . . ."

"Yes, yes," said Ben, cutting him off and flashing some imperious irritation. "Wesley, we've had this discussion before, that it's vital to have the flexibility to handle special orders for special customers . . . do you know what the turnaround time at American is these days?"

Wes opened his mouth slowly, knowing he wouldn't get a chance to answer. *American is nothing like us! They may as well be a bakery!*

Ben continued. "I've heard that they . . ." His intercom buzzed.

"Yes?" he said, irritably.

"I'm sorry to interrupt, Mr. Albertson," came Judy's deferential voice "but Ms. Galloway is returning your call."

Ben looked a bit flummoxed, thrown off his stride. *He's torn between continuing to roast me and taking the call. He hates to quit when he's got a good reaming underway.*

"Ah, yes," said Ben, drumming his fingers once on the desk and arriving at a decision. "Tell her I'll be right with her." Then, to Wes: "Wesley, we'll have to continue this discussion a little later."

"Sure," said Wes, rising. *Great. Now I can have this hanging over me, probably all weekend. I'd rather get it over with now.* He retreated from the executive area, back to the tepid comfort of his glassy cubicle. He sat in his chair and slumped, staring off unfocused, the papers and files and phone and computer monitor becoming an undifferentiated mass on his desk. *This is killing me. I'm trapped in a circle of days that I just exist through. How could I teach now? It's been too long since I got my degree . . . I may as well not have one. And Trish and I may as well just be sharing a house. Too much has happened, too much has gone wrong. The fire's been out too long.* The fluorescent light became uncomfortably bright, the office threateningly disorganized. *I'm small and weak and trapped . . .*

Danny was hovering at the doorway, his nervousness at interrupting The Boss causing the color of his cheeks to nearly match that of his rich, red hair. "Uh . . . Wes?"

Wes took a breath and sat up. "Yeah."

"Could you please have a look at this order? I can't find Mark . . ."

"Yeah, sure.*" I wasn't meant to do this kind of work. This is as good as I'm going to get at it and I'm not very good.* He rose heavily and followed Danny out the door. *Shit.*

CHAPTER 3

Melanie Becker entered her apartment that evening with her usual greeting.

"Kitty! Where's my Mimi?"

Melanie had adopted Mimi five years prior from a litter born at her uncle's farm. The feline trotted from the living room into the small entry area, meowing nonstop. Melanie bent, picked her up and cradled her.

"How's my baby?" she cooed, ruffling Mimi's short black fur as she walked into the kitchen. Mimi meowed, squirmed, and dropped to the floor. She rubbed around Melanie's ankles, alternating between meowing and purring, as Melanie put her purse on the counter and filled a tea kettle from the faucet, setting it on a front coil of the stove to boil.

The pair proceeded into the living room, where Melanie turned on the TV to catch the local weather. She hit the remote button to send the VCR into rewind, then returned to the kitchen, this time pausing to check her answering machine, which indicated no messages.

"Hmph. Nobody cares about poor Melanie."

"Yaoww!" complained Mimi from near her food bowl.

"Hungry, baby? Are we hungry?" There were a few bits of kibble remaining in Mimi's bowl, but she still seemed interested in the new cat food being poured into it. Melanie emptied the nearby water dish, refilled it, and set it on the floor, then picked a few soft treats out of a packet and tossed them here and there in the kitchen.

"So, how was your day? Hm?"

Mimi vocalized with excitement as she scampered from

one treat to the next.

"Oh, I'm fine," continued Melanie. "I had to talk to the weird people at Datamax today. *That's* always fun. It's like, 'Excuse me, are you speaking Martian or something? Are you completely clueless?' I'm starting to think they're calling from a psych ward somewhere, like, 'Hi, this is Gary at Datamax. We need some dynamite, a big, sharp knife, and a bunch of rope. Could you ship that overnight, please?' Huh. Weirdos."

The tea kettle made heating-up sounds. Melanie put the treats away, opened a cabinet and got out a medium-size glass jar full of dark flakes. She filled a tea ball from the jar and placed it in a large mug with a cat design on it. Mimi set to work on her fresh food.

"Baby, I wish you didn't have to be home alone so long. Maybe I should get you a friend." She paused thoughtfully, then smiled knowingly. "But first, Mommy needs a friend . . . a real friend this time." Her tiny hips swung into action as she chanted, "Melanie an' Wesley sittin' in a tree, k-i-s-s-i-n-g . . ." She stopped and leaned back against the counter, closing her eyes. Her voice dropped into a smooth whisper: "Ooh, Wesley, the things you do to me. Ooh, you're good, you're good, oh yeah . . ." Her eyes opened a slit and ran the tip of her tongue slowly around her pouting lips. She sighed and straightened up as the kettle's whistle began to rise. She turned off the burner and filled her mug with steaming water. A strong herbal fragrance arose almost immediately.

"Excuse me, baby, mommy's got to get comfortable." Melanie strolled out of the kitchen and into the bedroom, leaving Mimi to her kibble. She stopped for a moment to regard herself in the full-length mirror opposite the bedroom door. She turned this way and that, posing, plumping her hair. She looked at herself in a mildly critical way, then shrugged her shoulders and flashed a small, encouraging smile. "Oh, well," she sighed, turning away to sit on the bed.

Humming tunelessly, she pulled off her boots and tossed them aside. Then she rose to unzip her skirt and let it drop to the floor, stepping out with her left foot. With her right foot, she tossed the garment in the air, catching it and depositing it on top of a week's worth of clothing covering an old armchair nearby.

Melanie practiced what could be called "situational housekeeping" – the bare minimum when she was alone, a slightly more robust minimum when she was expecting company. She hadn't been raised with a family tradition of home care. Her mother's time had been consumed by work and then by addiction. Her father had never been anything but a source of chaos and mess. Much of what she knew about keeping house she'd picked up from television commercials. She vacuumed once a week, but her vacuum cleaner had a filter she was unaware of and was just redistributing cat fur at this point. Laundry was a weekly chore as well, with occasional extensions to that schedule. With some regularity she would slide a clothing item out of a stack, hang it in the bathroom while she showered, and give it a couple of spritzes of cologne.

She untied her shirt and let it slide off her arms onto the chair, then pulled off her camisole and laid it on top. At her age, and with the size of her breasts, she often did not feel the need for a bra. She enjoyed the continual light stimulation of her nipples against fabric, as long as it was smooth enough, and relished the knowledge that any hint of protrusion was irresistible to the male eye.

Mimi padded in, meowing and rubbing against Melanie's still-stockinged legs.

"Hey, boo'ful," said Melanie reaching down and scratching her fingertips through Mimi's fur from her neck down to the base of her tail. Mimi stretched her hind legs up, purring loudly. Melanie straightened up, tucked her thumbs into the waist of her pantyhose and worked them down to her feet. She stepped out and bent to retrieve the wispy mass from the floor. Holding it in both hands, she brought it to her face, closed her eyes, and inhaled deeply. "Mmm-hmm, that's what they like. That's what they like alright."

She tossed the fragrant fabric on the pile and moved to her dresser, retrieving a bikini set that had been hanging from the mirror. It was creature of the era, cut high on the thigh, coming down mid-cheek in the back, with an abstract neon multicolor design. As she strolled out the door, followed closely by Mimi, she turned briefly bit to twitch her hips and wink at her reflection in the mirror.

In the bathroom she made quick work of her makeup with petroleum jelly and facial tissue. Back in the kitchen, she raised the tea ball from the mug, shaking out a few drops before depositing it in the sink. She carried the steaming mug across the living room and placed it on a magazine lying on an end table next to the couch, then retracted the large vertical blinds and opened the sliding glass door to the small wooden deck. Mimi, who had been waiting by the door, trotted out and began to make herself comfortable in a warm spot where the wall met the deck.

The deck was furnished with a tubular metal lounge chair with worn yellow webbing and a small round metal table with a mesh top. Melanie picked up the mug, a pair of sunglasses, and a paperback book from the end table and took them out to the patio table. She retrieved a large, aquatic-themed beach towel from the floor just inside the door and draped it over the lounge.

She sat and stretched out, donned her sunglasses, took a sip of tea, and settled back, gazing at what passed for a landscape. Later in the season she would apply tanning lotion; at this point it seemed unnecessary.

Melanie's second-floor apartment was on the end of a two-story apartment building, part of a multi-building complex that had been utilitarian to begin with and was slowly sliding into decrepitude. The view back from her deck was to the western edge of the property, a grassy field that sloped gently away to a small scrub-covered creek that drained the area. A chain-link fence at the edge of the field marked the boundary of the complex. A wooden panel to her left screened her deck from that of the neighbor next door. To the other side, the view, partially blocked by a number of large, mature trees, extended to the main road serving the complex. The trees and the distance to the road meant that traffic noise was not usually an issue. Her deck felt secluded enough that, as the temperatures climbed, she would occasionally remove her top.

After ruminating with her tea for a few minutes she put the mug down and picked up the tattered paperback, a generic work of the sort featuring shirtless hunks and long-haired sirens. She got lost in it, relaxing, letting the sun's rays do their toasty work.

This evening's session was a short one. A bit after 6:00 she roused and reversed the process, bringing everything in and closing the door. Mimi went directly from the deck to the couch and took no time in resuming her evening rest. In the kitchen, Melanie set about microwaving some leftover lasagna for supper. She took a few more sips of tea, then poured the rest down the drain.

Moving to the bedroom, she removed her swimwear and hung it back up on the corner of the dresser mirror. From the top of the dresser she picked up her "comfort undies," her oldest, softest pair of white cotton panties. From the other corner of the mirror she pulled the faded, oversized T-shirt which served as her alone-nights nightgown. It was a thrift-store find featuring a cartoon character from her youth. She slipped it on and returned to the kitchen, where the microwave had just beeped.

She removed the plate of lasagna and carried it, along with a fork and a paper towel, to the living room, placing them on another magazine, this one on the aged coffee table in front of the threadbare couch. Nothing in the room, or in the whole apartment for that matter, matched. The one item she had pur-chased new was an "entertainment center," a vinyl-covered particleboard shelving unit. This housed a television, a VCR, a large boom-box with detachable speakers, and a collection of mostly hard-rock CDs. The living room furnishings were rounded out by an aged, rickety recliner, two mismatched end tables on either side of the couch, and a couple of very generic framed pictures on the walls.

Back in the kitchen, she opened the cabinet from which she had previously fetched the jar of tea. That jar was one of many that took up most of the middle shelf. There were a variety sizes and shapes, some with labels, some not. The con-tents of the jars varied markedly, spanning a range of natural colors and organic textures. On the bottom shelf were a few very basic spices, half a dozen bottles of nutritional supple-ments and, next to them, the same number of amber prescrip-tion bottles. Two were empty, the other four partially full.

Melanie removed three of the medicine containers, open-ing them in turn and tapping out one tablet from each onto the counter. She replaced the bottles and fetched a plastic tumbler from the adjoining cabinet. On the counter were two bottles of very inexpensive red wine, one of them half-full. She popped the cork and filled the tumbler to almost full, then scooped up the pills and tossed them back, washing them down with a gulp of wine.

Finally settled on the couch, with Mimi curled up beside her, she pushed Play on the VCR remote. She took another gulp of the wine and started into her meal halfheartedly.

The recorded program was a soap opera that Melanie had watched with her mother during its glory days in the early '80s. She had warm memories of that small slice of time in which her father actually worked so her mother could stay home after the birth of Melanie's sister, Miranda. Those sunny afternoons, with the welcome absence of her father, the splendid gift of time with her mother, and the lovely images of her baby sister nursing or napping, were the warmest memories of her life. Melanie became rather vocal during those moments of the show when she felt the characters particularly needed her advice. "No! Don't listen to him! He's a such liar! Oh, how could you, how could you . . . he's such a scum!"

By the time the show was over she had quit eating, with plenty left on her plate. The wine was nearly gone. Back in the kitchen, she shoveled the remains back into the whipped topping tub that she used as a leftover container and placed it in the refrigerator. On trash day she would go through and dispose of those food items that had been worn down by too many re-heatings. She put her plate and fork on top of the rest of the week's dishes in the sink. Running the dishwasher was another theoretically weekly task.

Just then, Mimi sauntered in and dropped a one-legged cricket out of her mouth and onto the linoleum.

"Oh, so we *did* find ourselves a little buddy!" laughed Melanie. "Having fun?"

Mimi was mostly making her own fun, since the cricket was too stunned and wounded to do much moving. She flipped over on her back, looking at the cricket upside-down, and batted at it with outstretched paws. Nothing from the cricket. Mimi sat up, facing away from the insect, and dabbed at her fur with her tongue, feigning uninterest. Then she sat still, keeping it in her peripheral vision. When the cricket finally gave a feeble hop, Mimi turned and leapt high in the air, landing with a thud and pummeling it wildly with her paws. She stopped and stepped back, then bent low to sniff at the motionless black form.

"You *do* play rough, little girl!" giggled Melanie. She paused, considering something. "Y'know, it's been a while since *I* had playtime. I think I'll do that tonight . . ."

She carried the wine bottle into the living room and refilled her glass, then closed the blinds, settled back into the couch, and started into the evening's lineup of sitcoms. Sipping steadily at the wine, she smiled occasionally but laughed little, and read her racy book during commercial breaks.

When the last show ended, just before 9:00, she sauntered into the bathroom, gazing vacantly into the cabinet mirror. She brushed her teeth and washed her face, then wandered into the bedroom, flipping on the underpowered overhead light. She pulled a boot box from under the bed and sat cross-legged in the middle of the mattress, tossing aside the lid to reveal a mass of fashion dolls, clothes, and accessories. Over went the box, out came everything, in a pile. She began sorting through it, laying things aside here and there. She picked up a doll whose mass of blond hair bore a striking resemblance to her own, selected a small brush, and spent a few minutes doing some styling.

"Lookin' good, girl," she said, smiling.

She answered herself in a tiny doll-voice: "Thank you."

"Sorry it's been a while. I get distracted but I know that's no excuse."

"That's okay, I stay busy. Gotta keep the boys happy!"

"That's my girl."

The doll was wearing an aqua teddy. Melanie added a pair of white heels.

"Ready for action!" said the doll.

Melanie propped the doll up against the boot box and picked up a male doll, already dressed in a shirt and slacks, to which she added a tie, jacket, and black shoes.

"Wes, what a doll!" she said admiringly, giggling a little at her play on words. She switched to a low-voiced caricature of a male: "Why, thank you." She picked out a tiny, heart-shaped candy box and held it to his chest, then walked him toward the female doll. He stopped, and Melanie said, "Knock, knock, knock!"

She picked up the other doll and said, "Coming!" while walking it toward him. "Oh, hi, Wes! What are you doing here?"

"I just thought I'd stop by. Wow, look at you, you're beautiful!"

"Thank you!"

"Here, I brought something for you." Melanie switched the box of candy to the female doll.

"Oh, thanks! I was just getting ready for bed. Do you like my outfit?"

"Oh, yeah, you really look fantastic! Can I come in for a minute?"

"Sure." They walked in a few steps. "Here, make yourself comfortable." They sat together on the bed. "Wes, do you think about me when I'm not around?"

"All the time. You are *so* beautiful. I wish I wasn't married, so we could be together whenever we wanted. I could make you so happy."

"Do you think you'll ever leave her?"

"I'm going to, soon. I'd do anything for you. I love you."

"Oh Wes, I love you too. Make love to me, Wes."

Melanie removed his tie and jacket, then her fingers faltered and stopped. Tears welled up in her eyes, rolled down her cheeks and under her chin. She sat, motionless, crying silently, letting the tears flow and fall, staring off into space. Finally, she dropped the female doll and raised her hand to the edge of her chin, collecting a large teardrop on her fingertip. She lowered her finger to the head of the male doll, letting the tear flow onto its mouth.

"Drink up, Wes. I hope you're thirsty."

CHAPTER 4

Wes worked most Saturdays, partly to catch up on the inevitable leftovers from the week and partly to avoid less palatable tasks around the house. Tricia didn't get much out of staying still. She was an energetic woman and her ready list of things to be done occupied most of their time together. *I can't fault her much for it; she certainly does more than her share of the work, and the house looks a lot better than it would if it were up to me . . . I'd probably waste the time channel-surfing or napping if left to my own devices . . .* a bit of self-knowledge that was reinforced every time Tricia and Posie left town to visit her family. Working at his job on a Saturday was routine almost to the point of being restful. Except for the occasional cleaning person or maintenance worker, he was alone, at least in his own department.

This Saturday was such a day. Weather was moving in; the clouds were low and dark and the wind gusted a bit, carrying intermittent sprinkles of rain. It was midmorning, and Wes sat at his desk, a second cup of bad vending machine coffee at hand. He realized that he had been reading the same line of a report over and over while his mind entertained fantastic images of Melanie in various stages of undress. He gave up on the report.

I wonder what her pubic hair looks like? Probably the usual small, dark triangle. But what if it's blond? That image struck him as being particularly erotic and he pictured her prominently displaying her golden thatch in various poses. He had to slide his hand down into his pants and adjust himself to allow room for a rapidly increasing erection. *Maybe she shaves it off* . . . was his next scenario, a feature of some of the newer porn movies he'd rented for late-night basement viewing. His fantasy-Melanie was very cooperative, indulging his desires for the most graphic poses. *As good as the fantasy gets, it's never as good as the real thing. It's like looking at a picture of a steak. Well, maybe a little better than that.*

He sighed audibly, stood, stretched, and wandered out of his office into the work area. The calmness and quiet were an enjoyable contrast to the usual workday noise and chaos. He meandered around the stacks of cardboard boxes and through the maze of carts and conveyor belts that had been his world for the past four years. *"Welcome to the wonderful world of corrugated fiber. Please allow me to show you around. Careful, kids, it takes years of experience to handle this material properly."*

The wind was picking up, occasionally rattling the big doors that led to the loading dock. A thunderstorm would be nice. A heavy spring rain to wash away the rest of the winter sand and silt.

His mind wandered back to MelanieWorld. *What does she really think of me? Is she as interested as she appears, or is that just kidding around . . . a tease? What could she possibly find attractive in me?* Wes was basically okay with his physique, and objectively it was what one would expect in a man his age: muscle tone down, body fat up, but still serviceable. But every time he was with Melanie, the thickness around his waist felt far more pronounced than he would have liked. *I've got to start doing sit-ups every day, even if I don't get any other exercise.* He had made this vow many times before; the resolve never lasted more than three days. *She's nice to me, but she's nice to most of the guys . . . still, she does make it a point to come see me almost every day. The thing is, what do women find attractive about men? Sometimes they like guys who are obviously good-looking, but then there seem to be all kinds of plain or even homely guys that they go nuts for.*

There's no consistency . . . it keeps you guessing. I don't think I know much more about women than I did in high school, and that was not very . . .

The lights went off. He was stunned by the total darkness that fell on him and he froze, his senses hunting for input.

"Shit," he whispered.

The hum of the lights and the distant whooshing of the ventilation system were gone, replaced by the ticking and clanking of fans spooling down and pipes adjusting. His eyes darted about, straining to adapt to the sudden change. The only light came from the distant green glow of the exit signs. *Where are the emergency lights?* He looked toward the loading dock doors but could find no outline of daylight around the edges. *They really weatherproofed the hell out of those suckers. Still, it must be pretty overcast outside.* Confirmation came in the form of heavy raindrops peppering the roof. *There's the rain I was wishing for. Well, I guess I'm going to find out how well I really know this place.*

He stretched his arms out to the front, just above waist high, and took a slow step forward, cautiously waving his hands back and forth. *Nothing. Where was I when the lights went out? I wasn't really paying attention.* He began to feel disoriented, as though the building as he remembered it was beginning to shift around him. A knot of anxiety began tightening up inside him and he angrily attempted to push it aside. *Fuck! Why should I feel afraid here?!* He crept ahead cautiously, waving about until he found something solid, something he could use to orient himself. *Vinyl dustcover . . . okay, this must be . . .*

There was a soft giggle off in the darkness. He froze again, fear slithering out to every corner of his body. *Oh God, what was that?!* His skin crawled with the painful prickling of hair. Images of his recurring nightmare began to form. *Hands rising toward me in the darkness . . . NO! I can't let the panic take me!* He could feel his eyes straining, darting about in the direction of the sound, but there was no light, no movement. His eyes hadn't had enough time to adjust for the light from the distant exit signs to be of any use. *Work your way back to the office. Get the flashlight in the bottom drawer.* He was about to move when a hissing whisper came from another direction:

"Wess . . ." *Oh God, oh no . . .* He was panting, sweating, trembling, bracing to fight. *I feel like just grabbing something and running at the sound, but I can't see a damned thing! I'd kill myself.* His racing nerves seemed to be sensing creatures approaching from all sides. He turned spastically to face the threats, straining for identifying sounds.

A light glowed behind him. His head jerked around and a shock vibrated through him. Melanie's face floated far off in the darkness, unmoving and unblinking. Hunched in a combat position, he turned slowly to fully face her. He moved his head slightly to one side, then the other, then forward, trying to comprehend what his eyes were seeing. His lips parted to speak, but his mind took a moment to catch up. The best he could manage was a whisper: "Melanie . . .?"

The light blinked out. Melanie's face remained briefly imprinted in his visual memory, then vanished back into the darkness. He was adrift again, and terrified. His hands were up and out defensively, his head twitched back and forth, his ears again straining for sound. Keeping his eyes on the general area where he'd seen the apparition, he sidled away slowly, feeling for something he could put his back to. Once again, from out of his subconscious came the nightmare hands, reaching for his throat, constricting his breathing.

His foot struck a box, and he gasped as he felt himself on the brink of falling. His arms jerked out for balance and the back of his left hand smacked a metal edge, adding a sharp jolt of pain to his fear. The panic was telling him to *run, get the hell out of here!* while his mind insisted that he *keep control or you'll kill yourself!* He moved again, with careful steps, his muscles coiled, ready for instant, violent action.

There was a flash of light close behind him and a sound that shot through him: "Boo!"

He whipped around, painfully startled, his wide-open eyes staring into the luminous face of Melanie, just a few yards distant. He was a hair-trigger away from lunging at it. "What . . . ?" he said in a clenched whisper, shaking with adrenaline

The face smiled. "Scare ya?" *It is Melanie!!*

"Holyfuckwhatareyadoin?" he gasped.

The light turned slightly, revealing as its source a small, mirrored compact. In that bit of illumination he saw Melanie fully resolve out of the darkness. In her dark jeans and wind-breaker and her hair up under a ball cap, she had been invisible in the shadows.

"You coulda killed me!" he gasped, trying not to shout. "What the hell are you doing here?!"

"I came to see *you!*" she replied in a matter-of-fact way, smiling. *Calm down. If you stay upset, you'll look like a fool.*

His heartbeat and breathing relaxed a notch; his shoulders uncoiled slightly. "*Man*, you scared me!" he said, managing a bit of a smile.

"I guess I did," she giggled. "Sorry. I just meant to have a little fun."

She looks like a commando, or a burglar. "What's with the outfit?"

Striking a pose, she held her arm out and turned the light back on herself. "I look like a robber, don't I?" She took a step toward him and arched an eyebrow. "Like it?"

The tension inside him began shifting to arousal.

"Oh yeah, you're a very attractive . . . robber. I'll have to hire you to rob me sometime."

She stepped closer to him, and, forming her free hand into a "gun," pointed her index finger into the center of his chest. "Stick 'em up," she said, looking into his eyes. *Oh, man . . .*

She glanced behind him, and then, using only her fingertips, pushed him backwards toward a work table. When he was firmly against the table edge, she set the compact down so that the light shone on them, then placed her cap beside it, shaking out her hair.

"Melanie . . ." he began. *This is very exciting. I'm very tense. Trish . . .*

As she unzipped her jacket, Melanie saw Wes flexing his hand, working through the ache of his injury. "Oh, are you hurt my poor baby?" she crooned. "I'm so sorry." She lifted his hand tenderly with both of hers. He felt disarmed. *How can I refuse?* "Let me kiss it," she said. She glanced again into his eyes, then back to his hand as she lifted it to her mouth. As her lips touched the tender area he trembled slightly. *She's kissing me!* Her kisses fell like flower petals, landing gently here and there.

She looked at him again, opening her mouth slightly and running the tip of her tongue slowly around her lips. It was a very stimulating sight. She went to his hand again and drew her tongue along its width. Then she worked back across, planting more pillowy kisses along the way, eyes shut, savoring the experience. A thrill shivered through him. *It feels like her kisses are pouring into me.* Little sounds of satisfaction came from her throat. He stared, his mouth open, fascinated and intent. *I've never felt anything like this . . .*

She pulled back slowly, her lips swollen and barely parted. She slowly unveiled her eyes to stare into his. "Mmm . . . I love your skin," she whispered, inhaling and licking her lips.

"Wow . . ." was all he could manage.

She let his arm down slowly, then pressed against him, putting her hands on his chest. She looked up at him with dark eyes, lips parted and waiting.

"Well . . .?" she said, invitingly. He bent to her and embraced her. They kissed openmouthed – soft, sliding kisses.

She wrapped her arms around him, up on her toes, pressing full against him, her breasts firmly into his chest. He ran one hand down the small, snaking curve of her back, stopping just short of . . . "Don't stop," she whispered into his mouth . . . and he continued down over the compact mound of her bottom. He was overwhelmed by the excruciating actuality of touching what he had so long fantasized about and lusted after.

She slid her mouth barely off his. "Nice ass, huh?"

No subtlety in this little dynamo! "Oh, yeah," he gasped. "Amazing . . ."

She reached over and snapped the compact shut, blanketing them in darkness once again. *Same building, same blackness . . . totally different feeling.* He felt pulsing energy flowing between the two of them as she clutched at his back, digging in firmly with her fingertips.

Wes reached up with one hand to the back of her head and they kissed and kissed, as hard as they could. *What is it about darkness that lets you do things you wouldn't do in the light?* Melanie broke free of his mouth, panting, then grasped his head with both hands, turning and tilting it to lap at his ear with the tip of her tongue, sending shivers tickling through him. His engorged penis, trapped in a downward orientation, formed a rounded bulge in his pants, a coiled spring aching to be released. *She's got to feel it pressing into her belly.* She moved her mouth onto his throat, planting wet, sucking kisses, running her tongue firmly into his flesh, biting just hard enough to create a jolt. He pulled away a bit. *Hickeys! I'd better not get any hickeys!*

Her hands found his belt buckle and flipped it open. *Oh my oh my oh my oh my . . .* He could feel her consciously slowing as she unbuttoned his pants and slid the zipper down. She brushed her hands up his torso to cradle his head with her hands once again, massaging his scalp with her fingertips. "Let go, Wes, relax," she whispered into his ear. "We both need this." He realized that his whole body was rigid and he felt himself obliging, letting the tension go as much as he could. *I do need this . . . I've been hungry so long . . .*

Her hands floated back down his chest to his waist and she knelt before him, slowly sliding his pants down to his knees. She feathered her hands lightly over his still-restrained organ . . . *Wow!* . . . then placed her open mouth on it and breathed hotly through the fabric. *Wow!!* Wes's mind was narrowly focused on the two of them, on the intense sensations that were vibrating though him. Melanie's delicate fingers grasped the elastic waistband of his briefs and pulled it out and down, allowing his eager appendage to snap into full erection. She slid his shorts down onto his pants, then pushed him back against the edge of the table.

The first touch of her tongue was electrically sweet. It started softly in the center of the shaft, then moved upwards to the rim of the tip. She flicked her tongue about with a delicate, wet point, turning Wes's mind inward even more to concentrate on the potent stimulation. She grasped the base with one hand and slid her mouth wetly down around the tip, opening her petite mouth as wide as she could. She began a rhythmic motion with her mouth and hand, letting her tongue slip back and forth across the underside of the head. *I feel like I could come any second . . . got to hold back . . . ride with it and let the pressure build.* The intensity of her touches seemed to be crossing wires in his head; he saw flashes of light and shapes shifting and turning. *I have never experienced sex this intensely before . . . inside my head like this . . .* She pulled off and moved her mouth up and down the underside of the shaft, her tongue-tip flying like a hummingbird's wing. The vibrations tugged at his swelling reserve of semen. *Can't hold off much longer . . . overpowering . . . steep glide path to orgasm.* He felt his muscles tensing in anticipation, building . . .

There was a sound somewhere in the darkness.

"Hello . . .?" called a far-off voice.

Wes's eyes snapped open. *Shit!* Melanie's touch disappeared. *No! So close!* He saw the beam of a flashlight from across the work area.

"Anybody home?" called the voice. *It's Alex, from systems.* Wes fumbled with his clothes, leaving his shirt untucked to help hide the bulge in his pants, trying to relax his erection so he could walk normally. He took a few awkward steps and was about to speak when the lights began to come on. As the ventilation equipment whooshed to life, he quickly looked around for Melanie, his eyes blinking to adjust to the glare. *She's gone.* Alex spotted him and waved the flashlight.

"Hi, Wes!" he called. Wes waved back. "That sure screwed me up!" continued Alex. "I've got to start over now! Sucks!" He waved again and left. Wes walked slowly back to his office, shaking with adrenaline and coiled tight with unspent sexual energy.

*   *   *

Tricia protested as Wes led her down the hall toward the bedroom that afternoon. "Posie . . .!" she hissed.

"She's downstairs playing games on the computer. This won't take long." *Must fornicate, even if it's with my own wife.*

It was almost impossible for him to get Tricia interested in sex anymore, except on the rare weekend nights when her mood took a brief trip back to the early days of their relationship, but sheer horniness was forcing Wes to be more persuasive than usual. His excitement took Tricia by surprise and quickly broke down her habitual reserve. They entered the bedroom, closed and locked the door, kissed hard and wet and undressed each other in a feverish hurry. *Wow, she looks damn good! How long has it been since I've seen her naked?* Tricia fell back onto the bed, pulling Wes on top of her. She had become as aroused as he was now, and she angled her hips to allow him easy entrance.

They went at it furiously. Wes sweated rivers. For the first time in years, they came together, in long, hard waves, and collapsed. He rolled off and they lay next to each other for a few minutes, not speaking. Tricia felt satiated but perplexed. Wes felt relieved and guilty.

*   *   *

At 2:57 a.m. the phone rang. Wes got it, feigning alertness as he usually did when awakened by a call. "Hello," he said.

There were the rustling sounds of someone listening for an answer before hanging up. The line clicked and went dead.

"Hm . . .?" grunted Tricia.

"No one there." *Answering the phone sure feels different when I have something to worry about. My own personal guilt-detector.*

It took him a long time to get back to sleep.

CHAPTER 5

Sunday, it was *"W-M-E-L, your all-Melanie station, all day, all night, playing your Melanie favorites nonstop."* Yesterday's events had been so strange and intense that Wes could replay them in his mind over and over without wearing them out. More than once, he found himself hopelessly lost during a conversation with Tricia. *Usually I can fake my way out if I haven't been paying attention, but I'm way gone today.*

For the first few years of their marriage, Sunday morning had been a time for sleeping in, followed by brunch, coffee, and a thick newspaper. Although church had been a regular part of Wes's life growing up, often tedious but overall not unpleasant, the freedoms of college life had tempted him into nonattendance and he never went back. Tricia had grown up in a family whose moral code and expectations of behavior rivalled that of any established religion, but churchgoing had never been a part of her life.

Over time, first with the arrival of Posie, then with Wes's laggard approach to home responsibilities, and more recently, his desperate situation at work, Sunday morning had become just another block of hours to be filled with tasks.

This morning's activity was one of his least favorite: Seasonal Clothes Rotation. It had been a tenacious winter, and the finally-arriving warm weather brought with it a need for the summer clothes that were stored in the basement, garage, and crawl space. Tricia had announced this fact in the middle of Wes's breakfast, as he idly sorted through the paper and replayed his extraordinary adventure.

"Wesley, are you listening to me?"

Wes took a short breath and gave his head a quick shake, sending Melanie back into the ether. "What? Oh, sorry . . ."

"What's so interesting in the paper today? You look like you got clubbed on the head." *On the head . . . no, stop it!*

"No, just feeling a little tired still . . . didn't sleep all that well."

"Well, you'd better pep up a little, because I need your help with the clothes today." *No, not the clothes! Everything I have fits in one closet. Why do they have four times as much space and still have to pack things away?*

"Okay," he said noncommittally, returning to the paper. *Jobs like that – packing and unpacking, endless laundry, climbing into the crawl space . . . they're guaranteed to put me in a fog on the best of days, and I'm already meandering through the mist.*

Posie, preceded by Turnip, clambered up from the basement, where she'd been on the computer since getting up. She wandered into the kitchen and gave Wes a glazed smile. "Hi, Dad."

"Hey, kiddo," he replied. "What have you been up to?"

"Stuff and whatnot," she said, pouring a glass of orange juice. "Mostly stuff."

Tricia struck before Posie could disappear back to the basement. "Posie, I want you to clean up your room. We're going to do clothes today. Take all of your dirty clothes down to the laundry room."

Posie's shoulders slumped, but she knew enough not to complain. "Okay, Mom," she sighed, shuffling off toward the stairs to the second floor. *It probably won't be fifteen minutes before Trish is snapping at her.*

Nine minutes later, there were sharp words flying from Posie's bedroom.

"I thought I told you to start picking up! Why are you lying there reading?"

"Mom, I was starting to, then I remembered I only had

one chapter left in this reading assignment . . ."

"Now is *not* the time for homework! Put it down and get moving!" *Well, that means no more putting it off for me, either.* Wes put the paper down and was rising as Tricia hustled into the kitchen. "I could really use your help now," she said testily.

"Yes, coming." He stacked the paper, rinsed his dishes, and put them in the dishwasher. *A shower would feel good . . . do some good daydreaming, but I'd better just get dressed and get to work now. Tricia could fly right through her irritation levels directly to blowup today.*

Soon, he was wandering in a trackless wilderness of clothing, with memories of his encounter with Melanie intruding at every opportunity. Fortunately, his sluggishness and inattention were not unusual under the circumstances and he got off with just a few exasperated reprimands.

At one point, as he was waiting to be handed another stack of clothing to place up on a high shelf, his head cleared enough to look at Tricia with some vestiges of spousal concern. *How much fun is she having? Is she enjoying life? She doesn't really seem to be happy much anymore. I don't ever see her laughing, really laughing. Her mood is never much better than agreeable. I wonder if she's been tempted at any point . . . if she's seen anybody . . . there must have been somebody along the way, some other teacher . . . but I can't imagine her ever going through with it.*

His usefulness in the process finally declined in mid-afternoon, and he was able to escape to the garage with the excuse of doing some vague – fictional – work. He leaned up against his workbench, which was piled high with miscellany, and stared off into space. *What am I going to do? What's going to happen when I see Melanie tomorrow? Should I call her . . .? No, no, there's too much strangeness right now, the way she appeared and disappeared . . . and what would I say? "Hey Mel, I was wondering if we could continue my blowjob*

*sometime soon . . ." or, "What kind of relationship are you
really looking for?" or, "How was it that you showed up just
when every single light in the building went out?" Man, I hope
she can keep her mouth shut. I could be out on my ass in a
minute if she blabs . . . although, no one saw us together, and
I'm not her boss, and it's not like dating doesn't go on at work
. . . yeah, "dating," we were on a "date" in the middle of the
work area, with my dick in her mouth. Man, how can I live
without great sex now that I've been reminded how terrific it
can really feel? I mean, it was amazing that Trish went along
yesterday but I know it won't continue. The fire's pretty much
gone, we know too much about each other. There's lots of fire
with Melanie, she was all over me . . . well, I'll just have to
wait until tomorrow and see what happens.*

*   *   *

Suppertime.

"Wesley?"

"Hm? . . ." *Shit. Caught again.*

"Posie just asked you a question. Weren't you listening?
What is your problem today?"

"Sorry. Just work." Putting his fork down, he rubbed his
face with his hands and took a deep breath. "Okay, sweetie,
what was it?"

"The book. Did you get that book you said you would? I
need it for tomorrow." *Shit!*

"Oh, no, I'm sorry, kiddo, I totally forgot. Are the
bookstores . . . no, I guess they'd be closed now. I wish you'd
reminded me yesterday." *I need to get my head out of my
pants.*

Naturally, Tricia was irritated. "You know, it's not as
though you participate a whole lot in her schooling. We know
you're busy, but I'd think something like just picking up a
book . . ."

"I know, I know . . . how about if I pick it up at lunch and
bring it out to the school?"

Posie brightened. "Yeah, yeah, you could just drop it off at the office. Thanks, Dad."

Tricia wasn't through. "When did you stop writing notes to yourself? That seemed to work pretty well for a while."

"I was writing so many notes that I couldn't keep track of them. I just gave up."

"Well, you've got to find something else, then. Your brain needs help."

Posie laughed. "Yeah, maybe you need a brain rotation, Dad. It's all worn out on one side."

"Hey, hey, what is this, tag-team insults? Leave my poor brain alone."

"Don't worry, Dad. If we ever find it, we'll flee in terror."

Wes could feel himself perking up. "I refuse to respond to that, on the grounds that it would definitely incriminate me."

Posie was sharp, too. "As your lawyer, I advise you to find a new lawyer. You can't afford me."

Tricia was watching the exchange, amused. Her irritation was fading quickly.

"How do I know you're a real lawyer?" continued Wes. "You might be an alien spy, scouting the Earth for invasion."

"That's strange, I thought that only lower life forms could see through my disguise."

Tricia laughed out loud. "Where do you two get all this? My goodness, Posie, I'm glad you got your father's sense of humor. I can't keep up with you." *That's nice of her to say.*

Posie clapped her hands to her head. "Oh no, Dad's sense of humor! I'll never be a member of the smart set at school now!"

Wes laughed. "You've been reading those vintage girl stories, haven't you?"

Posie cocked her head, smiling and batting her eyelashes. "Why Father, what a clever observation! No wonder everyone admires you so!" *This kid is great.*

Tricia shook her head and rose from the table. "I think you

should take this act on tour. We'd be millionaires."

"Hmm . . ." Posie mused. "How about 'The Amazing Posie Sargent and Her Trained Dad.'"

"'Trained?'" said Tricia wryly, as she rinsed her dishes. "Good luck."

"Well," said Wes, rising also "this is where I came in. Pardon me if I skip my own flogging."

"We'll forego the flogging if you clean the kitchen," said Tricia. "I still have work to do tonight."

"I am the Trained Dad. I live to serve." He began clearing the table.

"Wish I could help," said Posie, getting up and heading for the door "but I hear important homework calling to me."

Wes felt reflective as he worked. *I guess I have become pretty lax around here lately. Today just made it more obvious. Whatever happens with Melanie, I shouldn't let my family down, especially Posie.*

His burst of mental sharpness began to fade as he finished the cleanup. Thoughts of Melanie had crept back into his consciousness when Posie hauled her schoolbooks in and dropped them on the table. "Help me with my homework, Dad," she said, flashing him a cheesy grin. "Please?"

"Sure, sweetie," he said, smiling reflexively. *I should run out to a convenience store and see if they have any Fix-A-Brain.* Posie had a textbook and notebook open by the time he sat down next to her. "So, what are we working on tonight?"

"Algebra."

"Do you maybe need help with something I haven't forgotten everything about?" *Oh yeah, Mr. Professional Teacher here. Good attitude, you dope.*

Posie tossed him a look of mock disgust. "Thanks, Dad. That really helps."

Wes made a show of straightening up and squaring his shoulders. "Okay, sorry. I will now assist you in your studies to the best of my ability."

"Uh, yeah, right . . ." She worked for a few moments as Wes stared over her shoulder at the hieroglyphics on the pages. *This shouldn't look so foreign.* "I need to factor this," she said, pointing her pencil at a string of symbols that had the appearance of a knotted length of yarn.

Wes sighed. "Uhhh . . . here, let me look at the book."

She turned it toward him. "Don't you remember *anything* from when you were in school?" *Good question.*

"Nope," he replied, leafing through the book. "In fact, you shouldn't waste your time learning anything, either. You'll forget most of it, and what you do remember, you'll never use." *I shouldn't be so flippant about this. I know she likes to joke around, but schoolwork is important.*

Posie rolled her eyes. "Mom!" she called. "Will you help me with my homework?"

"What's the matter?" came Tricia's voice from the dining room, where she was working on Monday's lesson. "Is your father having another out-of-body experience?"

"Hey!" said Wes.

"No, he's having an out-of-his-mind experience."

"Double hey! Haven't I already had my daily dose of abuse?"

"Here, I'll figure that one out later," said Posie, taking the book back. "How would you solve for 'y' in this one?"

Wes studied the problem. *This stuff should be easy. What's happened to the rest of my brain?*

When they had slogged through the homework, Wes and Posie hit the couch to watch television for the remainder of the evening. Tricia continued working, correcting papers. *It's the lazy man version of "together time," but I sure don't feel up to anything else involving thought.* It was comforting to have Posie seated close to him on one side, with Turnip dozing on his lap. *This is nice. I'm a lucky man.*

He stopped by Posie's room when she had gotten in bed. "'Night, sweetie," he said, casting a shadow from the doorway. She was on her stomach, head half-buried in her pillow. Turnip, as was his habit, was starting the night near her feet.

"Dad?" she said, her voice half-muffled by the pillow.

"Yes?"

"Are you doing what you wanted to be doing? What you thought you'd be doing?"

He sighed. "No, I guess not."

"I didn't think so. Why?"

He walked into the room and sat on the edge of the bed. *That's a good question. She deserves a real answer.* "I guess . . . I guess I'm someone who reacts more than acts. I've never felt all that driven. I've ended up doing just enough to get by." He stopped to think and reflexively began to run his hand over her back. Backrubs had been a part of bedtime throughout Posie's youth but had gradually vanished along her path to adolescence. There was silence for a time.

"I think you used to be happier," she said. Wes's hand paused.

"Well, sweetie, I guess you're right." He resumed the backrub.

"Howcome?" *She's fading fast. Keep it simple and comforting.*

"Mostly just work. It'll get better."

"Dad?"

"Yes?"

"Is it true that tornadoes only spin in one direction?"

Hmm . . . "Uh . . . yes, I think so . . . at least in the Northern Hemisphere." *Kind of like water whirling down a drain, I think . . .*

"Mmph," she mumbled. He watched her face lose its daytime veneer of maturity and reveal the sweet child still beneath. "Dad?" she said, with tired lips.

"Yes?"

"Don't forget the book."

"I won't." *I'd better not.* Continuing the backrub with one hand, he picked a very small stuffed pig out of the pile on her bed and tucked it into his shirt pocket. *Pig equals book. Make a note before you go to bed.*

"Mm. 'Night, Dad." She rolled her head further into her pillow. Wes pulled up the covers, then bent down and kissed her hair.

"Goodnight, kiddo." He stood up and walked to the door, then turned and stopped, watching her drift away. *Couldn't I just be satisfied with this? A house, a family, a job? But I feel like I'm withering inside. With Melanie, I feel my blood flowing again.*

He slept deeply and without dreams. For the first time in many years, he awoke with a real desire to go to work.

CHAPTER 6

Monday, mid-morning. Wes had gotten the creaky mechanism of his department rolling as efficiently as was currently possible. He sat down heavily at his desk and stared blankly at its cluttered surface. *Well, here we are. What's going to happen when I see her today? Should I visit her at her desk? I never do . . . it would look strange if I did it now. What'll she do when she sees me? Has she told anyone? It's hard to believe it actually happened. I was so close to . . .*

He looked up to see Mark in the doorway, staring at him.

"Wes, you have the unmistakable look of a married man who's recently had sex. Now, it couldn't have been Tricia . . ." *Here it comes, more shit about Melanie.* ". . . so I'm guessing that you somehow improved your masturbation technique." *This I can handle.*

"My wife loves me," replied Wes, with mock sincerity. "She'll let me do anything I want, as long as she's bored enough."

"Wes, you kinky stud! Sex with your wife!"

Wes spotted the permanently plaid-shirted form of Steve, ambling either toward or away from one in an endless series of maintenance tasks. *He doesn't have much motivation to move fast in a job like his.* "Sorry, nothing personal, gotta run," said Wes, rising and moving toward the door, which was blocked by Mark. Wes paused momentarily, feigning thought. "Well, no, I'm *not* sorry and it *is* personal. Get the hell out of my way."

"That's better" said Mark, stepping aside. "I was afraid you were starting to like me."

"I'm sure you'll never let that happen." Wes strode off toward his slow-moving target. "Hey, Steve," he called. Steve stopped and turned, smiling good-naturedly through his large, shrublike moustache as Wes approached.

"Hey, Wes. Whatcha know?"

"Not much, not much. How you doing?"

"Oh, can't complain. Same old thing."

"I was wondering about that blackout on Saturday. What was that?"

Steve gave him his vacuous, I-sure-as-hell-don't-know smile. *I'm never going to find out what happened.*

"Got me!" chuckled Steve.

"Everything was out except the exit signs. No emergency lights came on. That can't be right."

"Yeah, that's what Alex was telling me. I checked a couple of them this morning and they were fine. Who knows? They're working now. Anyway, I gotta go fix a toilet in the executive can. With all the bullshit they put out in there, it could be a real mess with no crapper." He grinned at his own joke and Wes went along with a perfunctory chuckle as they parted. *I should have known better than to expect a useful explanation from him.*

Wes worked distractedly the rest of the morning and used an extended lunch break to buy the book that Posie had requested and deliver it to her school. When he returned to his office, an envelope with his name on it rested on his chair. *From Melanie, I bet.* He picked it up and sat down, opening the envelope and unfolding the note within.

> *Wesley,*
> *I would really like to see you. Can you come to my place right after work? I told you the complex I live in. Take the first right after you turn in and go around. The building is 3705, apartment 201. Come if you can and let me know if you can't.*
> *Thinking of you,*
> *Melanie*

Wes felt the twin thrills of opportunity and risk twining around each other. He sat still, holding the note, staring at it as his mind leaped and wandered. *Could I go, without fully crossing the line? I might have thought so before Saturday. If I was going to tell her, "No," that should have been the time.* The din of machinery and voices outside his windows faded to nothing in his consciousness. The humming, artificial light of his office bathed him in indecision. *If I don't go . . . I know I've been leading her on. I've been sending her the message that I'm interested in a relationship. Allowing her to do what she did, really, it was an admission that we're already in one. If I beg off this time, it will only confuse things and postpone a real resolution.* His shoulders slumped a little as he exhaled. He began folding the note. *I have to go, I have to see where this is going.*

Making the decision energized him more than he antici-pated. He worked hard that afternoon, with all of his efforts designed to get him out the door on time. He got a little uneasy around three o'clock, but Melanie didn't show up. He left the building at 5:07, whipping off his coat and tie and tossing them in the back seat of his car.

His trip to Melanie's was a study in sameness, driving from the drab grey industrial district that was home to HiTek through a run-down commercial area to the worn residential neighborhood that contained her apartment. *It must hard to afford any place at all, on her own, making what she makes.* He turned in at the sign, nestled into a small plot of untended plantings, that read, "Laurel Valley." *I'm pretty sure there's no laurel here, and only the barest hints of a valley. Plus, it sounds like a nursing home.* There were a number of buildings in the complex; he made his way slowly, checking the ad-dresses. *The grounds are mowed, anyway, even if the land-scaping has been neglected.*

Around 5:30 he parked in a visitor space and walked toward the entrance to her building. *What is this sensation? What am I feeling?* It was familiar, from years gone by. *I feel . . . anticipation. Thrilling anticipation. Yeah, it's been a while.*

He expected that he would need to get buzzed in, but the front door was stuck somewhere on its frame and he was able to simply walk in. *I'm guessing this isn't the most responsive management company regarding maintenance. Kind of like HiTek.* He chuckled to himself as he walked up the stairs, which were carpeted in a dingy beige and paralleled by handrails that were just a bit loose. *This beige is as close as you can get to not being a color.*

He walked down the hall to her apartment. Hesitating for a moment, he knocked, waited, and knocked again. There was no answer. He tried again, a bit louder. He could hear a cat meowing just inside. *Something wrong?* He suddenly had a vision of the police showing up and breaking down the door to find Melanie, nude, sprawled in a pool of blood, and hauling him off for murder. *Feeling just a little paranoid here.* He tried two strong raps, then put his ear to the door. *Just her cat . . . I don't like this . . .* He jumped at the sound of Melanie's voice, from behind him.

"Hey, mister, what's the rush?" He whipped around, trying not to look too startled, as Melanie strode toward him, carrying a couple of plastic grocery bags. Her outfit was modest: a plain cotton button-up shirt with the sleeves rolled to midforearm, tucked into high-waisted jeans. Wes had come to the realization, some years prior, that it was more the wearer than the clothing that had the most impact. *She could be wearing a burlap bag right now and still look hot.*

"Sorry I wasn't here sooner," she said. "I stopped for gas. I really didn't think you'd get off so early. You never do." *A light and friendly opener. Let's see what happens.*

"That's okay. Thanks for the note."

Smiling softly, she drew close and put her free hand on

his arm. "Thanks for coming. It really means a lot to me." She brightened. "Could you hold these, please?" She handed the bags to him and fished her keys out of her purse to open the door. *I'm carrying her groceries. Does this mean we're going steady?*

Wes felt a heady rush of excitement as they entered. *The two of us . . . alone.* Sunlight on the sliding door blinds created a muted glow. *First impression: small and dismal. Strange how they somehow got the white walls and beige carpeting to clash. The sunlight helps a little.* "Nice place."

"Thanks. Kitty! Where's my Mimi?" The cat trotted up to her, talkative as usual, and Melanie picked her up. "How's my baby?" Mimi meowed. "Look, baby, Wesley is here! Remember I told you about Wesley?" She turned to Wes. "Mimi is my guard-cat. She protects me when I'm sleeping."

"Uh . . . that must make you feel mighty secure," said Wes, petting Mimi briefly before she squirmed out of Melanie's arms. *That is one light-absorbing cat. You can barely make out anything but eyes.* Melanie detoured briefly to rewind the VCR as Wes set the bags on the kitchen counter. When she entered the kitchen she glanced at the answering machine and started to press a button but stopped herself and turned away.

Hmm . . .

"Do you have any pets?" she asked, unpacking the bags. *Okay, light conversation. Good. Work into the heavier stuff.*

"One cat currently. It just showed up, so we called it 'Turnip.'"

Melanie missed the wordplay. "We always had a dog, sometimes two," she said, efficiently putting away her purchases. "I liked the summers I stayed at the farm, there were animals everywhere. They had room to run, they could come and go. I got Mimi from there."

"We had the usual stuff when I was a kid: hamsters, fish, an iguana, a snake – which we actually kept for quite a while even though Mom didn't like it . . ." *Let her talk.*

"I can see you doing that."

"It did get out once but she never knew. We told her we were looking for lost homework, which was stupid but it was all we could think of at the moment." *I need to shut up! Just because I have a story to tell doesn't mean I have to tell it!*

Melanie laughed lightly as she crumpled the empty bags and tossed them in the trash. She walked over to where a cat calendar hung next to her phone and crossed something off. *"Invite horny co-worker for sex?"*

"Get groceries," she said, smiling at him and turning to the refrigerator. "Would you like something to drink? Wine? Orange juice? Some pop?" *I'd better take it easy, keep my head on straight. No wine.*

"Pop would be good, thanks."

Melanie opened the refrigerator door and pulled out a 2-liter bottle of store-brand citrus soda.

Okay, start vague. Let her get specific. "So, very interesting day, Saturday . . ."

Melanie smiled but didn't look up from pouring their drinks. "Wasn't that the weirdest thing? I was just stopping by to say, 'Hi,' and bam, there went the lights . . ." *Just a coincidence? No point pursuing it.* ". . . so I thought 'Hmm . . . this could be fun.'" She looked up. "I *did* get carried away. Sorry about the bruise on your hand."

"Oh, that was my fault. No problem. I'm just wondering . . . about what happened . . . with us . . ."

Melanie pulled open a bag of salted snack mix and poured it into a serving bowl. "Let's go sit down," she said.

They walked into the living room. Wes took a quick inventory of the furnishings. *Thrift store? Curb rescue? Hand-me-down? At least she's trying to get by, to make a home.* They sat on the couch, each a little awkwardly, not quite at the ends but not really together.

Melanie set the bowl and her drink on the coffee table and

turned toward Wes. He took a couple of sips, wondering how to proceed. "I'm really glad you're here," said Melanie. "Really, thanks for coming."

"Thanks for inviting me. I haven't been able to do much but think about you . . . I kept getting in trouble yesterday because I wasn't listening to anybody . . . I was so lost in thought . . ."

"Oh, I know, me too . . . poor Mimi, I stepped on her tail." She looked over at the cat, who was examining them from the middle of the room. "Didn't I, boo'ful? Hm?" Mimi blinked at her, and Melanie turned back, leaning toward him a little. "I've liked you ever since I met you, Wes. You've been a good friend . . . you're so easy to talk to . . ." *We're going to have sex.*

Wes put his drink on the coffee table. "You're very flattering."

Melanie moved closer, reaching out to lay a hand on his forearm. "It's the truth, Wes. You're really special. I've thought about you for a long time." *She might actually feel that way. I wonder how many times she's felt the same way about other guys.*

Wes could feel his heart rate increasing. "I've felt very close to you, too, for quite a while. You're a very special . . . woman. I'm sure you hear this all the time, but I'm very attracted to you. You're beautiful."

She smiled and turned away, as though the compliment was too big to accept, then glanced back. "That means a lot, coming from you. A lot of guys tell me I'm sexy, or they tell me I'm beautiful, but I can tell they mean sexy anyway. I feel like you're looking at all of me . . . I do feel beautiful when I'm with you." *Wow . . . am I really doing that?*

"I'm glad I can help you feel that way," said Wes. "You should feel that way all the time."

Melanie shook her head lightly. "That . . . just hasn't been working out very well lately."

"I'm sorry to hear that." *Kind of . . .*

"*I'm* not. I'm finally finding what I really need." She held one of his hands with both of hers. *Getting very close . . . aroused and apprehensive . . .*

"It seems like we're close to taking a really big step here," he said. "It's just that . . . I'm not all that free to . . ."

Melanie squeezed his hand. "I know what freedom is, Wes. I know you have responsibilities. But I also know what I see when I look in your eyes. I see a lonely man, a man who needs a lot more affection in his life." *She's right.*

"'Affection,'" he said. "That's a good word. It disappears without you knowing . . . it's really meant a lot, having you in my life. I've wanted to tell you how much I've enjoyed you coming around and talking to me in the afternoon. It's the best part of my day."

She looked pleased. "Mine, too." She held his hand tighter and looked down. They were quiet for a moment, then she spoke again. "I've been talking to you in my mind all day, saying the same thing over and over again . . ." She looked up, into his eyes. "I love you, Wes."

No, no, way too soon . . . "Melanie, you don't even know me."

"Well enough," she responded. "I've wanted to say that to you for so long . . . it's been so hard, seeing you every day, knowing how miserable you were . . ." *How long has she felt like this? How should I respond?*

"I've wanted to kiss you since the first time I saw you," he said, truthfully.

It seemed to mean a lot to her. "Really? You noticed me right away?"

"Oh, yes. You were . . . a vision." *A Nordic nymph . . . but I don't think that would mean anything to her.*

Melanie's eyelids dropped a notch and her lips opened as she moved even closer. Wes moved to meet her, pulling her against him as they kissed. *Her lips, her perfume, the feel of her in my arms* . . . The warmth spread quickly, glowing through him. They kissed a long, hungry kiss. Melanie pulled away with a gasp, her face suddenly infused with passion.

In one smooth motion she rose and turned to straddle him, sitting on his lap. Her fingers roughed through his hair, stimulating his scalp and neck, then toyed with his ears. Her gaze deepened. "I've been looking for someone like you as far back as I can remember," she whispered, covering his face with small, wet kisses. *Electric kisses. Feels so good* . . . He ran his hands in long strokes up her sides, around and down her back, along her hips and thighs and back up, circling in to brush over her abdomen with his thumbs, then flowing up and over the enticing hillocks of her breasts.

She reached up, taking his hands and guiding them to the top button of her shirt. *Here we go* . . . Trembling a little, he began to unfasten it as she stroked the backs of his hands.

"Relax, baby," she said. "Take your time." *This is wonderful! This is unbelievable!*

Sudden, unwelcome thoughts intruded. *Sperm. Egg. Pregnancy.* Wes hadn't had to consider birth control for twenty years.

"Melanie . . ."

"Yes," she whispered.

"Uh . . . what about . . . birth control?" *She didn't tense up . . . this isn't a problem.*

"I've been on the pill since I was fifteen. I had bad periods. We're fine." *Thank God for the Pill.*

He resumed the disrobing, opening Melanie's shirt down to her belt, then pulling the bottom out of her jeans and undoing the last button. He parted the cotton curtain, revealing a filmy black lace bra. The outlines of her erect nipples showed through the silky material. He wrapped his hands lightly around her waist and slowly moved them up, circling with his thumbs to feel the subtle peaks and valleys of her ribcage, the lacy elastic of her bra strap, and then the smooth hollows under her arms. *I can feel my touch working in her. I can feel the connections being made.*

"Ohh . . . your hands," she said, as if responding to his thoughts. She closed her eyes, looking inward. He moved his hands in and over the filmy cups of her bra, relishing the knowledge that they would soon vanish. Her breasts were even softer than he expected, contrasting with her nipples, which were large and very firm. He could see her focusing on his tender caresses.

Taking a breath, she opened her eyes and unbuttoned his shirt with deft and practiced fingers. He sat up slightly to let her pull the tail clear and she slid the garment off behind him. In stark contrast to her alluring undergarment, he was wearing an old, V-neck T-shirt. *Man, I was not thinking ahead! What a turnoff!*

Melanie looked anything but turned off. She moved her hands in smooth, broad circles all around his chest and stomach, up and over his shoulders, back down his chest.

"Ooh, you're a manly man!" she said teasingly. *She's so playful . . .*

Wes made a muscle with his right arm, jutting his jaw and lower lip in mock self-satisfaction. She squeezed his bicep, which actually looked huge under her tiny hand.

"Oh, my," she said. Her touch turned very light as she brushed her fingertips here and there about his chest and stomach. He let his arms drop and just watched her delicate motions, glancing up to see the look of relaxed concentration on her face. Her hands moved flat up the center of his chest. Her fingers curled over the neck of his T-shirt, gripping the material, massaging it lightly between finger and thumb, feeling the texture. She stopped, staring at her hands. Then, with a sudden jerk, she tore the shirt right down the middle, almost to the bottom. *Holy shit!* Before he could react, she curved her fingers into claws and raked them down his chest, hard, but not enough to break the skin, sending a shock wave of sensation shooting through him. An answering wave of brute passion swelled within him, but as he rose to take her, she stopped him, her hands on his shoulders.

She licked her lips. "Slow down, gorgeous. Let's really enjoy this."

I am enjoying this, oh yes I am. He stopped and breathed a couple of times, savoring his arousal. They shared an intimate smile.

Melanie reached down and tugged his T-shirt free of his pants, then slipped it up and off him. She brought the white-cotton mass to her face and inhaled deeply, looking into Wes's eyes with a knowing expression. "Mmmm . . . I want more of that," she cooed.

Wes reciprocated, sliding her shirt down over her shoulders. She dropped her thin arms, letting the garment slide easily onto the floor behind her. As he reached around her back, she bent forward and settled her lips onto the side of his neck, where she planted firm, wet kisses as he undid her bra. The action of the elastic snapping open under his hands felt wonderful, the warm expanse of skin inviting. He spread his fingers out, covering most of her back, feeling once again the rolling undulations of her ribcage. *She's so little. She feels so fragile.* She sat up. The bra came off like a wisp of smoke and he stared down at the small wonders that were her breasts.

"You have beautiful breasts," he whispered.

"Thanks. They're kinda small." *I wonder if she's serious. They really are beautiful, and they fit the rest of her figure, but maybe it's like with guys . . . everyone wants bigger tits or bigger dicks.*

"You'd look silly with bigger breasts. You'd fall over. These are perfect." *She probably hears the same thing from every guy she meets. And she knows that most of them are lying.*

"I'm glad you like them," she said.

He put his fingertips on either side of the entrancing

mounds, trying and failing to absorb the full, astonishing reality of actually touching them. Melanie closed her eyes and clasped her arms behind her back, arching slightly up and forward to accept his attentions. He brushed her breasts gently, curving around the sides and underneath, feeling for the sensitive spots that would give her pleasure.

"Mmm . . . mmhmm . . ." she murmured. He lightly massaged her erect nipples with his thumbs, then bent to kiss each of them in turn. He pulled at them with his lips and batted them with the tip of his tongue. A part of him felt that he could be fully satisfied continuing with these explorations, but other regions urged him to move on.

He planted a firm kiss between her breasts and then, with his tongue, traced a line up the center of her chest, onto her throat, and over the curve of her chin to her mouth. They wrapped their arms tightly around each other and pressed together. They kissed hard, their lips wet and parted. Her tongue darted out, probing into his mouth, finding his tongue and dancing with it. Their heads tilted and turned, searching for ways to get closer, go deeper, connect more intimately. He moved his hands up, massaging her neck, cupping the back of her head, tracing the outline of her ears, tugging on her earlobes, smoothing her cheeks, then using his thumbs to probe into the corners of her mouth, which was pressed passionately against his.

She pulled away and grasped his right hand, pulling it to her mouth. She brushed her lips back and forth, kissing and licking his fingertips, then licked his thumb hard, tongue full out, and took it all the way into her mouth. She made love to it like it was the most erotic thing she'd ever encountered, her eyes closed, her breathing ragged, her tongue rolling. The sight and the feel were powerfully arousing, and he felt a pounding urge to go further.

"Let's go," he whispered urgently in her ear.

"Yes," she gasped, sliding wetly off his thumb.

Wes bent forward and pushed up, holding Melanie against him as he rose. She wrapped her legs around his waist and her arms around his neck. He walked toward the bedroom, purposefully but carefully, not wanting to break the spell of the passion by tripping or ramming her into something. *Nothing like a knot on her head to stop this thing cold.* They passed through the doorway and made it to the edge of the bed. He stopped and held her for a moment and they looked at each other with hot, dark eyes. Cradling her with his arms, he bent and lowered her to the bed. She stretched out invitingly. He lay down beside her, up on one elbow, one hand under her head and the other caressing her face. He kissed her on her forehead, her temple, her cheek, her chin, on the bridge of her nose, on her waiting lips. He put his mouth close to her ear. "I'm feeling things I haven't felt for years," he whispered. "I'm feeling things I've never felt before." And it was true.

"You're a man who needs to feel," she said, stroking his shoulder and arm. "I see the tenderness inside you. Let me touch your tenderness." *Oh, yes* . . . She pulled him full on top of her, with her breasts pressed into his chest and her stomach flat against his. He could feel his erection pushing against her and knew that she could feel it too. He licked and kissed the side of her neck, then opened wide and planted his teeth firmly into her tender flesh as if to consume it. She gasped and threw her head back, signaling her willingness to sacrifice herself to his desire. He drew away, grasping with his lips as went as though pulling her flesh into his mouth.

He kissed his way down to her breasts, still astonishing in his eyes. He ministered to them with his lips, tongue, and fingertips, then proceeded to the sensitive skin of her upper abdomen. Touching so lightly that he could feel the fine down covering the surface, he traced lines with the tip of his tongue and planted delicate kisses all around. He rose enough to free both of his hands, then held her hips firmly, running his thumbs in rough circles over the texture of her jeans. He reached for the ornate buckle on her belt, but she pushed his hands away and slid out from under him. *Hm?* She swung her legs off the bed and stood, turning to face him. *Ah!* He turned as well to sit on the bed directly in front of her.

This time his fingers found the buckle and undid it, then the metal button underneath. As he ran the zipper down, the denim parted, revealing a glimpse of familiar black lace. He pulled her jeans down over the seductive curves that had fascinated him for so long. Directly in front of his eyes was a perfect, round little belly. *A doll version of womanhood.* He bent to slip the jeans to the floor; she rested her hands on his shoulders to step out. As he sat up, he caught the scent of her, sweetly musky, and it seemed to flow right to the center of him. His eyes closed briefly to savor it. *Ohhh . . . I love that smell. Are there really guys who don't? It's hard to believe. I love it I love it I love it!*

He reached out with his right hand and cupped the curve of her lower abdomen, resting his left hand on her thigh.

"You're beautiful," he said quietly, not looking up.

"I'm all yours," she said. *Heaven . . .*

Her panties were a minimal bikini style. *Almost as stimulating on as off . . .* The fabric was thin enough that he could see the texture of her pubic hair underneath. *So close . . .*

He sat back slightly, taking her in with his eyes, enjoying the sight for a moment. Her eyes were shadows of desire, her lips were full. *I feel like a kid at a birthday party, opening his presents.*

He tucked his fingers into the elastic and slowly pulled down. As soon as the waistband passed her hips the panties dropped to the floor and she stepped out of them. He sat forward, pausing briefly to kiss her trimmed patch. The scent of her arousal was even stronger now, mixing with her cologne to create a heady cloud which he inhaled deeply. *Narcotic.* He stood, bending down to meet her lips, letting his hands drop behind her to trace the contours of her hips and her bottom.

She reached around and dug her fingers tightly into his buttocks, pulling him tight to her.

They kissed and groped until Melanie broke free with a heavy exhalation and grabbed his belt buckle. She had it open in a flash, kneeling to the floor as she pulled the zipper down and guided his pants to his feet. He lifted each foot so she could pull the pants free and fling them to the side. She brushed her fingers along the outline of his erection, which showed clearly through the fabric of his shorts, then pulled his waistband out and down, dropping the underwear to the floor and tossing it aside as well. She grasped the shaft of his penis with one hand and lightly kissed the underside of the head, gazing up at him with a look of pure lust. As aroused as he was, and as tiny as her hands were, he looked huge. *I like this!*

"I want this inside me," she said.

"Yes."

She rose and he took her like a doll, turning and laying her flat on the bed, feeling powerful and exhilarated. Her legs parted and he was on top of her and sliding into her in one smooth thrust. Her vaginal walls were tight around his penis, but she was very wet, and he began stroking back and forth with strong, even thrusts. *Oh, man, I'm already so far along! I need to extend this.*

He pushed until his pubic bone was in firm contact with her clitoris, then began rocking with her, minimizing the stimulation to the head of his penis. *Take the long way around. A drifting ride to the waterfall.* He slid one hand under her neck and the other under her back, dropping his head to explore her skin with his lips, teeth, and tongue, then pulling back to contemplate her rising arousal. She wrapped her arms around him, her hands gripping and relaxing, digging in with piercing fingernails. She crossed her ankles firmly behind his lower back, adding further pressure to their exertions.

Wes closed his eyes and touched his cheek to hers, feeling her panting exhalations. They breathed to the rhythm, riding together in perfect symmetry. They floated on, lost in each other, lost to the world.

Finally, it was time. *I'm close. So is she. I need to get her there, I don't want to come first the first time.* He began subtly varying the angle and depth of his thrusts, feeling for the motion that would arouse her most. She gasped, then groaned almost imperceptibly deep in her throat. "Let it go," he whispered, "let it go."

As if in response, Melanie's moans rose in pitch and volume, taking on a sharp edge. She rocked her pelvis against him, pushing to make the thrusts stronger and deeper. Her muscles tensed all around him; her movements became strenuous and deliberate. She surged toward climax, eyes closed, fingernails clawing at his back, legs clutching him tight.

Here it is, over the edge! He felt Melanie's intense first wave of orgasm crash through her just before the explosion of his own overwhelming climax shut down his mind. He ejaculated in huge, almost painful contractions, his whole body rigid, his arms locking her to his body. He thrust spasmodically, maximizing the effect, riding the blast as long as he could. His consciousness opened back up enough to encompass the rest of Melanie's climactic experience. She, too, was prolonging it, enjoying the ride, drawing pleasure from every motion.

Waves of relief began to flood over him as his movements slowed, as the pumping lessened in intensity. His hands and feet were tingling, and he seemed to be breathing purer, softer air. He found himself floating in a wonderful, glowing closeness with Melanie. He relaxed his grip on her and held her tenderly as both of them began slowing to normal breathing. Wes felt his erection begin to diminish within her. As they lay together, without speaking, he felt as though he was bathing in satisfaction.

He brushed his lips over hers. "That was wonderful," he whispered. *What an understatement.*

"Yeah," she sighed, suddenly inscrutable.

"That's the best it's ever felt for me," he continued. *I certainly don't remember it ever feeling better. But then, you can't really remember something that powerful. You only know it as you experience it.*

"Me too," she said, eyes still closed.

I wish I knew what she was thinking . . .

He rolled off, onto his back, and they lay motionless for a few more minutes, letting all the aftershocks subside. He felt relaxed from head to toe. Already, though, at the edges of the contentment, the outside world was beginning to reappear. He was someplace he shouldn't be, and he'd have to start thinking about leaving.

He sighed inaudibly. "What are we going to do?"

Melanie's voice was calm and reassuring. "We're already doing it, baby. We're just enjoying each other. It doesn't need to be any harder than that." *Sounds temptingly simple.*

"You're an amazing woman. Where did you come from?"

"From good places and bad places," she said, a little more distant. *Hm? Better leave that one alone for now.*

He propped himself up on one elbow and kissed her. "I need to go."

She smiled a little. "I know. It's been wonderful. I think we've started something beautiful here. And . . ." She touched her patch of pubic hair. ". . . at least part of you belongs to me now." He felt a little twinge of discomfort. *Not sure what to say to that.*

"Yeah," he said, smiling a bit. He began to dress in the dim light as she lay there, watching him. *So this is what an affair feels like. Now I'm the burglar, getting ready to sneak off.* Mimi rubbed at his legs as he pulled up his pants. "Hey there, Miss, you weren't spying on us, were you?"

"She doesn't miss anything," replied Melanie, sitting up. "C'mere, you little weirdo." Mimi jumped up on the bed and lay down near Melanie to get petted.

Something on the dresser caught his eye. *Is that it?* He picked up a plastic makeup compact with a ribbed cover and held it up so she could see it.

"Good memories?" she said, smiling. *Memories, anyway. The strangeness will fade . . .*

He flipped it open and saw his eyes reflected in the small, lighted mirror. He turned his head toward her, leaving the light on himself. "Boo," he said. She giggled. He snapped it shut a put it down to resume dressing. *Well, I won't be taking this T-shirt home.* He held it up.

"Need some cleaning rags?"

She laughed. "Sure, throw it here." He tossed it to her and she slipped it on as he put on his shirt. She bent her head and sniffed it. "Mmm . . . it has that good Wesley smell." *Ugh.*

"Yeah, sorry about that." He sat on the bed to tie his shoes. She moved over to rub his neck and back. *Yess . . .*

"I love how you smell. Now I'll have this to remind me. It's your first gift to me!"

"Oh, right, I'm so thoughtful. Well . . . ." He stood up. She climbed out of bed and they walked to the front door. They embraced, swaying together for a few moments. *I wish I could have all this without the guilt. What's wrong with feeling this good?*

Melanie stretched up and kissed his cheek. "Take care, Wes. Thanks for coming." *Yep, I sure did come . . .*

He kissed her forehead. "It was my pleasure. You're wonderful."

"I do love you."

It's easy to confuse need and desire with real love. But I do truly care for her . . . "I love you too," he lied.

He stepped out into the hall and they gave each other a smile and a wave as the door closed. He scanned the parking lot as he left the building and walked to his car. *Yep, now I'm the criminal . . .*

CHAPTER 7

Hundreds of miles away, in an apartment that smelled of cigarettes, beer, and dogs, Melanie's sister Miranda shook with terror, her makeup-darkened eyes made even bigger and darker by fear.

"No, Daddy, please . . . !!"

Ron Becker advanced on her slowly, his blocky body coiled in rage. "Did you think I wouldn't find out?! After what happened last time . . . and here you go, out showing your body again and calling it 'dancing' . . . whore!" He lunged at her, lashing out with both clublike arms, throwing her against the wall. She sagged down and staggered away on rod-thin legs, fishing frantically in her pockets as he advanced.

"Here, here, you can have all the money, please . . ." She held out a wad of bills with both hands. The skin of his close-cropped scalp turned even redder, and he smacked the money away with one swipe of a meaty hand.

"Bitch! Fifteen years old and already selling yourself! When I get through with you I'm going to tear that place apart!" He laid into her with his fists, lost in fury. She covered up feebly, hopelessly, her long mop of auburn hair swirling about her head as though it was trying to curtain the horrible scene from her sight. When he had battered her body, he jerked her upright by both shoulders and stared into her eyes with a look of fire. "They might think twice about hiring someone who looks like *this*!" He smashed her across the face with the back of his hand, and she flew like a rag doll across the room. She felt as though she was underwater in a sea of pain. The room was blurry and distant, her father's sweating, ranting face miles away. From that distance came: "That's the last time, you little bitch!" and then, with a hollow thump of the door, he was gone and there was quiet. One small part of her mind was quite clear, and that part knew that he had no intention of starting a fight at the club where she'd worked. He was on his way to a bar to continue his drunk.

She lay slumped against the wall, with no strength to get up or even raise her head. She stared at nearby spot in the dingy carpeting, feeling her heartbeat pulsing painfully in her temples. Her eyes closed and her head sagged a notch further. All she could feel was pain and tears.

There was a familiar snuffling sound in her ear. Her eyes cracked open and the welcome face of the family dog appeared, looking worried about his unmoving mistress.

It was time to check the damage.

CHAPTER 8

And they were off. Wes began hustling during the day so that he could get away as soon after five as possible. This was unfortunate. He had always been able, when circumstances forced him, to make sure that a day's work, or even many days' work, got cranked out. But he was deficient when it came to longer-term planning and projects, and his focus on Melanie caused him to neglect those areas even more, at a time when his department was already close to crumbling. His management style was, in effect, to paint over cracks, and he was ignoring the fact that those cracks were widening dangerously.

Although he didn't realize it, he had begun to rely, over the past couple of years, on his nemesis, Ben, to goad him into action. When Ben chewed him out, he put it in high gear for a while. When Ben was mute, he drifted toward idle. Once in a while he lucked out and had improvements made for him, like the new software that the systems department had come up with the year before. They had installed it and trained everyone, and after a few days of confusion and inconvenience it had markedly improved the department's numbers, getting Ben off his back for months.

The problem was, Wes's opinion of Ben as a narrow-minded and overpaid priss was mostly accurate. Wes was getting occasional motivation but not real guidance from someone who had about as much business being in his position as Wes did in his.

Melanie resumed her afternoon visits to shipping, and they immediately turned from welcome respites to dreaded encounters. *It feels like we're doing a solo spotlight dance at the prom. I can't tell if she's acting more intimate now or if I'm just a lot more sensitive to her behavior. It seems like anyone could look at us and guess.* He found himself unable to play the part of normalcy, and after Tuesday he stayed in his office instead of wandering out to greet her, using the not-quite-untrue excuse of having to work harder to get off early. She still came around, and either hung out in the doorway or sat down for a few minutes. *Jeez, this looks suspicious too, but everything seems to look suspicious now. At least this way it's less likely that we'll be overheard. And she has always been a wanderer and a gabber – that's nothing new.*

He put off his arrival at home with fictitious, but not unusual, claims of working late. Tricia had long ago given up on him getting home in time for a family dinner, so she and Posie ate early and he either had leftovers or fended for himself. It was an easy deception, and he quashed the first stirrings of fear and guilt with similar ease, although they were never far from the surface. Of course, he was having great sex (*happy, happy neurotransmitters*) and great sex has justified sin in the best of minds, although not-so-great sex has often sufficed.

In order to mask or eliminate the various telltale scents associated with his activities he assembled a collection of countermeasures in his car: breath mints, alcohol wipes, deodorant, and clean shirts. He also purchased a small tube of makeup foundation to cover any potentially suspicious nicks and abrasions.

The sit-ups never materialized, but he did become a little more particular about what he ate. And instead of staying up late channel-surfing, he went to bed with Tricia, so he'd have more energy for Melanie. *Well, here's a nice bit of irony.*

He became very cautious about showering and getting ready for work. *I look like I've been mauled by a baboon on PCP.* Melanie was an artist with teeth and nails, and her handiwork lit up red after a hot shower. Wes found himself making greater use of towels and bathrobes, in what he hoped was a not-too-noticeable change from his normally semi-nudist tendencies. *Really no way of explaining away something like that. One bite mark would be all it would take for a conviction in the Court of Tricia. "No, really, someone brought their four-year-old into work and I picked him up and he just attacked me! Paramedics had to pry him off with the jaws of life. I didn't want you worrying about unsafe working conditions, so I didn't mention it. Sadly, it turned out that the little boy was rabid and they had to put him down." Nope, better just stick with the New Modesty.*

He hustled a little more to get to the phone, although Melanie never called. *I can't really tell her not to call – I don't think she'd appreciate being told what to do. I'll just have to rely on her judgment . . . she must know that it would cause trouble.*

He tried to remember what his routine had been pre-affair, how he had acted. *Jeez, it's hard to act "normal" . . . am I being suspiciously nice to Trish? Are my work excuses believable? Is Trish acting "normal?"* He was tempted to ask her if anything was bothering her so he could ease her suspicions with something from the list of explanations he was beginning to keep handy in his head: *They're speeding things up again . . . lost some good people . . . haven't been feeling all that well lately . . .* but he knew that just asking the question could be incriminating in itself.

It quickly became obvious that it would be difficult for him *not* to go to Melanie's apartment after work. He'd certainly made it clear to Melanie, over the time that he had known her, how dissatisfied he was with his home life, exaggerating frequently to gain the sympathy which she was so willing to give, so it occurred to him that he might have to lie to her about an obligation if he felt the need to get home early. *Jeez, things get complicated in a hurry . . .*

He also realized that he had never seriously considered

what he would do if he actually found himself having an affair with Melanie. He had been so wrapped up in the idea of the physical that he hadn't thought much about the emotional part, or what day-to-day life would be like with her. It became plain that Melanie had quite an emotional stake in their relationship, that she had risked being rebuffed by him when she initiated it, and that she continued to risk rejection because of his family commitments. *I'm really in it now.*

He contemplated all of this in the semi-secluded confines of his office late Friday afternoon while eating the reheated remains of a chewy vendo-burger left over from lunch (but with no potato chips, per his new diet).

"Hey, you screwing Melanie yet?" Mark was at the door.

Wes tightened up from the skin in. *Holy shit.* He recovered quickly, however, and looked at Mark with what he hoped was typical disdain. "Why, you waiting your turn?" *Man, I've really crossed the line . . . I'm living guilty.*

"Aw, I'd have to have a dick transplant first . . . from a whale! She's probably so loose she could fuck a watermelon."

"Why do conversations with you always head right for the gutter?"

"Do you think rich guys get dick transplants? I've never heard of it. But hey, why not? If they can transplant lungs and kidneys, you'd think they could slap on a nice, fat wiener. I wonder how much it would cost?"

"Check the insurance booklet. Maybe it's covered."

"Sure, you could claim that the stress from having chicks mock you all the time was affecting your work. 'What is that, an inchworm? Get that pathetic little thing away from me.'"

"Speaking of pathetic little things, was there something you wanted? Besides an audience?"

"Yeah, when are you going to get to those performance and wage reviews? Some of them are a month late, and the natives are restless. All you have to do is pull your hands out of Melanie's pants long enough to get them done."

This time, Wes nearly exploded. It was all he could do to reply evenly, with no chance of tossing back the humorous retort that Mark was certainly expecting. "Ben still hasn't approved my budget. I'll ask him about it."

"Yeah . . . well, when you see him, tell him I said, 'Mount my meatpole.'" Shaky as he was inside, Wes could still manage a surface chuckle. *Too knotted up to really laugh. It would feel good to really laugh again.*

*   *   *

The knots loosened only when he and Melanie were in bed together. The time between arriving at her apartment and becoming nude decreased exponentially over the course of the week.

That night, Melanie seemed a little down, and after they undressed, they got into bed and quietly lay beside each other, half under the covers. Melanie was stretched out on her back; Wes was lying on his side, facing her. The rush of words that had accompanied their new relationship was over.

He let his free hand roam lightly over her skin as she stared up through the ceiling. His fingertips traced the tendons of her throat, then floated down onto the small bony plate of her sternum. He circled about, then drew a line down the center of her chest, slipping his hand under the bedding to the soft flesh of her abdomen, where he made broad, light arcs with a flat hand. Drifting back up, he stroked and cupped her breasts, careful not to stimulate her nipples past arousal to irritation. She remained motionless but communicated almost imperceptibly that she was enjoying his attentions. Her eyes began to relax. *Hmmm . . . this might be a good time for an extended voyage south.*

Wes had developed an early and lasting interest in the art of cunnilingus, and his experiments with previous partners had led him to believe that he could properly entertain a woman. Tricia had appeared to enjoy it about as much as her predecessors, although she was somewhat less demonstrative during any sexual activity. That activity had, of course, tapered off to almost nothing over the years and Wes was both anxious to indulge in his special interest with Melanie and concerned that his performance could prove to be a bit rusty. Experience had shown him that too much time away from oral sex lessened the strength and endurance of his tongue and, to a lesser extent, his mouth muscles. *I'm sure I'm out of shape. Got to pace myself.*

He curved his hand around the far side of her chest and ran it down at a leisurely pace over her hip and thigh, pushing the covers past her knees, then turning back and slowly stroking up the inside of her leg. He brushed lightly through her pubic hair and traced his fingers down and up her other leg, passing over her abdomen to repeat the circuit, each time lingering longer and probing deeper in her tended garden. When his fingertips found moisture, he stopped his wanderings.

He massaged her clitoris delicately with one fingertip, dipping down occasionally to pick up more liquid. She closed her eyes, parted her legs, and assumed a meditative stillness, except for an occasional muscle twitch along the inside of her thighs. While continuing his manual persuasion below, he licked her nipples to full engorgement, flicking at them with the tip of his tongue. He played with her, varying the speed, direction, and pressure of his tongue and finger. Then he dipped deeply into her rapidly-filling reservoir and drew his hand up, painting a wet line over her abdomen and circling her aureoles with her own fragrant lubricant. *That smell . . .* He sucked briefly on his fingertips, tasting the deeply floral sweetness. *Must have more . . .*

"I love everything about you," he whispered. "I love your scent, the way you taste, the way you feel."

Melanie smiled a little, her dreamy eyes barely opening to gaze at him. "That's how I taste. That's how I smell. I'm glad you like it. I want you to know everything about me." *Can't get much more encouraging than that . . .*

Little Witch

He kissed her between her breasts, moved down almost imperceptibly to lick her skin, then followed this pattern as he traveled slowly down toward his goal. He paused briefly to stimulate her navel with his tongue, then continued until he reached her small furry thatch. It was a well-defined triangle whose lower tip ended just above her otherwise hair-free genitals. *Nature's directional arrow.* Wes ran his lips in circles through the springy curls, inhaling deeply through his nose, enjoying her warm aroma. *Time for a taste.*

He moved down to position himself between her legs, lying flat to get the best angle, his legs hanging off the end of the bed. She moved her knees up and apart invitingly, revealing glistening, engorged folds of delicate flesh. Wes inhaled again. "You smell wonderful, wonderful . . ." Her legs opened a little wider in response.

He began his explorations on the surface, licking up at a leisurely pace with a flat tongue from bottom to top, over and over. *Best to start slow, let her get settled in.* Then he added some variety, licking up slowly and then lightly flicking the edges of her labia on the way down. He began to point his tongue, slipping deeper and deeper between her fragrant petals on every pass. Then he pushed the tip of his tongue deep into the middle, into the wettest part, and licked up firmly until he found the nerve-rich mound at the top. He flicked his tongue off and into his mouth to savor its delectable coating. *Mmm . . . so gratifying . . . now the real fun begins*

He drew circles around her clitoris with his tongue tip, deliberately and delicately, then licked at it like a tiny ice-cream cone. He flicked it rapidly, doing his best to give the impression of a hummingbird's wing. *Here's where I need to get the endurance back.* Melanie adjusted herself on the bed, tilting her pelvis and repositioning her head on the pillow. She began stimulating her nipples with her fingertips. *Mmm . . . settling in for the ride. That's good.*

He worked his way down from her clitoris to her vaginal

opening, probing with the tip of his tongue, back and forth, around and around. He opened and tilted her legs just a bit more and pushed his tongue in as far as he could, wishing he could go further. *I need a longer tongue, too.*

He pulled back to play with the slick folds of tissue, massaging them gently between thumb and fingertip, pulling them open to reveal her enticing entrance to ecstasy. *Go in with a finger? Seems a little rude the first time.* He circled the opening with one finger, slid it up to apply pulses of pressure at the base of her clitoris, then popped up and over to give her a burst of sensation. He resumed his lingual exertions, lapping up and down through Melanie's pliant envelope. *Do I dare trespass further? Trish never lets me get past Mount Perinium but I'm not sensing any tension from Melanie. Might as well go for it.* He made a couple of brief, exploratory passes over the low mound of undifferentiated flesh just under her labia. She responded positively, rolling her pelvis up and pulling her knees back toward her chest. *She's into it.*

He put his hands on the undersides of her thighs, helping her hold position, then pointed his tongue as sharply as he could and settled it into the center of her anus. She gasped lightly and contracted reflexively but gave every indication of wanting him to continue. He pushed deeper, flexing his tongue. "Mmm . . ." she moaned. *A little earthy, a little tangy. Well, I guess we have a real relationship now . . . Mark would approve.* He gave her elastic pink ring a few more moments of attention, then lowered her legs so her feet once again rested on the bed. *No point pushing my luck. Back to headquarters.*

He moved his arms under her legs and grasped her thighs, resting on his elbows, to help him stay steady through the coming tempest. He went to work on her swollen clitoris, guided by the movements of her body, the variations in her breathing, and the subtle sounds in her throat. *I haven't lost too much. I'm think I'm still pretty good.* He tried a few of his favorites: licking purposefully up and down so that his tongue stimulated her clitoris on both strokes, planting the tip of his tongue firmly in the center of the mound and pushing it around, and gliding up slowly from underneath and then flicking off sharply.

When he sensed that she was ready to ride it in, he switched to steady, medium-to-heavy flicking, subtly varying the direction and pressure as she readied herself. She became more vocal as her climax approached, making a sound with each exhalation: "Aah . . . aah . . . aah . . ." Her pelvis twitched and rocked with increasing frequency; he held tight and moved with her to maintain contact. *Tongue's getting tired. Got to push it.* She clutched the back of his head with one hand, pulling him tight; he had to push back against it to avoid crushing his mouth into her genitals. He put everything he had into the effort, fighting the fatigue and pain to give her what she needed.

With one final, throaty gasp, her body went rigid, and he flailed away with all the speed and pressure he could muster. She was locked in an orgasmic paralysis, unable to breathe, fully lost in an overpowering onslaught of sensation. *Yes! It's working!*

When it seemed as though she would swoon from lack of air, she released just long enough to gasp, then convulsed again, a shade less forcefully. When that spasm ended, she managed to gasp twice, beginning to ease into her taper. Wes rode with her, relaxing the motion and pressure so he wouldn't irritate her sensitive tissue. When the last big wave subsided, she heaved a great sigh and collapsed from head to toe, letting her legs fall open like a book. *Wow, so great!*

He bent slightly to brush his lips and cheeks through her dark curls and plant delicate kisses on her swollen folds, listening to her panting as it gradually slowed. *I wonder if she has anything left. Her clit is still pretty firm, and her legs didn't collapse all the way. I'll keep going like I'm just doing cleanup and see if she gets another one going.*

He did a series of slow, full licks, just firmly enough to give her the option of a second go. *No indication that I should stop. I think she's thinking about it.* He pushed a little more firmly into the base of her clitoris and moved the tip of his tongue around. *Feels like I'm getting some response here . . .* He did a few broad licks over the mound and felt the tension of arousal returning to her body. She took a preparatory breath and brought her knees up just a bit. *Okay, here we go! Better make this one no-nonsense, wouldn't want to get her going and then leave her hanging.* He began flicking his tongue tip as firmly and rapidly as he could, keeping in mind that he'd have to sustain that level for at least several minutes, but she rocketed into her second climax almost immediately. *Feels like another good one, but more localized.* Again, he eased off the stimulation, letting her breathing and body movements guide him. This time, she collapsed with a gasp, her legs fully extending and falling flat on the bed. *Well, that's it for now. Good stuff.*

Wes planted more light kisses around her pubic area, then pushed up to lie beside her. They lay motionless for a time as he gazed at her face, which was nearly expressionless in its relaxation, her eyes still closed.

After a while, she breathed in a big lungful of air, opened her eyes, and turned to give him a quick kiss on the lips. "Thanks, baby. That felt wonderful." She turned away and rolled out of bed. Wes watched her wander off toward the bathroom, her hair delightfully mussed, her nude posterior swaying with what appeared to be unselfconscious seductiveness. *I am a lucky man, to be seeing this.* Then she was out of sight and it was time to leave. *Late getting home on a Friday night . . . that's pushing it . . . pretty unusual.*

While he was buttoning his shirt, Wes looked closely, for the first time, at the photo collage on the bedroom wall. A family snapshot caught his eye. *Melanie and her family, five or six years ago. She's a boy-magnet . . . smiling and posing in that self-consciously adult way that high school girls do. There's the sister that she's mentioned a couple of times. Cute little girl . . . serious . . . looks like Melanie, but hazel eyes, reddish hair. Mom looks like she was probably a high-school cutie too but was pretty worn down by this point. And Dad . . . interesting. Not a bad-looking guy, I think, but hard to look at. His expression, his body language . . . it's like he's been taken over by a malign spirit.*

Melanie entered, wearing her "good" bathrobe – a shiny black polyester kimono-style robe with a colorful dragon image on the back – and stood beside him. He pointed at the picture. "I was unexpected," she said. "Mom was eighteen. They'd been talking about getting married and I was the final push. Andie came along eight years later, Mom's way of trying to save the marriage." *So matter-of-fact . . .* "A year after this picture was taken, I graduated and moved here. A year after that, Mom died." Wes looked at her questioningly. "She was . . . she was on drugs. She died falling off a balcony. I tried to get Miranda to come live with me, but she thinks she needs to take care of Daddy . . ." She sounded like she was going to continue, but she turned away, moving to the bed and sitting on the edge. Wes continued to look.

"What was her name . . . your mom's name?"

"Christine."

"What did she do? Did she work outside the home?"

"Oh, yeah. She had to. Somebody had to keep us fed. She did all kinds of stuff, until she discovered coke. And then crack."

"And your dad?"

"Ron."

"Is he working now?"

"He hasn't for years. He got disability . . ."

Ron had joined the National Guard in the waning days of Vietnam, fearing that he would be drafted. It was a decision he regretted almost immediately. Through sheer (but unprove-able) carelessness on his part, he suffered a back injury severe enough to get him discharged with benefits. This was fol-lowed by years of surgeries, rehab, partial and short-lived em-ployment, and endless haggling over what the government owed him. Eventually he recovered almost fully, but because he was unbearably abrasive in his dealings with the bureau-cracy, he continued to receive benefits that he did not deserve.

Melanie shrugged and waved off the picture.

Most family photos could be titled, "Better Days." Maybe not this one.

She watched him from the bed while he finished dressing. When he was done, he sat next to her and put his arm around her. She leaned her head on his chest and spoke into his shirt. "Can I see you at all this weekend?" *Oh, no . . . if I go into work, I'll really need to work . . . but I should spend the week-end at home to help balance out all these late nights . . . keep them from becoming an issue.*

"I wish I could, but Tricia has all kinds of projects waiting for me that I've been putting off . . . I promised I'd get to them this weekend. *I can work Sunday if I decide to go in, in case she happens to try a repeat visit to work tomorrow morning.*

Melanie tensed and turned toward him. "That . . ." She choked off the thought and started over. "Why don't you just . . ." She stopped again and sighed. Her shoulders dropped. "I know. I'm sorry . . . I don't want to put pressure on you." She nestled into him. "I just know how much I'm going to miss you. It'll be almost three days until we can be together again."

Oh, man . . . I'm getting guilt on both ends. She sounds lonely already . . . should I try to see her? . . . no, I need a break, clear my head a little . . . this week has been pretty intense. "I know, I'm really going to miss you, too. I'll try to work something out so we can be together next weekend." *This won't get any easier. Better go.* He got up, and she rose with him, taking his hand. They walked slowly to the door, where they turned and embraced.

She feels so small . . . her apartment looks so dark and lonely . . . is this really what her life's been like? He bent and whispered, "I love you," in her ear.

"Oh, I love you, too, so much" she said passionately, rising up as tall as she could and throwing her arms tightly around his neck. "I've needed someone like you, for so long."

Wes had to try gently, a number of times, before he could unhook from Melanie, survive the final goodnight kiss, and make his exit. The door closed on the saddest face he could ever remember seeing.

CHAPTER 9

Saturday got off to a bad start. Wes was sitting on the couch in the living room, sipping coffee and looking through the paper, letting his brain do a weekend slow start, when Tricia came up from the basement.

"Wesley, I thought I'd gotten it through to you that I don't want rags in with the regular wash." He looked up and stifled a gasp. *The ripped T-shirt!* "Now, I know this looks pretty clean, but . . . what's the matter with you? It's not *that* big a deal."

Think fast! Wes shook his head. "No, no big deal. I just thought I'd thrown that one out." *Lame, but what can she say?*

Tricia looked at him a little oddly before turning back down the stairs. "Honestly, a person would think that I ride you mercilessly."

Wes stared toward the basement door, thinking hard. On a couple of nights he had really pushed the time with Melanie and in his haste to leave he had skipped putting on his T-shirt and had smuggled it into the house inside his jacket. *Maybe I picked it up by accident. Her place is becoming a bit of a mess . . .*

As soon as he could, he slipped down to the utility room and found the shirt on top of a few other scraps of fabric in a plastic bucket near the laundry basket. He reached in and picked it up and was immediately struck by the hint of a familiar scent. *Melanie's cologne! Did Trish not smell it? And if she did smell it, how could she think it was anything but an unfamiliar cologne? . . . but she'd have said something, wouldn't she? I can't imagine her smelling it and not saying anything . . .*

His strange encounter with Melanie the preceding Saturday began to gurgle up. *I'm off-balance. I don't know what's going on. I don't know what to think of her.* He stared at the T-shirt. *I should get rid of this . . . no, if Trish is suspicious, she'll be even more so if she sees that it's gone. I'll wait a few days and wash it with some other rags.*

He couldn't shake the feeling of unease that the incident had created. *I should call Melanie. If she's trying to send me a message with this, I want to know what it is.* In the afternoon, Tricia went out to the supermarket. Wes ascertained that Posie was wrapped up with the computer in the basement and went upstairs to the bedroom. He closed the bedroom door and made the call, halfway hoping that there would be no answer.

The phone on the other end was picked up on the second ring. "Hey, baby . . ." cooed Melanie's voice. *How . . . oh, she has caller ID.*

"Hi," he responded, trying not to sound like he was keeping his voice low.

"So, can you come over? I tried calling you at work . . ."

"I know, there's so much to do here. She just went out for a few minutes."

Melanie moaned with disappointment. "I miss you, baby . . . don't we miss our Wesley? Hm? Hm?" Her voice sounded like she had turned her mouth away from the receiver. Wes heard some noise on the line, then a meow, which segued into the thrum of purring. *I am not going to talk to her fucking cat!*

"Hello?" he said, still trying to keep his voice down. There were two more meows, then more static. Wes sighed and rested his head on his free hand. *Come on . . .*

"I'm back, baby," said Melanie. "Talk to me."

How can I work around to it? "Well, I miss you, too. I just wanted to see how you're doing." *And, also, find out if you're stalking me.*

"Oh, I'm okay . . . just cleaning the ol' apartment, watching some TV . . ." *She has even less of a life than I do.* ". . .

I'll probably go get some groceries . . ." *Maybe she'll run into Trish. They can swap recipes.* "Oh, wait!" she exclaimed. "This is funny . . . this morning, I got up and went out to start some tea, like I always do, and then I went in and reached through the shower curtain and whipped on the water, and Mimi just came *flying* out of there like a rocket! She was so scared she couldn't even meow, and she hid under the couch until I was almost ready to leave! Boy, did she move!"

"Wow, must have given you quite a start." *Conversation so light, it might be filled with helium. How am I going to get around to the question?*

"Oh, yeah! I sure was awake after that! I've never seen her go in there before. She must have been chasing a bug or something. Anyway, how about you?"

Ah, the Standard Jobs list. "Well, I'm doing some paint touch-ups, inside and out . . . cleaning out the garage . . . a lot of yard work, haven't done much of anything this spring . . ." *Mention the T-shirt. I'd be using rags for some of these "jobs."* ". . . say, remember that T-shirt that you, uh, altered?"

"Mmm . . . I sure do." She had switched immediately into her bedroom voice. "That was fun."

"Well, it was the oddest thing . . . I was looking for rags – for the painting – and I found it in the laundry . . . the T-shirt, I mean . . ."

There was a pause on the other end. "So?" she said, her voice losing its seductive tone. *This is beginning to sound really stupid.*

"Well, the last I can remember seeing it, you were wearing it . . . it just surprised me . . . I hadn't remembered bringing it home . . ."

There was a longer pause. *This is not good. This is not good. What should I say? Quick, go on to something else . . .* But, before he could speak, Melanie coolly broke the silence.

"You called to ask me about a . . . T-shirt?" *Dammit! Was it that obvious?*

Before he could respond, the line went dead. *Shit! I shouldn't have called! She's right, that was stupid. I'm being paranoid! Should I call right back? Deny it? Admit it? Apologize? No, I'd probably just get myself in more trouble . . .* He heard Posie coming up from the basement and felt as though he should get out of the bedroom. *I'm not usually holed up in here with the door closed.* They met on the second-floor stairs.

"Hey, kiddo, what's up?"

"Nothing . . . who were you talking to? I wanted to use the modem, so I picked up the phone to see if anyone was on it." *Great, any other time she'd just try to log on without bothering to check at all. I wonder how much she heard.*

"Oh, just someone from work . . ."

"A secret admirer?" She wiggled her eyebrows. "Whispering behind closed doors . . ." *She's too observant for her own good. Better just go with it.*

"Oh, yes, one of many. I'm admired by pretty much everyone who knows me."

"Dad?" She sounded serious.

Uh-oh. "Yes?"

"I think you work too much."

Whew! "This is true. Thank you for noticing. You *are* my ace detective."

"Expect a bill," she said, as they parted ways.

Wes wandered down into the living room and slumped into the couch. *Okay, what's going on here? Melanie is a frisky, sexual young woman . . . basically, an alien being. She'll probably do a lot of things that will mystify me and I'm so tense about getting caught that I'll take them wrong. Saturday was just a coincidence, and the shirt . . . well, I don't have the best memory in the world. If she did slip it in the house somehow . . . well, that would be really disturbing. Even if she was just having fun with me, the idea of her breaking in . . . oh, just stop it . . . let it go, let it go . . .*

The sound of the garage door opener, heralding Tricia's

return, gave him a start. *Jeez, I'm getting to be like some cartoon character . . . "Look, it's Mr. Jumpy!" "Yeah, let's go scare him! It's easy to scare Mr. Jumpy!"* He heaved up off the couch. *Time to haul grocery bags. Then, at least, I won't be lying one hundred percent about working this weekend.*

As often happened, the large influx of groceries caused Tricia to desire to eat out, which always suited Wes just fine, since he hadn't been able to permanently hand off the job of kitchen cleanup to Posie. *It sure seems like I did a lot more around the house when I was a kid.*

Later that evening, Wes felt a strong need for some temporary numbness, so when the women went to bed, he retired to the basement for a beer-and-TV session. It didn't work. *Used to be that enough beer made anything at least minimally entertaining . . . in fact, the more stupid the program, the better. Now, drinking just makes everything dull.* After three hours he quit trying and shuffled up to bed.

He'd just finished settling himself in when the phone rang. He lurched to get it before it could ring twice.

"Hello?"

He heard the weak, tearful voice of Melanie. "I'm sorry, Wes. I love you. Goodnight." She hung up before he could think of something to say. *Good thing. Not feeling real sharp right now.*

"Hm?" queried Tricia sleepily.

"No one there."

"Mm."

Wes felt a small sense of relief in his belly. *At least I don't have to worry about her stewing for the rest of the weekend.* His last thought, as he plunged toward unconsciousness, was less soothing: *She called to say goodnight just as I got in bed . . .*

*   *   *

Cold moonlight streamed in through the window, painting the bare room with a palette of dead gray. The walls were malevolent: they hemmed him in and hid his pursuer. . . . *fear*

fear fear fear . . . The murky shadow of the doorway gaped at him like a monstrous mouth. *Run! She's coming!* With great effort, he lurched toward the door and into the bowels of the house. His struggle to move suddenly unleashed a terrifying momentum and he began to career through the cavernous structure with almost no control, aiming for doorways, slamming off walls, feeling her approaching from the upper floors. *She's getting closer . . . I can't let her get me!* A half-open door appeared ahead, a dim light glowing within. In an instant he was through it, stopping for a dizzying moment at the top of a long, steeply sloping staircase. *The basement . . . go!* He scrambled down the steps, but again his body worked against him, hurling itself too fast, tumbling and sliding. He could see, in brief flashes of vision up the stairs, the shape of his tormentor as she began to follow him down. He struggled to get a handhold, a foothold, but the stairs began to break into fragments, and he realized, to his further horror, that *they're made of bones! Finger bones! Hand bones!* The walls, the ceiling, everything around him began to stir and shake and break up into calcified shards. He was sliding into a deep pit of rattling remains; he lost sight of the phantom. *Her hands could be anywhere! They could come at me from any direction!* He crashed to a stop, half-buried, clawing and thrashing in a hopeless effort to pull himself up. Swimming in a huge pool of bone, he sensed her approach, now from below. *No! She'll pull me under! Got to pull myself up! Get out!* He felt bones tumbling up through bones, wrapping around his ankles like manacles and tugging him inexorably down. He tried to scream but he couldn't. He grabbed and pulled at the . . . *blanket? I'm holding a blanket!*

He panted and blinked, staring at his hands.

A light came on. "Wesley!" *It's Tricia! I'm on the floor, tangled in the covers.* Her face loomed over him from the bed. She was fully awake, and angry. "What in the world is wrong with you? You're thrashing around like a speared fish!"

He sighed, took a deep breath, and began to work out of his trap. "Jeez, I'm really sorry, Trish . . ."

"How much did you drink?" she said, making a sour face. *Good. Blame it on the beer.* "You smell like . . . like . . ."

"Like a beer tanker on a reef?" he said, rising. This amused Tricia just enough to take the edge off. "I know, I know . . . I kind of lost track . . . sorry I woke you again."

"Well, go sleep on the couch if you can't control yourself."

"Good idea. I want you to get your rest."

He paid another visit to the Monster in the Mirror and to Raoul's for refreshments before retiring to the living room couch for an uneventful rest of the night.

*   *   *

Sunday, Tricia really did trundle out the List, with enough on it to keep Wes busy for three lifetimes. It felt good to him, though, working around the house and having something known and normal to concentrate on.

As he was sweeping out the garage, after moving everything moveable out to the driveway, Posie wandered out with a broom. Her hair was back in a particularly tight ponytail, which she thought helped her to look like she was working hard even when she wasn't.

"Hi, Dad!" she said, smiling cheerily.

"Hey, kiddo. Careful with that thing . . . it might be dangerous in unpracticed hands."

"Ha. I am not amused." She began to sweep in a very perfunctory manner.

Wow, voluntary work from Posie . . . the Apocalypse is truly nigh. "So," he began "how are you . . ."

"Dad?"

"Yeah?"

"Were you really talking to a cat yesterday?" *Oh, man . . .*

"Uh, yes . . . well, I wasn't really talking to it, but this person I work with thinks it's funny to put a cat on during our conversations."

"'This person?' Must be a woman" she said, with a crafty look in her eyes. *What is this, a cop show? She'll keep coming back until I'm trapped in a web of lies.*

"Well, yes . . . so?"

"'So?'" she replied, with a big-eyed, this-is-so-obvious look. "You're *married*, remember?" *Oh, jeez, I've got to put a stop to this.*

"Sweetie, I work with men *and* women. I can't just talk to the men, I have all kinds of people reporting to me."

"People with talking cats?" *I can't win with her.*

"Oh, stop it with the cats. You just came out here to rile me up."

"Hm," she said, glancing at her broom. "You're right." She looked back at him with a big, phony smile. "Well, I'll be going now." With that, she spun around and walked back into the house, abandoning the broom as she went. *It's kids like her that make me wonder about reincarnation . . . where does she get all this stuff?*

He worked steadily and hard the rest of the day and slept that night without incident.

CHAPTER 10

Monday, Wes reached his office at his usual 7:52 start time and pulled up short. *Office door's unlocked. I know I locked it on Friday. I always lock it when I leave on Friday. The cleaners never come in here, plus, nothing's been cleaned. Who would. . .* a chill shot through him . . . *unless Ben opened it, snooping for something . . .*

He advanced through the door and turned on the lights. *No, he's such an anal little ferret . . . he'd lock it back up and leave without a trace and then hammer me later with whatever he found.* He reached his desk and looked it over. *That's one of the disadvantages of poor housekeeping . . . someone could ransack the place and I'd never know it. None of the drawers are ajar . . . I always close them all the way.* He scanned the file cabinets, all with piles on top. *Looks pretty much the same. What could anyone want? The stuff they usually need is outside the office, where Mark or his gofer can get at it.* He sat down and reached out to turn on his computer monitor. *What?!*

On the glass of the monitor screen, faintly visible in the glare of the lights, was the smeared image of a phallus, running erect from lower left to upper right, with testicles at the base. *It's like a kid would smear a drawing onto a car window. It was Mark, that bastard. He must have gotten hold of a key somehow and did it after I left Friday night. He probably spent all weekend laughing about it. Now I'll have to think up a suitable revenge.* He got glass cleaner and some paper towels out of a supply closet and began erasing the graffiti. *It's certainly a cut above the standard bathroom-wall drawing . . . I didn't think he had any creative talents, unless he draws this sort of thing a lot, which I could believe.*

Wes was still at his desk when Mark, whose shift started later so he could stay until the last package pickup, wandered into the office at 10:05. He began with a high, nasal parody of a grade-schooler's voice: "G'morning, Mr. Sargent . . . get any this weekend?" He dropped back down to his normal low moan. "My wife says she'll buy me a subscription to Playboy if I stop bothering her for sex . . ."

Wes just stared at him for a moment, which didn't seem to bother Mark at all. *Well, let's get this over with. It has to be him.* "So, Mr. Sketch Artist, when are you going to start signing your work?"

Mark appeared genuinely caught off guard and gave him a look that changed quickly from bafflement to sarcasm. "I guess when you start making some fucking sense, you fucking fruitcake." *This isn't a typical Mark response, not if he'd done it . . . better give him a no-frills opening to confess and then move on.*

"You mean you didn't do that little screen decoration?" He nodded in the direction of the monitor. Mark glanced at it with a puzzled expression, then back at Wes. *He's going to slam me again. He didn't do it.*

"Are you seeing little green snakes in your shit again? Are you getting phone calls from dead relatives? I think you need a vacation, Wes, someplace where they have one-way mirrors."

"All right, shut up. It was obviously some other twisted asshole. I thought you were the only one here."

"Oh, no, Wes, there are lots of us, we're all around you, watching you all the time, taking pictures of you in the bathroom."

"Out! Go make someone else's day miserable."

"Fucking weirdo . . ." muttered Mark as he departed. *Well, weird is the word for it. I thought for sure it was him. I suppose it still could be, but I've never seen him play this kind of game before. Okay then . . . Melanie? . . .* He put his face in his hands and sighed. *Well, she's beginning to seem like someone who could get a door open if she wanted to . . . but that drawing . . . was it supposed to be some kind of carnal love-note? Some sort of voodoo-sex thing? Was it supposed to be funny?* He sighed again. *If she did it, will she be expecting some kind of response? But she may not have done it, so I'll have to bring it up obliquely.* "So, Melanie, honeybunch, I sure liked that cock you painted on my computer! I was simultaneously amused and aroused. Let's fuck." He rubbed his face roughly. *Like I don't have enough to think about already.*

The pressures of the workday soon forced Wes's mind away from such concerns and, strangely but thankfully, Melanie was absent once again from their afternoon chat time. As soon as he walked out of the building, however, he was overtaken by a surge of apprehension at seeing her again. *It's starting to feel like she's stroking me with her hands to distract me from the tentacles she's sticking into my belly . . .*

On the way over, he tuned his radio to the oldies rock station for some distraction. Out came the unsettling introductory notes to a song he hadn't heard in years. *"You're Paranoid"* . . . *Kenny Love . . . the Clever Children album.* He was transported back to his dorm, playing penny poker on a Saturday night, the stereo cranked.

> *I like to watch you through your window at night*
> *Don't want to scare you so I stay out sight*
> *I know your skin crawls but I'm not here at all*
> *You're paranoid, aren't you?*
> *I'm often near you when you're lying in bed*
> *I move as fast as you can turn your head*
> *You think I'm deadly but nobody else can see*
> *You're paranoid, aren't you?*
> *You're paranoid, aren't you?*

Little Witch

It never stops, my friend
You see beginnings where there should be ends
You're paranoid, aren't you?

Am I paranoid? I'm sure confused, I'm not thinking straight. It feels like Melanie is creeping around all the edges of my life.

He entered the building still feeling adrift. The more he tried to settle on how to handle his perplexing relationship the more confused he felt. He knocked on the apartment door. A moment later he heard Melanie call, "Come in!" He entered, curious and cautious, and stepped into the living room. The sight brought him up short and instantly washed away all of his doubts and apprehensions.

The vertical blinds on the sliding-glass door were pulled open. Sunlight streamed in and marked out a glowing rectangle on the floor. Melanie was nude, lying belly-down on a beach towel in the center of the radiant pool, facing away from him. Her chin was in her hands, her elbows on the carpet. Her bushy blond mane looked as though it was illuminated from the inside. Her wonderfully round rump rose up like twin balloons just taking flight.

She turned her head just enough to look at him, raising one of her feet into the air as she did so. "See anything you like?" she said, smiling enticingly.

"Oh, yeah," was all Wes could muster as he moved toward her. *Should I carry her to the bedroom? Strip right here? Feels a little risky with the blinds open.*

"It's warm in the sun. You won't need all those clothes."

Okay, strip right here. Glancing out toward the deck, he realized that they were completely hidden from prying eyes, but the thought of someone watching them intrigued him briefly as he undressed. *What would they do about it? Complain? No, probably just watch and enjoy it. That could actually be a little fun.* He was undressed in no time, his clothes in

93

a pile off to the side. He stood, looking at her for a moment, trying to decide what to do next.

Melanie stirred, pushing herself up to hands and knees. She turned her head and looked at him sideways through a thick veil of hair. "Anything come to mind, smart boy?"

Wes was momentarily speechless. *My fantasies . . . how could she know . . . no, she's just playing, just teasing.* "Hmm . . ." he said, with mock concentration. He glanced down at his rapidly stiffening penis, then back at her. ". . . I'll let you know if I come up with anything."

Melanie twitched her bottom enticingly. "Please hurry, sir. I'd hate to have to take care of this all by my lonesome."

Wes stepped behind her and knelt between her legs. She spread her knees wider and tilted her bottom up to better accommodate him. *This is more amazing than a thousand fantasies all at once.* Even in the shadows cast by the streaming sunlight his gaze was met by an exceptional view: the petal-like pink folds of her labia, topped by the delicate radial ridges of her anus. The areas of her skin directly in the sunlight shone with a fine, almost invisible down.

He put his left hand on her hip and grasped his penis with his right. He used the tip to stimulate her clitoris, then slid it up and down to collect and distribute the scented liquid that was rapidly accumulating. When the level of lubrication felt sufficient, he centered himself into her vaginal opening and moved his right hand to her hip. He pushed gently, probing, a little deeper each time. *This has got to be about the ultimate. My dick feels like a steel rod. I wish we were taping this.* He quickly achieved full penetration, firmly blanketed by her warm wetness. *Okay, take it easy now . . . let's really enjoy this.* He maintained control, as much as he could, savoring every stroke. He began playing with the tempo, the depth, the angle, trying to make it feel as good for her as it did for him. *Seems to be working . . . she's making little This Feels Good sounds in her throat.*

Following his old fantasy script, he bent forward and reached under to cup the small hanging globes of her breasts. Her nipples felt as fully erect as his penis. He let go briefly to load his fingertips with saliva and then returned to further stimulate them. Settling into a slow, easy rhythm, he bent his head close to hers and whispered into the mass of light golden hair. "You do amazing things for me."

Melanie responded between pants: "So . . . do you . . . so good . . ."

She sure has brought pleasure back into my life . . . powerful sensations that I'd forgotten about, if I ever felt them before . . . He drew his hands up and circled his fingertips into the delicate hollows under her arms, taking care to apply enough pressure to stimulate without tickling. Then he pulled up further to trace the outlines of her diminutive, angular shoulder blades.

He straightened up, hands returning to her hips, bending backwards a bit to get the full, sex-fantasy view of his penis, glistening with her lubricating fluid, entering and withdrawing. *I feel like I could star in a porno movie . . . It's been a while since I felt this potent . . . I feel like I could go on indefinitely if I was careful. I want to make this last as long as possible.*

He suddenly realized that their sunlit tryst was being reflected in the glass of the sliding door. *Wow, there's the movie!* He could see her face, chin up, eyes closed, mouth open, panting. She licked her lips, then grimaced with mounting tension, dropping her head so all he could see was a radiant waterfall of hair. *I want to burn this into my memory. I want to be able to replay it forever.* Melanie whipped her hair back, gasping, her eyes slitted open. Wes rode the edge, desiring more than anything to stay in this wonderland as long as possible.

Melanie's moans and twitches heralded her approaching orgasm. *Okay, keep it going, give her what she needs . . .* He got into the position and rhythm that seemed to be working best for her and kept at it steadily. Her breathing became uneven and shallow, her exhalations more vocal as she pushed back against him. His body's requests that he ejaculate began to increase in frequency and stridency. *Careful . . . careful . . .*

Her fingers dug into the carpet. Her body shook, then tightened into trembling rigidity as she climaxed. Her powerful vaginal contractions bound and released his penis. *Time to let go . . . before she's too far through her own.* He shifted his stroke slightly for maximum stimulation, and within seconds plummeted off the edge into the electrifying thrill of ejaculation. His mind shut down for the first couple of contractions, then opened back up enough to allow him to revel in the scenario once again. *I'd be hitting the wall if I wasn't inside her . . . I feel like a sperm cannon . . .* He could feel Melanie beginning to relax, her orgasm trailing off as his passed its peak. *Man, this is going on a lot longer than usual . . . feels like I found a spare tank in there.* His breathing slowed and deepened. Tension began to leave his body as the pumping inside his groin gradually tapered off. Droplets of sweat dripped off his nose and onto her back, which, along with her head, was swayed down in relief. He stayed inside her until all motion inside him had ceased, then slowly pulled out.

After a few seconds passed, she rolled to the side, propped up on one elbow, and patted the middle of the towel with her free hand. "Here," she said softly. "Lie down here."

That would feel good. I am so drained . . . He shifted and turned somewhat clumsily, stretching out next to her on his back. He looked up into her face, smiling contentedly, and she looked back at him with a dreamy, calculating expression. *She's got something else in mind. I hope it isn't more intercourse . . . I am totally spent.*

Melanie pushed up and over to straddle him, reassuming her hands-and-knees position. Her hair hung around them in a glowing tent. She looked at him with tranquil eyes, but he could tell that there were wheels turning inside.

"I can't begin to tell you what you mean to me, Wes. I know people talk about all my boyfriends, but with you it's so much different. You've always been good to me, talked to me, never came on to me." *I was too timid. I'm sure no gentleman.*

A small grimace twitched across her face. She looked down the length of their bodies and curved her hips forward and down toward the center of his abdomen until only a few inches remained between the two of them. As Wes looked down, he saw a thick mixture of his semen and her vaginal fluid begin to drip down onto his belly. *What the hell . . .?* Melanie adjusted slightly to fill his navel with the thick, warm liquid, which spilled out and began to run down his sides. *I can't keep up with this woman.*

She tweaked muscles here and there and the flow stopped. Then she rocked backward to sit on his legs and, using both hands, began spreading the rivulets in circles over his abdomen. What she was doing flashed into his head just as she spoke: "I'm making my mark," she said, looking at him slyly. "You're just too good to lose, Wes. I can't have anyone else sniffing around you."

Well, yeah, if Trish sniffs this stuff, she'll throw me out the front door . . . no, through the front door! The sunlight warmed the mixture on his skin, creating a strong, primal scent in his nostrils. *Wow, there's a cologne for you! Eau de Fluide.*

Suddenly, he had a tremendous urge to escape. *I can't just pack up and bolt . . . not with how upset she was at not being able to see me over the weekend . . . but it feels like my body is going to make tracks on its own . . .* Without really thinking about it, he spoke. "I . . . I know this isn't right, I really want to stay longer, but I have to . . . I really wish I could stay, but . . ."

Melanie stopped him with a smile and a pat of her hand. "It's okay, baby. I feel wonderful, and a little tired. I know you're busy. I think I'll probably have something to eat and just go to bed." *Wow . . . a miracle.*

They disengaged and rose slowly, his stomach wrinkling a bit with its sticky-dry coating. "Do you want to clean up first?" she asked. *I want to, but I want to leave even more.*

"Thanks, I'd better get going." Melanie left for the bathroom as Wes began to get dressed. *I'll have to hustle into the shower and then get these clothes downstairs in a hurry and think of some reason to wash a load as soon as possible.*

Melanie came back out in her kimono robe just as he finished. Mimi twined in and out of her legs as she walked, vocalizing and purring. Melanie wrapped her arms around Wes and breathed in heavily through her nose, smelling him. A deep growling sound resonated in her throat. "I saw a TV special on wild Melanies . . . turns out they're very territorial." Mimi was now vigorously rubbing against Wes's legs, stretching up on her toes. Melanie looked up at him, a shadow passing under the light blue of her eyes. "I hope I don't have to share you much longer."

"Me too, me too." *What have I gotten myself into?* She let him out the door with a simple kiss and a smile. He sped out of the parking lot.

It's like she's hypnotized me, put a spell on me . . . I'm losing what little control I had over my future. An uncomfortable sensation began to creep over the front of his stomach. *Ugh . . . feels like this stuff is seeping through my skin and into my muscles . . . like little fingers . . . or worms . . .*

He drove home like a fighter pilot and rushed through the house and into to the bathroom with a cursory greeting and lame mention of a "chemical spill at work" to explain his unusual shower time. He was under the hot water and scrubbing away with a washcloth before his mind slowed down enough to think clearly again. *It feels like there's something growing inside me . . . like I could scrub the skin right off and it would still be there.*

He flung the washcloth down and dug his fingertips into

his abdomen. *I want to just gouge out this flesh, dig down to clean tissue . . .* He raked up hard from the tops of his thighs to his ribcage, raising long, red welts, then dropped his hands to his sides and slumped, sighing heavily as the water continued to wash over his skin. *Why couldn't I have stayed safe? Life wasn't so bad. If I'd put as much energy into my marriage and job as I am into this affair, I might have really improved things. Now I'm on the outside looking in . . .*

CHAPTER 11

Jeremy loved Miranda, and Miranda loved Jeremy. He was seventeen, she was fifteen. Theirs was the kind of pure, heart-to-heart love only known by those who are truly falling in love for the first time. They had both been in relationships that had seemed meaningful – and actually had been in their own ways – but this was the first falling-into-the-ocean-of-each-other experience for either of them.

It was a pleasurable and mutually beneficial relationship. Miranda got access to a car, the false IDs (Jeremy knew people) that she needed to dance at the clubs, and a tender and attentive companion who would absolutely never touch her in anger. Jeremy got a girlfriend guaranteed to make all of his friends jealous, a partner who made him want to be his best self, and enough non-intercourse sex to keep him satiated. (Because she experienced so many fevered requests for copulation from the men she entertained, she had become absolutely firm in her unwillingness to cross that line. She had a sense that the time would come with Jeremy, but it was not something that preoccupied either of them.)

For a few days after a beating (longer, if there were facial injuries involved) Miranda would refuse to see Jeremy at all. When they'd first met, she had rushed to him immediately after an attack and had spent a lot of time talking him out of confronting Ron. Jeremy was a big boy, and tough enough to get by in the circles he ran in, but she knew that he didn't have her father's potential for animal rage and surely would go down in a real fight. So, following a beating, she would make excuses to not see him, which was made easier by the fact that they attended different schools. She would hide under makeup, sunglasses, and long sleeves at school, and recuperate in the relative calm which usually followed her father's violent outbursts.

It had been a week since she'd been punished for her choice of jobs, and she'd consented to have Jeremy pick her up after school. During the winter they would meet at a side door to keep her walk as short as possible, but on nice days in the spring she would have him drive around front so she could show off to her friends. Jeremy was a good-looking young man, with regular, well-defined features and rich brown wavy hair that required almost no attention, the kind that made many women secretly jealous. His wardrobe was influenced by the popular teen-oriented TV shows of the day, a welcome change, in Miranda's eyes, from the slacker look he favored when they first met.

"Oh, he's here!" she said excitedly, breaking from a small group of friends and dashing toward his ten-year-old Firebird as he pulled up. He leaned toward her and swung the door open just before she reached the car. She heaved her backpack behind the seat and jumped in, grabbing him around the neck and kissing his mouth repeatedly. "Oh, I've missed you I've missed you I've missed you!" she gasped, between kisses.

"Me too, me too," laughed Jeremy. "Let's get out of here." He disengaged himself from her enough to straighten up and blast out of the parking lot. "Where to?"

"Oh, I really don't care . . . take me to the mall. You can buy me something to eat. Oh, it's so good to see you again. I'm so sorry I've been so busy."

"Yeah . . ." He looked over at her, studying her face, which looked happy but a little nervous. If he saw anything, he didn't comment on it. "It's okay, Andie. You're always worth the wait."

They got pizza at the mall's food court. She bolted it down, babbling nonstop, while he ate more serenely and watched her with soft, happy eyes. Afterwards, he bought her a frozen yogurt cone and they went outside to a relatively secluded spot near a loading dock. The area had just been mulched for the season, creating a cushioned carpet. There were a few low, scrubby bushes that were struggling a bit to come back from the winter.

Jeremy sat cross-legged in the thick mulch, leaning against a concrete wall, and held her in his lap with his arms around her as she licked at the yogurt, which was beginning to drip down the cone. They relaxed in the warmth of the evening sun. He pulled her hair back to kiss her temple and the side of her neck, closing his eyes so that he could fully enjoy the sweetness of her lightly perfumed skin.

She paused between licks to speak, matter-of-factly. "I need to work again."

Jeremy sighed and hugged her closer to him. His lips tried to form words that his brain wasn't providing. She squeezed his arm in return. "I know . . . I know you don't like me being up there, but Daddy and I run out of money so fast, and I'm always the one who has to talk to the bill collectors. I hate that. Besides, I have you to drop me off and pick me up, and the bouncers really watch out for me. It's not so bad."

"I just feel like I should be doing more for you. You shouldn't have to be doing something like that, as young as you are."

"Hey, I'm . . ."

"I know, I know, I'm sorry . . . you're sure old enough to decide what you want to do, and you're a lot more mature than most girls, uh, women your age, it's just . . . I really should be making more money . . ."

"Don't you *dare*, Jeremy!" she said sharply, turning to look at him and nearly dropping her cone. "You stay straight! I don't want to hear that you've been into anything with that asshole Pat and his butthead friends." Jeremy, who was work-ing Saturdays and some evenings helping a family friend at his auto-repair business, had made a relatively impressive amount of money dealing marijuana in a brief period prior to connecting with Miranda. However, Miranda had the kind of visceral opposition to drugs that embeds itself in someone who has seen a loved one destroyed by them, and she was intent on keeping her sweetheart clean.

Jeremy winced. "Oh, don't talk like that, okay? Those words don't sound right coming out of your beautiful mouth. And I won't do anything stupid . . . I just wish . . ."

"Well, if you end up in jail, I'm never seeing you again," she lied.

"Then come live with me. My folks really like you. They . . . I told them about your dad."

"When?! How could you *do* that!" She jumped to her feet and spun around, glaring at him, her melting yogurt starting to run over her hand. "That is *my* business, not theirs! *I'll* decide who to tell . . ." Her anger overtook her. She balled her free hand into a fist but couldn't bring herself to strike him. "Oh!" she snorted. She abruptly turned and stalked off, flinging her cone against the wall.

Jeremy was quick to catch up with her. "Andie, I'm so sorry. I'm really, really sorry. I didn't think you'd mind, with Mom and Dad. You seem like you get along so well, you're like family. Mom always wanted a daughter."

Miranda slowed to a stop. She looked at her hand and raised it so she could lick off the sweet streamers that were covering it. Jeremy hovered, wondering if he should touch her or not. After a few licks, she wiped her hand on her pants, sighed, and turned to fall against him. They wrapped their arms around each other.

"I love you," she said to his chest. "I know you wouldn't do anything to hurt me."

"No, no, I sure wouldn't. I love you so much. I just want you to be happy. I want you to be with me all the time."

She turned away and tugged at him, guiding him toward

his car. "Me too. I just can't, right now. What I really need is for you to help me."

"Okay," he sighed. "You know I'll be there for you."

They walked toward the parking lot, holding each other, almost comical in their size difference. Her arm went around his belt; his lay across her shoulders.

"When Daddy goes out tonight, I'll call you to come. I'll leave a note for him that Simone picked me up, she got her license. You can hang around if you want, but I know you don't like it. I'll call you when I need a ride. If it's a slow night, I'll just work a couple hours and get home before he does. If it's busy, I'll sneak in after he's passed out. He won't remember anything in the morning."

They arrived at his car and he leaned back against it and held her gently by the shoulders. "But what if he finds out again?"

She stared off to the side, thinking, then shrugged and shook her head. She glanced up at him with a small, determined smile. "Let's go."

CHAPTER 12

Tuesday morning, Wes sat hunched at his desk, rubbing his stomach. *This vendo-coffee is making me sick. I should start bringing coffee from home again.* He chuckled ruefully. *But that would involve discipline and forethought. Scratch that idea.*

As he stared into the cup, a thought rolled into his consciousness on its own. *I've got to quit Melanie. I've got to get my life back to normal before it crashes. Which could be soon. I'll do it tonight.* The decisiveness of the thought was a comfort to him. *I'll just start in and play it as it goes. Too many possibilities to really plan it.*

As he drove to her apartment that evening, he tried to keep a happy ending to the whole thing in his mind. *She's very understanding and sees the stress I'm under. She wants what's best for me. We quit seeing each other outside of work, and she's okay with that.*

She greeted him quietly, almost perfunctorily. *Better get the lay of the land first.* He looked at her as they walked toward the living room. "So, how was your day? I missed you this afternoon." She didn't seem particularly interested in answering.

"Oh, alright. Long." She wandered over to the sliding-glass door and began closing the blinds, shutting out the evening sun. Wes sat on the couch. *This doesn't look promising. Calmly "up" would be the best mood to start with; quietly "down" is not good. Things could easily turn sour if I started talking about backing off: anger, bitterness, tears. I'll have to get her out of this funk before testing the news on her.*

She brightened by just a flicker as she walked toward him. "I was thinking . . . it would be nice to go out one of these evenings . . ." She stopped talking and sat down in the recliner, in a way that wasn't quite right, as though her motor had come unplugged.

Her knees just sort of gave way . . . "You okay?" He sat forward, ready to get up.

"Ahh, just tired," she replied, not moving. Mimi jumped up in her lap and began circling and kneading, making a bed.

She looks pale under her makeup, especially around the eyes. He felt tender concern well up in him and moved to kneel beside the chair. He grasped one of her hands lightly, touching her forearm with his other hand. She felt lifeless; her eyes stared ahead dully.

"Doctors say I don't eat right. Guess I need some pills. More iron. More vitamins."

"Where are they? I'll get some."

"I'll get it," she said, starting to rise.

He sat her back down with very little effort. "You look terrible. Where are they?"

"My purse . . . no, I'm out. Look to the left of the stove."

He went into the kitchen and found the shelf with the supplements. "Which ones?" he called, turning in her direction.

"Get me a 'B', an 'E', an iron, and a folic acid. Please."

As Wes began removing the appropriate containers he noticed, near the back of the shelf, Melanie's medication bottles, all turned with the labels facing away. *Okay, this could tell a tale.* He reached for a bottle, then paused. *If it was something she wanted to share, she would have told me already. For whatever reason, she's not ready. Whatever else is going on, I should respect that.* He continued to gather the requested supplements. *Odd time to grow a conscience.*

He took the pile of pills and a glass of water to her. She tossed the handful back, swallowing them in one large gulp of water. *She looks like a nursing home patient. There's no way*

I can talk to her now. Doesn't look good at all. He smiled at her encouragingly, sighing to himself.

He helped her out of the chair and over to the couch, briefly discomfiting Mimi, where they held each other in tepid silence. *Well, this is obviously not going to be a decision-making evening. Or a sex evening. Or a much of anything evening. She feels so small in my arms. It's weird to see her like this . . . none of her usual sparkle. Man, I'm tired of thinking so much . . .* He looked down at her quiet, expressionless face. She was staring off into the distance.

She's hurting, in ways I may never know. Now what do I do? I don't even know what our relationship is supposed to be right now.

When it was time to go, he left her lying in the recliner, covered with a quilt. *It's like tucking Posie in when she's sick. She looks so weak and alone. But I think there's something going on deeper inside.*

The rest of the week was much the same. Melanie's energy level recovered somewhat, enough for her to go to work, but her mood remained flat. Their bedroom adventures became confined to lower-effort oral and manual variations. Wes's determination to end the relationship circled into a holding pattern.

Friday brought another request for a weekend rendezvous, but this time he had a real, solid excuse: he'd been volunteered by Tricia to help paint a friend's house, a task that would very likely take most of the two days. Her expression as he departed that evening was that of quiet anger, rather than sadness. *It's beginning to look like she won't be satisfied with any excuse. She really expects me to leave Trish for her, and soon . . .*

He assumed that she would be fully recovered by Monday, but she was about the same, and not much improved on Tuesday. *Is this it, then? A cold marriage, a stress-filled job, and a sickly mistress? It's a wonderful life.*

CHAPTER 13

Wednesday, Wes racked his brain for a reason not to see Melanie that evening. *I really need a break, and this late-every-night thing is starting to wear a little thin at home.* The best he could come up with was the fictitious necessity of attending an information and registration meeting to get Posie into a summer soccer league, something Posie had talked about but decided against. *Seems like my best bet is to go with a Posie excuse. Melanie seems as determined for me to keep Posie's affections as she is for me to lose Tricia's.*

He'd made up his mind to catch her as she left work, but she made an appearance at her old afternoon time. When he trotted the story out, he got a mildly positive response.

"That's fine. I have to work a little late anyway to get my forty hours . . . I took a long lunch today. They're going to have me file some stuff." *That's strange. She fights harder than anyone I know to keep her lunchtime to a minimum. She hates working late. Oh, well, it gets me off the hook.*

*   *   *

Tricia was in an unusually upbeat mood when he arrived home and seemed uncommonly happy to see him.

"Oh, good, I'm glad you came home early tonight." So, on time is "early" now. *I'm glad I decided to skip Melanie's, looks like there's a chance to earn a few relationship points here.* Tricia took him aside in the hallway. "You know, it's Posie's birthday this weekend and I haven't shopped at all. She's invited some friends over, so we have to get party decorations and I don't even have any presents yet. I was just fixing some dinner for her and then I was going to the mall. Want to come?" *Excellent. Easy, positive activity.*

"Sure, love to."

"Well, get changed and I'll finish her dinner." She smiled and bustled back into the kitchen. Wes went up to the bedroom and began shucking his work outfit. *Why couldn't it be like this more often? It seems like we spend most of our time just tolerating each other. If we could be a little happy like this half the time, it would make all the difference to the marriage. Well . . . and more sex.*

The trip to the mall was a delight. They chatted easily about home and work, although Wes kept his turns brief and used them to paint a vague picture of burdensome conditions beyond his control and to apologize once again for his late hours. Tricia lightly brushed it all aside, regaling him with a backlog of humorous anecdotes from her seventh-grade English classes.

". . . but he really does try. His nonfiction book report was on a car-repair manual! And it was actually interesting! What a fascinating boy . . ."

They had supper in the food court. Wes had Italian, Tricia had Chinese. *She's very pretty when she's happy. Actually, she's still a beautiful woman . . . I guess it's possible to take anything for granted after a while. The happiness just adds a sparkle that's been missing for so long.*

"You're going to be beautiful your whole life," he said, toward the end of the meal. It was the first unasked-for compliment he'd given her in a long time, and she was surprised and delighted.

"My, thank you . . . what brought that . . ."

"I was just thinking how blind a person can be to something he sees every day. You really do have the kind of face that'll always look good."

"That's very nice of you to say," she said, smiling as she gently shook her head "but those little lines keep creeping in . . ." *Perfunctory self-criticism. But she's really pleased.*

"Smile lines," he responded. "You're gorgeous."

"Oh . . ." she said, glowing.

"I've thought about how most people have a particular age when they look their best. Of course, there are a few, like you, who look great straight on through . . . well, except for that one picture of you in fifth grade . . ."

"It was the mumps, I tell you, the *mumps!*" she said, laughing.

This is the woman I loved, who loved me . . . and I think I still do. "Anyway," he continued, "you have to feel sorry for the people who look best as infants, or toddlers . . . the glory days gone before they have a clue . . ."

"*You* were a cute baby . . ."

"Yeah, I know, it's been all downhill from there." He shook his head in mock dismay.

"Oh," she said, smiling warmly as she reached out to touch his cheek "I've always loved this face. I think you're very handsome." *Is she being straight with me, or is she just in a good mood? Can't tell. Either way, I'll take it.* "Well, thank you, ma'am, for your comforting imitation of sincerity. My ego thanks you, and my id wants to know if you're wearing underwear." Tricia let go with an open laugh of real amusement.

"You have *such* a sense of humor," she said, rising to start the shopping portion of the evening. Wes jumped up to do the table-clearing. *Politeness counts when you're on a date.*

The party decorations were a fairly quick purchase; the hunt for presents began.

"Thirteen-year-olds!" exclaimed Tricia. "Worse yet, soon-to-be fourteen-year-olds! Everything they see they want, but everything you get for them is all wrong. Well, you just have to get something and ignore the complaining." They had picked up a somewhat generic sweatshirt in a department store and were on their way to look at jewelry when Wes saw the gates of Hell opening in front of him.

Melanie!

She was walking toward them, looking in a store window, a few seconds away from spotting him. His mind went into hyperdrive: *Duck aside? No place to go. Trish would balk if I rushed her. No way to avoid Melanie. Stall, look ahead, like you don't see her. Handling Melanie: act cordial, put a little extra spark in your eyes just for her, add a shrug like you can't help being here. Handling Trish: stay a little closer to her than to Melanie, maintain obligatory physical contact.* He wished that he and Trish weren't holding hands. It would look suspiciously amicable to Melanie, and he was beginning to sweat. But it was too late.

"Well, hello, Wesley." Melanie's voice had a strong shading of trouble in it. Wes pretended to notice her for the first time.

"Oh . . . hey, hi, Melanie." He gave her the look and the shrug while Tricia's focus was on Melanie, but he found himself looking into cold eyes. *Could be a bad scene later.* Tricia dropped his hand, which was quickly becoming slick with sweat. He glanced at Tricia, who had plummeted out of her good mood. He gestured feebly in Melanie's direction. "This is Melanie, she works in customer service." He put his hand to Tricia's back, which stiffened in response. "And this is Tricia, my wife." *Why would I say, "my wife?!" Of course she's my wife!* "You two may have met at a Christmas party," he continued, grasping to stay afloat.

The women exchanged brief smiles and cool hellos. *Let's make this as quick as possible. I have to start repair work with both of them.*

Melanie turned to him, arms crossed, barely smiling. "So, Wes how was your meeting?" *Shit! She's calling me on it! Story needs to suit both sides . . .* He felt as though his face must be turning Guilt Red.

"Oh . . . it ended up being canceled. I guess they'll re-schedule it." *Please stop . . . don't say anything about soccer, or Posie.*

Tricia moved half a step away, breaking contact with Wes. Her voice was strained. "I can go on if you two need to talk about work."

"Oh, no, that's fine," said Wes, hurriedly. "We can talk at work tomorrow."

Melanie looked at Tricia. "It was nice to meet you."

"Yes, you too."

Melanie glanced briefly and angrily into Wes's eyes before striding away rapidly. When Wes looked back at Tricia, she was also walking away. He had to trot to catch up. *Start right away. Assess the damage.* "So. Where to next?"

"Home. I have some work to do. I'll finish shopping tomorrow."

"Well, let's just try one more place on the way out."

"Do what you want. I'm leaving." *Big damage.*

The ride home took a long time. Wes's conversation-starters were met with curt, conversation-stopping replies. *What could she have seen? How would it have been any different if I wasn't involved with Melanie? Man, and things were going so well tonight . . . now it's worse than before. Should I try calling Melanie? Run out for gas or something and make a call? I'd sleep better if I could at least find out how mad she was and could start apologizing.*

Once they were home, leaving for any reason seemed like a bad idea. *I need to be here to take my lumps when Trish feels like starting . . . and I can't think of a reason to go out that wouldn't seem suspicious under the circumstances.*

Tricia stayed pointedly busy the rest of the evening. Wes felt awkward, trying not to hover or follow her but not wanting to disappear in case she decided it was time to unload on him. The couple of times they passed in the hall she acted like a fifth grader who was trying not to catch cooties from inadvertent body contact. He gave up on initiating a conversation and settled in the living room, pretending to read the paper, so he could observe most of her comings and goings and at least give her the chance to make eye contact. When she finally did, it was to announce that she was going to bed. Since it was half-an-hour earlier than usual, Wes was unprepared and was left drifting in the hum of the refrigerator. *I couldn't leave fucking well enough alone, could I? Now what do I have? Two women who are really pissed off at me. I'm so bad at this . . .*

He went downstairs and channel-surfed until he fell into a tiring slumber on the couch.

CHAPTER 14

Melanie was not watching television.

She was crouched on elbows and knees in the living room in front of the sliding door, dressed in the lacy black bra and panties that she'd worn the first time she and Wes had sex. The lights were out. Moonlight filtering in through the slats in the vertical blinds painted thin bands of white over her coiled form.

Mimi padded up, curious. "Mrr?" asked the cat.

"Not too loud, Mims," whispered Melanie. "I'm hunting tonight." She remained still, peering out into the living room while Mimi sat down and licked at her paws in boredom.

Melanie took a deep breath through her nostrils and narrowed her eyes. "Do you smell that?" she said, still whispering. "There's definitely something out there. I'm going to have a look." She rose to hands and knees and crept out quietly. Mimi made a little sound in her throat and followed, trotting back and forth. Melanie swung her head slowly from side to side, looking intently into the shadows. She stopped in the middle of the room and sniffed again. "Where is that coming from? It seems so familiar . . ."

She continued off through the small entry to the front door, where she sniffed carefully along the bottom. Mimi did the same. A look of recognition came to Melanie's face. "Smell that? It's just like I thought. That . . . I hate to use the word, but that bitch is here."

Back they went, turning this time into the kitchen, where Melanie snuffled about over the floor. "No . . . no . . . not here . . ." Melanie smelled Mimi's food dish. "Eww . . . how can you eat this stuff? Well, you seem pretty happy . . . wait!" She froze, looking toward the closed door to the bedroom. Light shone through the thin gap along the bottom. "No! Not in my bedroom!" Her eyes narrowed in a look of menace. She crept slowly toward the door, focused on the thin strip of light. She paused when she reached it, sniffing vigorously along the bottom. Mimi scratched at the door, trying to push in.

"Back!" whispered Melanie tersely, pushing the cat away.

"Mai!" responded Mimi, in protest.

"She's in there. I go first." Melanie reached up and slowly turned the knob, then gingerly pushed the door until it swung open to reveal the source of the light. The small table lamp on her nightstand illuminated two dolls sitting in chairs on the floor. Her Wes doll was clothed as it had been previously, in coat and tie, and was facing the door. Facing him, with her back to the door, was a female doll with black hair that had been crudely hacked short, clad in a small brown paper bag out of which had been cut jagged openings for the head and arms.

"So, there you are," hissed Melanie as she sauntered in, still on all fours. "Look, Mimi, Tricia-bitch is here." She glanced at the male doll as she reached the little tableau. "Don't worry, Wes, I'll take care of this." She knelt behind Tricia. "So, Missy, what do you have to say for yourself?"

There was silence for a moment. Melanie bent closer. "I'm talking to you, whore. I suggest you turn around." Silence. Melanie's face tightened with rage. She grabbed the doll's torso with one hand and violently twisted the head around with the other. The face was a mess of magic marker – black circles around the eyes, blobs of red around the lips and on the cheeks, eyebrows that created a thick, savage "V" in the middle of the forehead, and an opposing, frowning "U" dropping down from the mouth. She settled the doll back in its chair, then sank to her belly to look it in the eyes.

Her voice became conversational. "Ooh . . . bad face day,

Trish? I just don't see what Wesley ever saw in you. But, hey, he's a guy. Who can figure 'em out?" Her face hardened. "The answer, bitch, is *me*. *I* can figure them out, and when I do, they belong to *me*." She moved forward until their heads almost touched. "And when they belong to me, it's time for everyone else to disappear."

She lay still for a moment, her eyes drifting. Then she energetically popped up to her knees. "Still, there's something you ought to see before you go." She cocked her head to one side. "What, not interested?" Rage flared in her again. "I INSIST!" she shouted, snatching up the doll. She ripped the head off and flung the body violently against the wall, then grabbed Wes and stood up. She put the ravaged doll head near the edge of the nightstand and tipped the lampshade so that the light shone on the bed. "Now, keep your eyes open, whore, and you might learn something."

She flopped on the bed on her back, clutching Wes to her chest. "Oh, Wes, baby, I'm sorry you had to see all that. You okay, honey?" She held him up close to her face and stroked his head. "Now, let's just forget that nasty ol' Tricia is here and relax. What would you like to do?" She held him close to her ear. "Ohh, yes, that sounds wonderful. You do such good things to me."

Melanie put Wes to her side , slipped off her panties, and tossed them across the room, then lay back and opened her legs. She picked up her Wes doll and positioned it so that its head was touching her clitoris. Moving the doll in small circles, she began writhing and moaning in mock arousal. She worked the head down and into her labia, increasing her vocalizations as she went. "See, bitch?" she hissed. "He's a good man. You shouldn't have treated him like that. It's your own fault."

Melanie quickly played out a porn-video version of rising passion and overwhelming orgasm, then brought Wes back up into her arms. "That was wonderful, baby. Here, let's give the bitch a sniff."

She held Wes's head in front of Tricia's. "Mmm . . . fresh and funky, right? What does yours smell like, an outhouse at a construction site? Wes would pass out if he went down on you."

She brought Wes back and held him up to her face. "Now, you sleep while I say goodbye." She kissed him once and tucked him under the covers, then rolled over on one elbow to address the head on the nightstand. "Wow, pretty wild, huh? I'll bet it's been a long time since you saw action like that. You'd probably need to set your dried-up old ass in a tub of oil before you could saddle up." She looked off in the direction that she had thrown the doll body. "But then, your dried-up old ass has already taken a powder. You must be getting lonely."

She sat up on the edge of the bed and opened the nightstand drawer. From it she retrieved a sandwich bag containing dark, dried crumbles. She inverted the head, picked out a small portion of the dried material, and carefully dropped it into the opening. She tore off a small bit of a cotton ball and sealed the opening, then held the head up so they were facing each other. She put her other hand up to her mouth as if whispering a secret.

"Catnip. Time to make new friends." She hurled the head out the bedroom door and heard it ricochet away as Mimi streaked after it.

CHAPTER 15

Thursday morning. Posie was upstairs getting ready for school. Wes put his breakfast dishes in the dishwasher and wiped the sink and counter with the dishcloth. He turned to wipe the table. Tricia was standing in the doorway, leaning on the wall, her arms folded. *Here it comes.* "Oh, hi," he said, putting one hand to his chest. "You startled me a little." He began to wipe the table.

"So, when were you planning to tell me what's going on?"

Careful! Stay calm . . . see what she knows . . . strike the right tone. "What do you mean?" he responded, as evenly as he could. *Don't sound too baffled or too indignant. That'll just make it worse.*

"How long were you planning on being 'late from work' before not coming home at all?"

Options . . . start with generalities . . . "I told you, sweetie, it's been worse than usual. A lot of people have quit . . . *it's sounding lame . . .*

Tricia straightened up and walked into the room. She leaned back against a counter, arms still crossed. "Why is it that you get phone calls from work when you're supposed to be at work?

Who would . . . no one said they tried to call . . . "What? When was this? I was probably in a meeting . . ." *No! Not at six p.m.! Stupid!*

"Yeah, right" she said, with angry sarcasm. "Last week, Posie said 'What's wrong with Dad? Is he nervous or something? It's like he's talking to himself.' Don't make me sound like an idiot here."

She's getting angrier. Have to give a little . . . He sighed and shook his head. "Look, you're right . . . I haven't been fair to you and Posie . . . my priorities have gotten all screwed up." *Got to keep it vague. I can't give her an opening to directly accuse me.* Tricia was quiet, staring, waiting for more. "I . . . I'm sorry, really . . . I didn't realize things had gotten so bad between us." *Take a chance.* "Last night, when we went out, it felt so good to see you happy again. You're such a beautiful woman . . . you have a face that was meant to smile." *A glimmer . . .* "It felt like it used to feel, and I was wishing it could be that way all the time. I felt so bad when you got upset." Her lips tightened as tears started to roll down from her eyes. She looked away. *Might get out of this. Keep going.*

He moved toward her, arms turned out apologetically. "Let me get myself straightened around. I didn't realize things were this bad. You deserve a lot better." He reached up to touch her arm, but she pulled away, shooting a red-eyed glance at him.

"Don't."

Wes dropped his hand and sighed again, keeping a careful watch on her face. *Her move next. Stay cool.*

She turned away to pick a napkin out of the napkin holder. She swabbed out both eyes and blew her nose loudly. "Wesley," she said, snuffling, "I want to tell you something. Not because I'm mad, which I am, but because it's true and I've been thinking about it for a while."

"Okay . . ."

"In a way, you've never gotten much past fifteen. Emotionally, I mean. You got stuck somehow . . ."

Careful . . . don't commit . . . "What do you mean?"

"You're like an adolescent in a man's body . . . you still get turned on by the same things that turned you on in junior high. I've seen the kind of women you look at. They're barely more than girls. Like that . . . Melanie."

Am I that obvious, that transparent? "If I'm looking at

anyone, it must be just automatic . . . a lot of guys . . ."

Her irritation was quick to return. "A lot of guys are pigs! Don't compare yourself to them!" She paused and changed to a more resigned tone. "I don't know what's going on with you these days, or what you're doing, but something's wrong and I think you'd better decide what to do about it." *She suspects, but she's giving me an out. A chance to shape up before an outright accusation. And she's not sure exactly what's going on. She hates to be wrong and sound stupid. Wrap it up.*

He nodded. "Okay," he said, quietly. She looked at him with a mixture of disappointment, sadness, and suspicion. He moved to hug her and she let him, briefly. He kissed the top of her head as she moved away, out of the kitchen. A wave of remorse washed through him. *She's angry because she's lonely and frightened and I'm lying to her. She needs affection too, but she won't cheat to get it.*

He made sure to kiss her goodbye when she left for work. The tension between them had returned to an uneasy simmer.

CHAPTER 16

When Wes looked up from his desk that afternoon, Melanie was leaning against the door frame, arms crossed, staring at him. *Oh shit, here comes the second barrel! Take the initiative.*

He started to rise. "Uh, Melanie, I . . ."

She broke into a smile and waved him back down. "Relax, baby. I'm not here to bite your head off." She sauntered over and sat on the edge of his desk, which he knew would look suspicious to any passersby, but perhaps no more than having a serious personal conversation in full view. "Was I mad last night?" she said. "Yes. Am I mad now? No. I know that plans change and I know you don't have much control over what goes on at home. It was just . . . I was just walking along and suddenly there you were, with her, holding her hand . . ." *I knew it!* ". . . and it just tore me up, because it should be *me* that you walk around with and hold hands with . . ." *Looks like another escape . . .*

"I know, I felt awful meeting you like that. I'm trying to keep her from being suspicious until the time is right. But she must have sensed something . . . she thinks there's something going on now . . ."

Melanie's face turned more serious. "There *is*. Maybe she should know. Maybe it's time that you told her."

This is not what I wanted to hear. Get to something solid. "Well, Posie . . ."

Melanie interrupted, annoyed now. "It's not doing Posie any good to live with parents who can't stand each other." *Why did I have to exaggerate that so much?* "It would be better for her to know the truth. She'll find out eventually, anyway." *She's so naive. How can you explain parenthood to someone with no experience?*

He sighed and glanced around, stalling. "It would be a lot better if Trish left me. I think she's thinking about it . . ."

"Well, give her something to think about" snapped Melanie. "Tell her you're moving in with me."

I'm not ready for this . . . show some weakness. He slumped, resting his forearms on his desk and bowing his head a bit. "I'm scared," he sighed. "I'm scared I'm going to lose my daughter." Melanie's face softened and she touched his shoulder lightly. *It worked.*

"Oh, baby, don't worry. It'll work out. I just know you'd be so much happier with me . . . so much happier sleeping in the same bed. Posie loves you; she'll still love you. Besides, the court won't let Tricia keep you apart." She bent a little to catch his eye. "We're so good for each other. I just want to get started with our life together."

Wes nodded and smiled a pretend smile, briefly glancing at her. "Yeah," he said, "me too." *Our life together . . . what kind of life will we have outside her apartment? We don't look like a couple, we look like bedmates. There aren't that many things we both like to do, or would even look natural doing together . . .*

"Well," said Melanie, brightening "even if we aren't going to start our lives together tonight, we may as well keep practicing." She winked and walked out.

Great, she's forgiven me. How do I leave her now? I can't walk out on her when she's down and I can't quit her when she's up. Any more stress and I'm going to implode and explode simultaneously.

*   *   *

That evening, Melanie poured two tumblers full of wine and brought them into the living room, where Wes was sitting on the couch. *She looks better today. More energetic.* She handed one to him and sat next to him.

"To us, forever," she said, tapping plastic against plastic.

"To us," repeated Wes, forcing the words out. Melanie took a long gulp. Wes took a sip. *Gack. This should be labeled "faux wine."*

"Mmm . . . do you like it?" she said. "Try a big swallow."

The things we do for lust. Oh, well, beats being fully conscious. He got up his nerve, held his breath, and knocked it back where he wouldn't taste it quite as much. He swallowed heavily and smiled as best he could. "Mmm . . . that's really something."

Melanie smiled and took another drink. *Odd, she didn't swallow.* She moved closer to him, her eyes gleaming. She tilted his head back and put her closed lips on his, motioning for him to open. *Oh, boy . . .* He parted his lips and she pushed in, pursing her lips and letting the wine flow slowly into his mouth. *Wow . . . it does seem to taste better this way . . .* He let it trickle down his throat, starting to feel some warmth inside. *I guess it's true . . . drink enough of any wine and it becomes good wine.*

When her supply was spent, she pulled away and nodded at his glass. "Your turn." *Well, why not?* He took a mouthful and they came together, Melanie tipping her head back and opening her mouth. He put his lips between hers and let the wine dribble out carefully. *Remember, she has a much smaller throat . . .* She sucked on his lips and gulped at the wine, apparently deriving great satisfaction from the activity. When his mouth was emptied, she licked his lips thoroughly, then ran her tongue inside along his gums.

She held up her tumbler. "Bottoms up!" *Oh, shit. Well, no point insulting her taste in wine . . .* They tossed back the fairly large quantity of remaining wine and set the glasses down on the coffee table. *"Coffee table" . . . there's an anachronism . . .*

"So," she said, rising, "why don't you go in the bedroom and get comfortable? I'll join you in a minute."

Yep, that sounds just fine. He stood up and they parted ways, Melanie going off into the bathroom. Wes wandered into the bedroom, feeling the warm rush of the wine. *Well, here we are. I may as well enjoy what I can, while I can. Let's get right to it.* He shucked off his clothes and lay stretched out on his back in the middle of the bed. The room glowed with curtain-filtered sunlight. *Sex is good.*

He heard the bathroom door open and looked up to see Melanie appear in the bedroom doorway, dressed in a stunning aqua outfit designed for the male mind: ribbed bustier with open cups, G-string panties, thigh-high stockings and garter belt, rhinestone choker and bracelets, and spiked high heels. Wes's head reeled in amazement. He propped himself up on his elbows for a better look as his penis began rapidly unfurling. *Other men would pay large sums of money for this . . .*

She moved her feet apart and put her hands on her hips in a mock-heroic pose. "Ready for *action*!"

"Yes, I guess you *are*! I wish I'd dressed for the occasion . . ."

She strutted to the bed. "Oh, you wore your best outfit. I know it fits *me* pretty well . . ." She sat beside him and went right to work with her mouth. Wes lay back on the pillow. *This is very good . . .*

When she had him well under way she reached down and shucked off her heels, then straddled him on the bed. She reached between her legs, pulled her panty string out of the way, and gently lifted his penis into position. Then she slid down and back until he was completely inside her. Wes sighed with great satisfaction. *This . . . feels . . . wonderful.* Melanie began rocking back and forth slowly – forward until he was almost out of her and then back to take him all the way in. Her hair hung down in a familiar blond cascade, brushing his face and his throat.

"You're very good," he whispered, knowing it was a cliché but really meaning it.

"Only because you make me feel so good."

He knew she was flattering him; she was just good. Still, he wanted to fully participate in this dream-world come to life and he began to thrust up as she slid back. He cupped his hands around the sides of her bustier, feeling the thin, silky fabric and the stimulating protrusions of the ribbed ridges, then moved up and in, circling over the exposed breasts that were thrust slightly up and forward by the bustier's open cups. Their pelvic motions settled into a steady rhythm as he delicately massaged her tender flesh, brushing her silky skin and softly stimulating her nipples.

They rocked together, slowly. She bent low, and her breath streamed hot against his face as she traced the lines of his eyebrows, nose, lips, and chin with her fingertips. He was really building now, tightly focused on the approaching explosion. She began to contract and relax her vaginal muscles with each sliding cycle. Wes gasped at the sensation. *Penis hugs! This girl really is talented.*

She grasped his wrists, pulled them up over his head, and pushed them down firmly into the pillow. She stopped moving and they lay, motionless and tense. She dropped her head, touching her cheek to his. She spoke close to his ear, her breath creating a tickling charge inside him.

"Wesley," she whispered.

"Yeah?" he breathed.

"What scares you?"

Something quickened in him. He came alert. A door swung open inside.

"You do, sometimes." *I can't believe I said that.* He could feel his heart beating faster.

"Good," she said. She tightened firmly around his penis and held it for a moment, sending a powerful wave of desire through him. He gasped. She relaxed inside but stayed seated against him. "You *should* be scared, Wesley. I'm a scary woman." *That's for damn sure!*

She squirmed her hips around in a tight circle, letting him

fully feel his ache. "Isn't this a pretty picture?" She stroked into his ear with the tip of her tongue. "I'm sure Tricia would think so."

He started, but not enough to escape her grasp. She held him to the bed. A wave of panic rose up from his middle, but he was so close to orgasm that when it reached his groin, it stiffened his penis to the point of discomfort. "What? . . ." he gasped weakly, his throat tight.

Her head rose up slightly, her face still close to his. "Hush, hush. We're just playing now."

He felt dizzy; the room turned around a little. He was desperate to orgasm and began to thrust against her again, grunting quietly down in his throat.

Her hands tightened around his wrists and she pressed her body full against his. "Not yet, baby." He lay still, panting with the effort.

Slowly, she opened her hands, maintaining fingertip contact with his upturned wrists. She sat up halfway. "Be a good boy now," she admonished, looking firmly into his eyes. She slowly rocked forward to slip off his penis, causing waves of sensation to pulse through him and very nearly push him into ejaculation. *Ohh . . . so close . . .* She swung her leg over to kneel beside him.

"I . . ." he began, turning his head toward her. She stopped him, holding a finger to his lips.

"Uh-uh," she admonished. "I said be good."

He rolled his head back to face the ceiling, his hands still above his head. His heart was pounding, his mind racing.

Melanie began flicking her fine little fingers across his upper body, like butterflies fluttering across a vast plain, contrasting her ethereal fineness with his relative bulk. Barely touching his taut skin, she flicked this way and that, around his abdomen and up to his chest. She brushed over his underarm hair, right on the borderline between tickling and arousing, then continued up the sensitive areas of his inner arm.

Feels like she's setting up an electrical field over my whole body.

She grasped each of his arms just below the wrist, crossing one over the other. Maintaining control with one hand, she slipped the other under to cradle his head. Her grip firmed and she looked at him in a disquieting way, with the barest hint of a smile at the corners of her mouth. Once again she arched forward, dropping her head to the side of his face, letting her breath stream across his cheek as her lips approached his ear. He felt powerless to move, and he dreaded what she would say.

Her words hissed into the center of his mind: "You need to be tied up." He gasped, twitching slightly but staying within her controlling hands. In his primal depths, lust and fear writhed together. Melanie maintained her contact for a moment, waiting for him to settle, then rose up over him, letting her hands fall away. "Stay," she said.

He didn't respond – he had nothing to say, but trembling assent was in his eyes. He had entertained thoughts of bondage in his fantasies, but the reality of it was stimulating him much more than he had imagined. As if she sensed this, Melanie floated her hand down to the base of his rigid penis and brushed a fingertip, like a feather, along its full length, creating an intense spasm.

She turned and sat on the mattress, then bent down to reach under the bed, returning with a shoebox. She tossed the lid aside and sorted through the contents, pulling out a shapeless handful of fine fabric and displaying it to him. It was a pair of her pantyhose.

"Smell," she said, holding the crotch to his nose. The smell of her filled his nostrils as he breathed deeply, her natural scent combined with a hint of her cologne. The wispy softness of the stockings played over his throat and cheeks, adding another dimension to the sensation. "Feels good already, doesn't it?"

"Yeah . . ." he barely whispered.

Melanie reached up and looped one stocking leg around his wrists, tying them snugly, then fastened what remained around one of the metal rods of her headboard.

She picked out another pair and paused briefly, her eyes glittering darkly, to kiss him lightly on the lips. Then she slid off the mattress and tied one of his ankles, pulling it to the corner of the bed and securing it underneath. She picked a final pair out of the box. Letting part of it drape over his chest, she moved down slowly, letting the delicate fabric brush over his genitals and down his free leg. She restrained the leg, then stood at the foot of the bed, hands on her hips, head slightly to one side, relishing the tableau.

Powerful crosscurrents surged through him. The fear produced by his restraint threatened to spiral into panic while at the same time highlighting his state of extreme arousal. *"A hunger you can't feed is ten times the need." Where did I read that? Man, do I need it right now!*

Melanie broke from her pose and sauntered around to the nightstand, sliding open the small drawer and producing another bit of fabric. She dangled it in front of him. *A sleeping mask.* Crawling back on the bed and straddling his stomach, just out of reach of his aching erection, she slipped the mask over his head and positioned it carefully over his eyes. *I didn't know it was possible to feel this naked.* He felt her lean forward, felt her hot breath on his cheek as she leaned to the side. She sucked on his earlobe, then shot the tip of her tongue deep into his ear, creating a sparkly tickling sensation that shot all the way to his feet. He gasped and shuddered.

"First is story time," she breathed. "Do you want me to tell you a story?"

Wes nodded eagerly. "Yes," he said. *I'd say 'yes' to anything right now.*

"You know what I'd like to do to you someday?" she whispered, kissing him very lightly on the temple. "I'd like to slip into your office . . ." She kissed him again, now on his cheekbone, ". . . and hide under your desk . . ." another kiss, moving just a trace, ". . . and undo your pants . . ." kiss, ". . . and lick you slowly . . ." kiss, ". . . up and down . . ." kiss, ". . . and slide you down my throat . . ." kiss, ". . . up and down . . ." kiss, ". . . and make you harder and harder . . ." kiss, ". . . and you'd have to sit there the whole time, and talk to people . . ." kiss, ". . . until you were going crazy . . ." kiss, ". . . and then . . ." kiss, ". . . maybe . . ." kiss, ". . . if you behaved yourself . . ." kiss, ". . . I'd let you come."

The words, and the visions that the words conjured up in his head, were powerfully erotic and, coupled with the hypnotic rhythm of the kisses, pushed him to the edge of restraint. He squirmed and moaned.

"Did you like that story?"

"Yes, yes."

"Good. Now it's play time. Tonight, we're going to play with . . . touch." He felt motion on the bed and heard her retrieve something else – *another box?* – from underneath it. Her voice returned, close by, to whisper: "I'll let you know if something is going to be relaxing or exciting, so don't worry." He could hear the sounds of things being moved in a box. "This will be relaxing."

A silky cloud brushed onto his chest and circled it. *A fur mitten, something like that.* The softness traveled up one arm and back down the other, swirled around his throat and face, then slid down the side of his chest to his hip and down his leg. *It's lighting up my whole body, bringing sensation to every corner.* The pressure firmed a bit as the cloud reached the sole of his foot, preventing it from tickling. *That's wonderful, wonderful.* Then it moved up the inner surface of his leg, barely brushing his testicles as it crossed over to his other leg, down and up and then enveloping his genitals, floating around, dusting, flicking, creating sparks of pleasure. Then it was gone. *I'm floating . . . my skin is alive.*

"Exciting," she said. There was a gentle whooshing sound, and a cool mist shocked the center of his torso. *A spray bottle, like a plant mister.* The spraying sound repeated, slowly and regularly. A rain of microscopic droplets fell, exhilarating him and tightening his skin. His nipples tingled, firmly erect. His breathing shifted to shallow gasps. *Tied up, sightless, my mind is hungry for input. It's grabbing every sensation it can get.* The misting subsided. He began to feel chilled.

"Relaxing." He was momentarily chilled by a downdraft, then blanketed by the warmth of a large, plush towel. *Ohh, that's nice.* The towel covered him from his neck to just below the knees. *I'm making quite a tent down there, I imagine.* His groin muscles were tightening and relaxing in pre-orgasmic contractions, causing his penis to bob up and down under the towel. *It's a circus tent! "And now, if you'll direct your attention to the center ring . . . "* The towel lifted, and then his extremities were patted dry. *I'm the captive, but I feel like the one being tended to.* Then the towel was gone. A slightly longer pause this time. *What could . . .?*

Her voice was throaty: "Exciting." Something touched the top of his chest. A light, unmistakable sensation of cold metal. *A knife!* He gasped, tension shot through him, fear uncoiled from the shadows. "Settle down, baby," she crooned. He felt the blade tip up until only the sharp edge was in contact with his skin. Then it moved, snaking down over his abdomen, toward his . . . *oh no, oh no . . .* then it lifted. Nothing for a moment. His eyes were twitching frantically under the mask. *Where . . .* Suddenly, the hard edge was back, across the base of his throat.

"Uuhh," escaped involuntarily as his muscles went rigid. *Bleeding hands reaching out of the darkness . . .* "Melanie . . ." he croaked. The blade lifted.

"Nothing's happening, honey. We're just feeling things, remember?" His heart thumped like a drum as he pushed the panic back down. "Now, just feel it, don't think about it." The blade returned, this time at the side of his throat, and ran in a delicate arc over to the other side. *Blood . . . so close to my blood.* The sensation ended. Nothing for a moment, slight movement on the bed. Then . . .

"NO!" *The base of my penis!* His limbs convulsed against the restraints. *Wait, wait, it's only* . . . Melanie's pointed tongue slid slowly up to the tip of his throbbing erection.

"Really felt *that* didn't you?" she said. He felt her lips part as they surrounded the head and slipped down around the shaft.

"Oh . . . yeah . . ." *Please let this be it.* With tongue and lips she quickly lifted him to the trembling peak of orgasm. With practiced fingers, she retrieved his testicles from their pre-orgasmic shelters, skillfully tugging them out and holding them with gentle firmness. Her mouth went down, down over his erection, her tongue sliding back and forth. *Oh, good . . . good . . .* Her lips slid up and off, sucking as they went.

"Just one more thing, gorgeous," she crooned. "I want a little souvenir of tonight." The cold, sharp pressure of the blade reappeared at the base of his testicles.

"NO!" he croaked. "NO!" As he struggled against the stockings, her mouth plunged down on his erection and began working in earnest. His mind whipped back and forth between the hot wetness surrounding his penis and the sharp knife edge pressing against his scrotum. His pelvic muscles locked tight, and the tightness shot out to all corners of his body, setting him into a vibrating rigidity. All other thoughts and emotions vaporized as the first giant spasm of ejaculation exploded. Sparks of light flashed in his head, bands of color uncoiled and leaped as he pumped furiously, grunting, drenched in sweat. The knife was gone, his testicles were released – all that remained was the sweet sensation of her mouth, carrying him on and on through one shuddering contraction after another. He felt like a speedboat skipping over the waves at two hundred miles an hour, gradually slowing as he approached shore. Finally, the end drew near and Melanie slowed her movements to guide him to a post-orgasmic landing. The contractions faded slowly into twitching aftershocks. *That was beyond intense . . . like sex heroin . . . she's a sex witch, shooting me up . . .*

He could feel her leave the bed and then the restraints on his ankles give way and disappear. As he moved his legs together she gently lofted the sheet and pulled it up to his waist. Next his wrists were released and he brought his arms down to rest at his side. She sat next to him and bent close, whispering, "That was wonderful." His lips were too relaxed to respond. She removed the sleeping mask, kissed him on the forehead, and smoothed his hair back. Then she lay next to him, up on one elbow, and stroked up and down his chest. He drifted into an ocean of relaxation washing through his body.

He kept on drifting . . .

CHAPTER 17

Wes jerked awake with a grunt. *Birds . . . morning birds . . . dawn!* He whipped over to look at the clock. *5:43!* "Omigod!" he whispered hoarsely, bolting out of bed and startling Mimi into doing likewise.

Melanie stirred. "Huhh . . .?"

"What happened?! We slept through!" Wes began frantically pulling on his clothes, his mind racing. *How can I possibly explain this?*

"Oh, I'm so sorry, baby," said Melanie, examining the clock. "I just wanted to lie with you for a little while . . ."

Can I use a work excuse? . . . what could possibly last that long, and why wouldn't I call? . . . Accident? . . . too complicated . . . out drinking? Drunk? Big trouble there, but not as much as this . . . and I really was drinking! Jeez, was it that damned cheap wine? He was dressed in a flash. *Should I call from here, see what's up, start the story? Where would I be calling from?*

Melanie had departed for the bathroom and returned, clad now in an old white terrycloth bathrobe. "What are you going to tell her?" she said, crossing her arms.

"I don't know," he replied, his eyes darting, his body a mass of nerves. *Alright, drinking, I was drunk, I'm calling from a friend's house.* He looked at the phone with dread. *I've got to do this. It'll be better than walking in cold.* He picked up the receiver and punched the buttons. *Get right on top, get it started . . .* The phone on the other end was picked up after one ring.

"Hello?" came Tricia's voice. *She's been crying. Big*

emotional charge.

"Trish, I'm so sorry . . ."

"Where are you? I've been up since one-thirty . . ." *Huge anger. Very bad.*

"I went out with the guys, I should have called . . ."

"Where are you right now?!"

"I'm at Mark's, I guess I had too much . . ."

"Oh, I don't care. Just get home. No, I don't care what you do . . ." The phone slammed dead. *Okay, at least she can quit worrying and get started on the anger. And I know sort of what I'm walking into.*

Melanie had been standing off by the door, scowling slightly, arms crossed under her breasts. "What'd she say?"

Wes ran a hand roughly over his face. "She's really mad."

She came to him and put her arms around him. "Oh, baby, what are you going to do?"

He gave her a brief hug back. *Got to go.* "I've got to go, got to straighten this out."

She held on to his arm as he pulled away. "How long are you going to put up with this? Just tell her . . ."

"Soon, soon . . . I just don't want to split up like this." *I don't want her to know about you, ever . . . talk about mad . . .*

It was almost a 20-minute drive to his house from Melanie's apartment with no traffic. *I just want it to be safe and boring again. Just go back. No Melanie, no affair, just Trish and Posie and work. I just want that back. Trish doesn't deserve this shit . . . It'll be a struggle to spend time with Posie if we split . . . I'd better get ready to get hammered . . . I'm going to take a lot of punishment on this one.*

He pulled into the driveway and ran to the front door. *Locked.* He unlocked it and stepped in cautiously, looking around the living room and dining room. He walked toward the stairs, eyes darting about for Trish. Dressed in a robe and slippers, she appeared at the top of the stairs, arms folded, her eyes and nose red from crying.

"Hi," he said, as apologetically as possible. She said nothing as she began to descend, so he continued into the kitchen and leaned on a counter. *Better give us a little room to maneuver . . .* She entered after a moment, sniffling.

"I'm really . . ." he started, but she cut him off with a motion.

"You had better just play it straight with me and tell me what's going on."

"I told you, sweetie . . ."

"Don't 'sweetie' me, and I hardly think you 'went out with the boys' and didn't call until six the next morning. Give me a little credit."

Stick with it. Time to gamble. "Okay, I'm sorry. Call Mark if you want . . ."

"Oh, right, I'll really believe that weirdo." . . . *Good, she won't call . . . sounds like she wants to believe the story . . .*

"I don't know what's wrong with me. I know I said I'd straighten things out . . ."

She raised her hand again. "I just can't do this anymore," she said, close to tears. "Whatever's going on, I just can't do this." She paused, drawing on some inner strength. "I want you to go. Now, before Posie gets up. I'll tell her you had to leave on business. You go and figure out what you need to do and let me know. I'm tired of wondering and waiting. I want to get on with my life."

Better take it. Sounds like the only real option. "Okay," he said, starting for the basement.

"The suitcase is already on the bed. And your garment bag." *Good. Best to get out fast.* He turned and walked up the stairs, down the hall and past the closed door of Posie's room. A pang of regret shot through him. *Better not think about it now. Work it out later.*

The small but efficient portion of his mind devoted to trip-packing took over. He grabbed stacks of underwear and socks out of drawers and transferred them to the suitcase. Tricia was hovering around the bedroom door, snuffling, occasionally blowing her nose. Into the case went his gym shorts and swim trunks. *Swim trunks? That looks stupid. But they're already in.* He picked out his favorite casual shirts from the closet, still on hangers, and set the whole pile in the suitcase, folding them over once to fit.

He hooked the garment bag on the closet door and hung in it the drab jackets, shirts, and slacks that he wore to work. In the large, zippered pockets he put a pair of sneakers and some ties. *Almost done. Now that the decision is made, I've got to get out. Can't stand having her look at me like that . . . all that pain and anger.* He stepped into the master bathroom and reached under the sink for his kit bag, quickly piling all of his toiletries into it. He made room for it in the suitcase, which he zipped shut. He closed the garment bag, unhooked it, and folded it half to carry. *Run the gauntlet and get out.*

"I'm sorry, Trish . . ." *Have to say something.*

"Just go," she said, soggily.

He passed her and walked toward the stairs. *How many times I've walked through here, happy . . . stop thinking! This is bad enough already!* He turned as he went through the front door for a final look at Tricia, who had followed him down the stairs. *I hope I look as regretful as I feel.* Tricia's wounded look remained unchanged. Wes hustled to the car, tossed his bags in the back seat, and pulled out. As he shifted into drive, he glanced up at the door to see if Tricia was standing there. It was already closed.

He pulled out of the neighborhood and back on the route he'd just traveled. *I guess it's back to Melanie's. I won't be able to beg myself back into the house until I get things resolved with her.*

The morning traffic was starting to thicken a bit as he drove back to the apartment. *Well, Melanie's getting part of her wish: I'm out with Trish and in with her. I just haven't told Trish about her. Like I really need to. Trish knows. She just didn't force it any further, maybe to leave a door open for reconciliation. I hope so.*

And what the hell happened last night? It was like I went into a coma! The wine, the crazy sex . . . but I've certainly had more to drink and not passed out. Did someone want to force the issue? Me? Melanie? Both of us? I feel like there's stuff going on that I'm not conscious of.

*   *   *

Melanie opened the door. She still had her robe on but had showered and done her hair and makeup. Her face softened into a look of warm concern.

"Oh, baby, come on in . . . are you okay?"

He sighed, dropping his bags inside the door, and they held each other. Mimi appeared and rubbed against his legs, purring. "Yeah, I'm okay," he said quietly. *At least I won't have to pretend to Trish that nothing's wrong. But I can't let her find out where I'm staying, or who I'm staying with. That would be the last, last straw. And I don't want that to happen.*

"Does she know about us, then?"

He shrugged. "Kind of. She was already mad enough . . ." Melanie looked disappointed. *Can't deal with any more right now.* "Listen, the important thing is, we're together now. And we both have to get to work. We'll have plenty of time to talk tonight." *Careful. This is an emotional upheaval for her as well.* He held her head gently with both hands and looked into her eyes, smiling as warm a smile as he could muster. "We can spend the night together, just lie in each other's arms." *Gulp.* Melanie's face brightened.

"That's right. This is our home now. So, I guess it's time for my handsome man to jump in the shower and get ready for work!" Something occurred to her. "Oh, and this!" she said, bustling into the kitchen. As Wes wandered in, she pulled her hand out of her purse, holding up a key attached by a ring to a flat red heart ornament.

"Ah," he said, accepting it with a weak smile. She seemed

very pleased with her new sense of domesticity. *I feel like I'm playing house here . . . alright, just get on with it. I've got to screw my head back on and make sure I don't lose my job, too.*

There was no good way to refuse when Melanie made it clear that she wanted to ride to work in his car. *Fucking swell. I really need everyone at work knowing about this.* Fortunately, they used different doors to enter the building – Melanie at the front and Wes around the side near the loading dock – and no one was within visual range when he dropped her off after as brief and inconspicuous a kiss as he could get away with. *Now the question is, will she blab? As social as she is . . . but I kind of don't think she will, right away anyway.*

Exiting at the end of the day was not as successful. A few people leaving at the same time glanced their way as he opened the car door for her. *Well, that's that. It'll start through the gossip chain on Monday.*

* * *

Wes cringed a little as they entered the apartment building. *Feels odd tonight . . . this is home now . . . seems like there are a lot of hours to fill before bedtime. Things can sure change fast.*

"Honey, we're home!" laughed Melanie, breaking with her routine as she opened the door. Then she fell right back in, feeding Mimi and glancing at her machine. *Still not ready to share everything with me.*

Melanie apparently believed that she was a natural cook and threw together a chicken dish involving onions and cheese. Wes felt awkward as he tried to help with the dinner, having to ask repeatedly where things were and getting in the way when he attempted to assist, so he ended up a spectator as Melanie bustled about, chatting, doing her best impression of wife and homemaker. The meal was not all that tasty. *Trish can cook rings around her. But then, how many people have affairs so they can eat better?*

They had what already felt like perfunctory sex after dinner, then spent the rest of the evening on the couch, watching TV. *Well, here's something else we can do together, something we're both good at. Man, talk about fast changes . . . our first night together, unlimited time, and we stare at the tube.* His stomach maintained a feeling of bloat the entire time, churning uncomfortably on occasion. *That chicken feels digestion-proof. I barely made it through sex . . . too much movement makes me feel seasick. Whatever weird magic she has, it must stop at the kitchen door . . .*

It took him a long time to get to sleep. Whenever he drifted close, his mind weakened and filled with longing and regret. *Trish . . . Posie . . .*

CHAPTER 18

During the time that Wes and Melanie were lounging in front of her television, another drama was unfolding in the city that was home to Melanie's sister and father. In a part of that town that would never undergo gentrification, Ron sat at the bar of a dive named Rocky's, smoking cheap cigarettes and calculating how much longer he could afford to drink. It was one of a handful of establishments that he had on an informal rotation. He was a surly and combative patron and had been banned more than once at more than one place. His solution was to spread the pain of his presence enough to keep him in grudging good graces.

He was well into his drunk and storm clouds were rolling in on his brow. "Fucking losers!" he grunted, referencing the game on the TV over the bar.

The bartender, Greta, was a no-nonsense woman who had worked there for as long as anyone could remember. She was keeping an eye on him but knew enough not to engage.

A group of three regulars had come in some time after Ron and taken up residence at a corner table. They could be troublemakers in their own way, tending more toward irritating tomfoolery than belligerence. Jimmy, in particular, had a knack for button-pushing that his friends found reliably hilarious but that his targets found unfailingly annoying. He was familiar with Ron's weaknesses and decided to have a little fun. Glancing at his pals, he tipped his head in Ron's direction and got up. The others rose and followed him as he ambled casually to the bar and rested his arms a couple of steps from his quarry.

"What?" said Greta, sensing trouble.

"Shots," said Jimmy, making a small circular motion with his finger. As Greta reached for the glasses, he added, "And one for Ronster here. He's having a bad night." Ron continued to stare at the television as Jimmy turned toward him with smile. "Ronster! Long time."

Ron grunted, barely turning his head. He didn't like being called "Ronster," especially by Jimmy, but he liked free liquor, so it was a wash. "Jesus!" he exclaimed, his full attention back on the game.

"This is what happens when you trade your best guys for sacks of shit," said Jimmy, glancing at the screen. "They must have been high."

Greta had poured and distributed the shots like a magician performing a well-practiced card trick. Jimmy lifted his glass, followed by his compatriots, and then after a moment, Ron.

"To those fucking losers," said Jimmy raising his glass toward the television.

"Losers!" echoed the friend next to him. Ron said nothing. They all tossed back their drinks.

There was a lull in the conversation. Greta hovered nearby, even more watchful than usual.

"Actually," continued Jimmy, "I'm a little surprised to see you here."

"Oh?" said Ron, warily, turning his head just enough to look at Jimmy.

Greta's eyes sharpened.

"It's just that, you know, with your family in show business . . ."

"Jimmy!" snapped Greta. Ron rose, glowering, and faced Jimmy. "Ron, now..." she cautioned.

"What the fuck are you getting at?" said Ron, slurring a bit.

"Pete!" said Greta, over her shoulder, getting the attention of the burly co-worker near the other end of the bar.

"Hey," said Jimmy, backing up half a step and spreading his hands. "I can't help it if I see people here and there."

"Jimmy, shut up!" she said, as forcefully as she could.

"Where?" growled Ron, inching closer. "When?"

Pete loomed into the situation. Ron was big, but Pete was massive, like a bank safe with arms. "You guys can shut it down or take it outside," he said, wrapping one hand around the handle of a baseball bat positioned under the bar.

"All I'm saying is that I was at Pole Kats . . . when was it?" said Jimmy, turning to his companions. "Last week sometime?" They nodded, smirking. Jimmy turned back to Ron, who was now right on the edge. "Quite a show," said Jimmy, "I'm sure you're proud."

"You . . ." snarled Ron, grabbing a handful of Jimmy's shirt.

In an instant, Pete had clamped one massive hand around Ron's wrist and pulled out the bat with the other. "Goddammit, you are all out of here! Now!"

Ron had once been on the receiving end of that same bat; he decided to vent his wrath on a more pliant subject. He let go of Jimmy's shirt and relaxed enough for Pete to release his grip. Jimmy beamed with satisfaction. His friends made minimal efforts to quell their inebriated laughter.

"Pole Kats, huh?" growled Ron. "We'll see about this." He paused briefly, still glaring at Jimmy, not quite ready to let it go. He pointed a finger at Jimmy's face. "I don't need you getting into my family's business."

Jimmy was about to take a swing at that low-hanging pitch but was warned off by a very stern look from Pete. "No," he mouthed, waggling the bat.

Ron, who was paid up due to his lack of tab privileges, turned abruptly and steamed out the door. He knew where his daughter would be.

*   *   *

Jeremy and Miranda were hanging out at his family's

house, sitting on a couch in the living room, grazing on the household supply of snacks and watching TV. Jeremy had sunk down and stretched out his legs to rest them on the coffee table. Miranda was curled up in a ball with her head on his shoulder and her arm draped over his chest, maintaining as much contact with him as possible. Jeremy's mother, Diana, was next door in the dining room, poring over a table full of work papers from her realty practice. Diana always felt a particular comfort when Jeremy and Miranda were nearby. She genuinely wished that she could convince Miranda to move in with them, a view shared by Jeremy's father, who worked nights as a press supervisor for one of the city's main newspapers.

Miranda truly did feel at home. She felt cared-for in a way that she never had with her own family. The burden of responsibility that she had felt as long as she could remember was magically lifted whenever she walked through the door.

Jeremy sipped the last of his soda, pondered briefly, then made a move to get up. Miranda patted his chest. "Mm," she said, in the shorthand of lovers. She hopped off the couch, stepped around the coffee table and headed toward the kitchen. Her route passed through the dining room, where Diana looked up and smiled. "Hey," she said.

"Hey," replied Miranda, smiling as well.

"Need anything?"

"No, just a drink, thanks."

"Okay, let me know." As she so often did, Diana thought of the empty bedroom upstairs, vacated when Jeremy's older brother left for college. She knew that it would be a sore temptation for Miranda and her son, living in such proximity, but the thought of seeing that sweet girl tucked safely into bed filled her with tender longing. She had to restrain herself a little when greeting Miranda or seeing her off. She always wanted to squeeze her tight and tell her that she was loved, but she always settled for a quick embrace or a smile and a wave.

She didn't want to overstep.

Miranda entered the kitchen. The lights were on, as they always were in that household from dusk until the last person went to bed. It was of many subtle things that made the home feel prosperous and inviting. The refrigerator itself, with its patchy coating of taped and magnetized pictures, notes, and memorabilia, felt like an invitation: there was plenty room left for a picture of her and Jeremy, or with the whole family, or something as simple as a note she could write, a reminder that they were almost out of butter.

She swung the door open to reveal a thriving family's store of food and drink, with shelves that had to be constantly rearranged to accommodate new supplies. It contrasted with the dismal emptiness of her home's fridge, which was hardly worth opening unless one desired cheap beer. She pulled out the can of soda and let the door swing shut. This home could be hers. And yet it couldn't be hers.

She passed back through the dining room, this time just exchanging brief smiles with Diana, and made her way back to Jeremy. She paused for a moment to open the can for him; he took it with a smile. "Hungry?" he said. "We could order pizza."

"Oh, no, I'm fine," she replied, patting her belly, as she sat down beside him.

"'Kay."

She curled up and nestled into him, inhaling his unique combination of cologne and deodorant, with just the slightest hint, reassuring to her somehow, of his sweat. They drifted, as happy as they could be.

*   *   *

The shock of heavy pounding on the front door rudely interrupted the domestic reverie. It was a sound that telegraphed trouble. Jeremy and Miranda instantly knew who it was and shot up from the couch. "Daddy!" she gasped. Jeremy reflexively moved in front of Miranda, momentarily unsure what to do.

The pounding stopped, then resumed again almost immediately. Diana strode out of the dining room toward the door.

"Mom, don't!" barked Jeremy, to no effect. Diana sensed that something was up but was not one to shy from a challenge.

"Here," said Jeremy, pulling Miranda toward the study, just off the living room. "Get in the closet," he hissed as they entered, pushing her toward a set of folding doors. She opened one, revealing the closet's role as a clothing storage annex.

"Get in!" he snapped.

Jeremy's mother had arrived at the front door and peered through the peephole. She could see Ron, agitated, as he unleashed another volley of pounding. "Who is it?" she said loudly, although she was quite certain she knew.

"Where's Miranda?" shouted Ron.

"She's not here. You need to leave."

"O-pen-this-door!" he said, accenting each syllable with a beat on the door.

"I'm calling the police!" she barked, and it was not an idle threat. She turned and strode rapidly toward the kitchen.

In the den, Miranda had pushed the clothing aside and stepped in, leaving the door open just enough to watch Jeremy as he darted around the desk and yanked open a bottom drawer. He tossed a wooden box on the desk, opened it, and pulled out a 9-millimeter pistol. Miranda gasped, clapping her hand to her mouth. The gun belonged to Jeremy's father, who had shown him the basic operation of the firearm and taken him target shooting a few times. Jeremy snatched a loaded magazine out of the box and snapped it into place. "Oh, no no no no . . ." whispered Miranda into her hand.

Jeremy moved cautiously to the door of the study. The pounding had stopped. He could hear his mother making the call to the police. He took a few cautious steps into the living room, toward the front entry.

An explosion of shattering glass shocked him. Ron had hurled the bowl of a concrete bird bath through one of the tall windows on either side of the front door.

"Jeremy!" screamed Diana, from the kitchen.

Ron kicked a couple of large glass shards from the window frame and began squeezing his way through, shredding his shirt. He stumbled to one knee as he gained entry, then lurched to his feet. "Where is she?!" he bellowed.

Jeremy, overcoming the shock of the intrusion, made a hasty attempt to charge his weapon. He had forgotten how tight the pistol's slide was, and on the first two attempts his fingers slipped and the slide snapped forward before a round could be chambered.

Ron took advantage of this delay to make his way into the living room, circling around Jeremy on a path toward the study. "Miranda!" he shouted.

Finally cocking the pistol, Jeremy raised it in the two-handed grip his father had shown him, aiming at Ron. "Get out," he snarled. Ron had almost made it to the recently vacated couch, where he paused. "Now!" shouted Jeremy, gripping the pistol. Although his father had explained the importance of keeping his finger off to the side until ready to fire, in the confusion of the moment he was pointing the gun at Ron with his finger in firm contact with the trigger.

As drunk and enraged as Ron was, he immediately recognized the acute threat he was facing: a nervous amateur with a gun. He stood as still as his sobriety would allow and raised his hands off to his sides, palms forward.

"Put that thing away, son."

Jeremy kept the gun wavering in Ron's general direction. "You need to go, now."

"Where's Miranda."

"She's not here. Get out."

"Do not lie to . . ." The gun went off. Jeremy had squeezed the trigger just a hair too much. Startled by the first shot, he reflexively squeezed again, firing a second time in rapid succession. The first bullet passed through the outer portion of Ron's right thigh, barely grazing the bone. The second round splintered the spindly leg of an end table just to his side.

"Jeremy!" his mother shrieked from the kitchen, this time in panic. To Jeremy, it sounded as though her voice was coming through foam padding, as the sharp noise from the gunfire had partially deafened him. Simultaneously, Miranda screamed from the den. Ron groaned with pain and fury. As he sank to the side, he reached out to support himself on the damaged table, which collapsed under his weight. He grunted and snarled, fighting to stay upright.

Jeremy, shocked at what had just happened, backed away, taking his finger off the trigger and pointing the gun at the ceiling.

In a flash, Miranda darted from the den and raced between Ron and Jeremy toward the front door. "Andie!" shouted Jeremy.

Ron roused himself, roared with rage, and using what leverage he could with his good leg, grabbed the end table and hurled it at his fleeing daughter. A moment sooner and she might have been knocked to the floor by the projectile, but it smashed on the side of the arch leading to the entry area just after she had passed through. Jeremy's mother, still on the phone with the police, had stretched the cord enough to see into the living room. "Miranda!" she screamed, not knowing in the moment how best to protect the girl. But Miranda was hearing nothing. She had to get as far away as she could, as fast as she could.

"The police are coming!" Jeremy's mother shouted at Ron, who was awkwardly making his way to his feet. "Get out now!"

Jeremy sidled toward the entry area. He set his feet, blocking Ron from the front door. "No," he said, not sure how loudly to speak over the thready note of tinnitus now sounding inside his ears. "You stay where you are. If you try to go after her I will kill you." He focused, breathed, straightened his arms, and sighted the gun on the center of Ron's torso. Approaching sirens wailed.

Ron's pant leg was beginning to glisten with blood. He sank to the floor and fumbled with his belt, intent on fashioning a tourniquet.

Out in the darkness, Miranda ran and ran.

CHAPTER 19

Saturday morning. Wonder if I'll be able to get away to work.
He was at the table, eating unfamiliar cereal out of an unfamiliar bowl, uneasy at being away from his comfortable routine and environment. *I don't like having to think about everything, about what we'll do and where we'll go and who makes the bed . . . or how I can get out of this and go home.*

Melanie decided that they would go to a park. "It's supposed to rain tonight and tomorrow. Let's go get some sun." *Okay, not going to work today. Didn't think it was much of a possibility.*

They drove a bit, to a park on the edge of town that was usually less crowded. They stepped out of his car, into the sunshine and quiet, and began a slow stroll on a path. *Feels good to be out of that cave of hers.*

"This is nice. Good idea," he said.

"I like the sun. I like getting a good tan every summer . . ." Her voice trailed off and she squeezed his hand. They walked in silence for a few minutes. *I wonder if I'm really what she was looking for . . . what does she want out of life? What does she think she can get from me? I have no idea. She's become such a fragile little thing. Maybe I'm just noticing because I've been spending so much more time with her. It seems like she used to be more robust. There's not a whole lot of her to begin with. If she lost just a couple of pounds it would show.*

Melanie spoke. "I don't think I told you . . . I'm going to be gone Monday and Tuesday, I'm taking vacation to visit a friend I haven't seen for a long time." *Good, some time to myself.* "Those are her days off, that's why I have to go during the week. I'm actually leaving tomorrow afternoon." *Good, good . . . I can concentrate on work, maybe figure out what to do about Tricia, about this whole mess . . .*

They were at the park for a long time. They walked all the paths, played on the playground equipment, tossed things into a pond, and lay together in the sun. *At least we can feel a little good, for a little while . . .*

After a late lunch out, a forgettable movie, and a late supper, also out, they returned to the apartment, undressed, and lay together under the covers. Melanie turned to him. "Wes, I know how you must feel. I lost my mom, moved away from my sister . . . and my dad . . . I've felt alone for a long time. I could forget about it for a while, with a boyfriend, but you're the first man who's made me feel like I have a family again, like I have a home . . ."

Wes's heart softened, and he held her closer. "You deserve a home, and happiness." *Everyone deserves a home, and happiness. But I really don't think I'm the man for her.*

"It feels so good, just having you hold me," she said quietly.

"It feels good to hold you." *Felt good . . .*

They lay in silence and dozed off.

*   *   *

The phone rang. *Hmm? Dark out. Rain starting.* Melanie fumbled with the phone, then picked it up. Wes waited for the verbal signals that would tell him who was calling.

"Hello? . . . Andie! . . . What? What?!" *Her sister.* A longer pause. "He . . . omigod . . . okay, okay, we'll be right there . . . never mind, never mind, just stay there, we'll be right there. Okay! We're coming!" She slammed the phone down and leapt out of bed, energized. "Miranda's here. She's at the bus station. We need to go."

In the car, Melanie caught him up on the situation as best she could. "Miranda started dancing at clubs about a year ago." Wes looked at her in bewilderment. "I know, I know, she's way too young. Believe me, I've tried talking her out of it. But she found out how much she could make, pay the bills, and still go to school. And really, I think she likes it, she likes the attention. Our dad, giant asshole that he is, takes the money and, if he's drunk enough, beats her up. I guess he broke into Jeremy's house, her boyfriend's house, and Jeremy shot him."

"What?! How bad is it?"

"Well, he's not dead, so not bad enough, except that that would be big trouble for Jeremy. But no, he's just in the hospital, shot in the leg. Supposedly he'll go to jail when he's released."

They drove through the rain, with the wipers going and other cars making swishing sounds as they passed. *It's like waking into a hallucination, an adrenaline dream.*

Wes was thoroughly suburban. The thought of going downtown at night induced a sense of foreboding, and thinking about the kinds of people he might encounter at a bus station at night made him feel even more unsettled.

He thought back many years to his only lengthy bus trip. *Miserable. Seemed like everyone smoked, and that one guy kept going in the little bathroom to smoke dope, like we couldn't all smell it. And the guy next to me with the really long fingernails . . .* He shuddered a little. *Train travel was so much better. I do miss that . . . sitting up in the dome car at night, with the train swaying along, watching the lights off in the distance . . .*

A truck speeding by and splashing the windshield brought him back. He shook his head and glanced over at Melanie, who had lapsed into silence. *When you enter into a relationship like this, you take on the other person's whole life, not just them . . .* She was staring straight ahead, distracted and nervous in the passing glare of the streetlights and dim glow from the dashboard, her hands gripped tightly in her lap. Her eyes and face revealed a mind in turmoil. *She's off some-*

where. Looks like she's replaying scenes from her past . . . scenes that caused her to flinch involuntarily now and again. He noticed that she was rocking back and forth in her seat, almost imperceptibly. At one point, she said, more to herself than to him, "That son-of-a-bitch . . ." *She's really getting wound up. I should see if I can ease the pressure a little.*

"Melanie? How are you doing? What are you thinking?" She stopped rocking and took a breath, glancing briefly in his direction.

"Too much . . . too much . . . I'm flying around in circles." She shook her head. "This is just bringing everything back, stuff I've tried to forget about for so long." *Twenty-three years old and she feels like she's lived for a long time . . .* She spoke to herself again: "That bastard . . ."

I need to word this delicately. "How was it with your dad, when you were growing up?"

A dozen emotions rolled across her face in quick succession. "Oh . . . he was . . ." Dark, heavy things roiled around in her head. It was too much, and she grunted it off. "Don't want to talk about it . . . not now." She sighed, stared out the window and returned to silence. *There's a lot I don't know about her.*

They pulled into the parking lot and dashed through the rain to the terminal. *Feels like we're on a commando rescue mission. I wouldn't mind having a gun.* Inside the building, they were awash in the same fluorescent glare that greeted Wes every day at work. *Kind of a similar atmosphere, tired people who'd rather not be here . . . although a few actually look more energetic than my crew. Could be worse.*

Across the garishly lit room, nervously seated with her back to a wall, a small girl wearing a purple nylon jacket with orange and yellow trim over washed-out jeans spotted them almost immediately. She shouldered a large backpack and shot out of her seat toward them.

"There she is!" said Melanie, rushing to meet her. Wes

followed. As so often happened with Melanie at work, all the male eyes followed Miranda as she raced into her sister's open arms.

"Oh, baby . . ." said Melanie, hugging her tight.

"Let's get the hell out of here!" said Miranda, in a stage whisper. "I need to be dusted for fingerprints . . . I can't believe the slimeballs who sat with me on the bus . . . and *that* guy . . ." She jerked her head back toward a fish-eyed tatter of a man who was staring at her. ". . . I mean, where's a fucking bouncer when you really need one?" *Well, she talks like a stripper, whatever that means.* She glanced at Wes. "You Wes?"

"Yes. Pleased to meet you." *Hug? Shake hands?* He held out his hand, and she disengaged from Melanie to give it a quick shake.

"Me too. Let's go." She lifted her bag toward Wes as they started to move. "Here. Be a man. Thanks." Wes took it and walked a few steps behind as they headed toward the door. Melanie held Miranda's arm with both hands.

"Did he hurt you again, baby?"

Miranda responded with no attempt to lower her voice. "Not this time, but yeah, pounded me flat a couple of weeks ago." Wes could see Melanie wince at her sister's bluntness. "Good thing I heal up so fast. If he'd gotten hold of me this time, though, I think that would have been the end of it."

The sisters burst through the terminal doors before Wes could get ahead to hold them open, and the three of them raced out to the car, which he unlocked as quickly as he could. Melanie and Miranda both got into the back, so Wes jumped in behind the wheel, put Miranda's bag on the front passenger seat, and pulled out of the parking lot.

In the rear-view mirror, Wes saw Melanie look inquisitively into her sister's eyes. After a momentary pause, she leaned in and whispered a concerned question. Miranda responded with irritation.

"No! Jeez, thanks a lot! Dad thinks I'm a hooker and you think I'm a junkie!" She looked at Wes in the mirror. "What, do I look like a total loser or something?" Before he could respond, she was back at Melanie. "I'm a little stressed out, okay? Is that so hard to understand?"

With the addition of Miranda, there was a whole new dynamic in the car. *It feels like I'm seeing a relationship that's basically unchanged since childhood: caring, argumentative, loving, complex . . . Melanie's kind of like a big sister to Miranda and kind of like a mother.* Wes decided to keep quiet, since the females were ignoring him and it was difficult to participate in the conversation from the front seat. They huddled together, Melanie's arms around Miranda, and their talk became hard to follow through the sounds of the rain and the traffic. All he could pick up was what seemed to be a lightning tour of all of Miranda's major emotions: one minute confessional, then with a bitter edge in her voice, followed by weeping, then giggling wildly. *I can see why someone might mistake her for a drug user . . . but she's just a kid who's really struggling with life. Posie can be almost as hard to follow sometimes.*

He heard Melanie ask about "Jeremy," and caught part of Miranda's response: ". . . could have killed him . . . I called him . . ."

Toward the end of the trip, Miranda finally spoke for his consumption as well as for Melanie's. "Oh, listen, I heard this joke on the bus. Okay, so there was this parrot, and it could talk, and this lady wants to buy it but she says 'It doesn't swear, does it? 'Cause I don't like swearing.' And the guy at the store says 'No, definitely not,' so she takes it. And it's fine for a long time, but one day the parrot gets tired of the same old food all the time and he says, 'I'm tired of this fucking shit!' and the lady gets really mad and puts him in the freezer for an hour for punishment. So, when he gets out he's, like, really cold and the first thing he says is, 'Hey, if I got an hour for saying *that*, what did that turkey say?'" She and Melanie broke up into another giggling fit, as Wes chuckled dutifully. *That's actually not bad. Better than most people who try to tell a joke.*

In the apartment, Miranda went right to the refrigerator. Wes looked questioningly at Melanie as he held up Miranda's bag. She motioned toward the bedroom and followed him in.

"I really hate to do this, but would you mind sleeping on the couch tonight? She's scared and needs to talk. I'd feel a lot better if I could be close to her." *Wow. Kicked out twice in two days. But she's right, of course.*

"Of course, no problem at all. You two need to be together."

"Thanks," she said, smiling.

He put the bag on the bed and followed Melanie out. She entered the kitchen as Miranda exited, carrying a glass of soda and a bag of sour cream and onion potato chips.

"I'm going to make some tea," announced Melanie. "Does anybody else want some?"

"No," said Miranda, settling down on one end of the couch.

"No, thanks," said Wes. *Stay with Melanie? I'd rather talk to her sister, find out what's going on. Actually, Melanie might appreciate it if I did.* "Should I talk to her?" he asked.

"Oh, yeah, that would be nice."

He strolled into the living room and sat on the couch. Miranda was partly tipped back in the recliner, munching one chip after another, fidgeting and staring distractedly into her glass. *Let's take a chance on the direct route.* "So, you ran away . . ."

She glanced at him, then away. "Yep, sure did. Dad's on his own now. Maybe he can get up and dance when his leg heals."

"Dance?"

"With makeup I can pass for eighteen. My boyfriend got

me an ID . . . there's serious money at the clubs."

"Go-go dancing?" *"Go-go dancing?" What am I, eighty?*

"Whatever. Yep, that's what I do, when I can. I mean, he knows we can't make it on just his disability. Who keeps food in the house and the rent paid with him out of a job all the time? Did he think I'd be babysitting? I mean, I'm not knocking it, but you can't support a family." *This girl has had to grow up way too fast . . . what a difference between her and Posie . . .*

She glanced over at him. "Your dad ever work you over?"

"No . . . no, he hardly even spanked me. *He had other ways of hurting people . . .*

"Well, mine did. It's hard to keep on loving someone like that. I sure as hell tried. But he went too far this time. I can't let him get hold of me again. No choice."

Wes shook his head a little. Melanie looked out from the kitchen. "You want anything, Wes?"

"No, thanks. I'm fine," he said, smiling her way. *She sounds anxious to keep me happy. I'm doing her a favor by not getting riled up over this intrusion.* He turned back to Miranda, who was drifting away again. *These two are going to be in the next room, in the same bed . . . holy cow, talk about a fantasy situation . . . no, no, I shouldn't even fantasize about it, and no way would it really happen. And it shouldn't happen. Still, the possibilities . . .*

Melanie entered with her tea and walked over to the couch. "Well, Wes, what do you think? She's okay as sisters go, huh?" Miranda looked askance at her.

"Yes," he replied. "I believe she adequately fulfills the requirements of sisterhood." Melanie giggled; Miranda rolled her eyes.

"Gee, you guys must have a great time together. You deserve each other. I'm so glad I came."

It was Melanie's turn again. "I know why you're really glad . . . because I'm such a good landlord. You can afford the rent."

"Ha! You should pay *me* to be here! I'm probably the most excitement you've had in a long time!" She turned back to Wes. "No offense. I'm sure you're . . . very exciting."

"You're too kind . . . I can only try my best."

Melanie rose from the chair. "Well, I think we ought to get some sleep. How you doing, Andie?"

Miranda yawned. "Tired. I think that bus was designed to keep people awake."

Melanie looked at Wes. "Do you need to get anything? . . ." She nodded toward the bedroom.

"Uh, yeah," he said, rising. He brought his suitcase and a pillow out to the living room and changed into his gym shorts and a T-shirt while Melanie and Miranda used the bathroom and bedroom to get ready. He caught a glimpse of Miranda as she walked from the bathroom to the bedroom, but she hadn't changed yet. *Probably better that I don't know what she wears to bed.*

Melanie came out in her old nightshirt and sat on the couch with him. "I sure appreciate you being so nice to her, and driving downtown to get her, and sleeping out here tonight. I feel bad, with everything you've just gone through . . ." She put her head to his chest and hugged him.

"Really, it's okay. You're a good sister. It's nice to see how much you care about her. She's lucky to have you."

She smiled up at him, pleased. "You *are* wonderful. I love you." They did a goodnight hug and kiss and then Wes was settling into the couch in the dark, covering himself with an old afghan, feeling better than he thought he would. *Why is it that couches are almost always more comfortable than beds? I've done my best sleeping on couches over the years.* He opened his eyes and let them drift around the darkened room. *It's hard to believe I'm really here. What a strange life . . . I feel like a cork in the ocean, just drifting along, weathering the occasional storm, thinking, in my foolish, corklike way that I can change direction if I want to. Maybe I'd feel better if I just relaxed and gave up that illusion. Seems like a pretty sad way to live, though.*

The proximity of his housemates wormed its way up into his consciousness. *Only a few feet away, as the crow flies . . . or, in my case, as the pig snuffles . . . are two of the most enticing creatures I've ever met. What would happen if I just sort of wandered in and lay down? He could feel himself starting to drift off. . . . they don't really wake up, but start snuggling up to me, soft and warm . . .*

CHAPTER 20

Sunday morning, Wes escaped. Melanie and Miranda started talking as soon as they got up and showed no signs of slacking off, so when he floated the idea of going into work it was accepted with hardly a pause.

The hum of his office lights in the stillness of the building was comforting rather than irritating. Even as behind as he was, he was glad to be in familiar surroundings in a familiar routine. He could almost enjoy the coffee.

He poked at and shuffled the mind-numbing backlog of paperwork. *Reports to read and write, numbers to submit, applications to review . . . delegation has always been a weak point with me . . . I feel like I'm doing too much and too little at the same time.* He put his elbows on the desk and stared off into space. *What would I be good at? Would it have been any different if I'd found a teaching job? Or would I have ended up being just as disorganized and ineffective?*

He worked hard, but by noon he'd had enough, and left feeling that he'd only peeled away a thin layer. The final clouds in a train of rain were just scuttling off to the east.

As he entered the apartment, he saw a folded piece of paper taped to the entry wall where he would see it. "Wes," it said, written in Melanie's workmanlike cursive. *Maybe it's a "Dear Wes" letter. Yeah , I think not.* He pulled it off and opened it.

> *Wes,*
> *Sorry, baby, I still had to leave today to visit my friend. She's going through hard times, otherwise I would*

cancel. I was going to call you, but I know you have a lot to do and I didn't want to bother you. I hope you had a good day. My dad called from the hospital looking for Andie, but I don't think he thinks she's here yet. She has a lot of friends and she's run away before and stayed with them so that's where he'd look first. I don't think he'll be out for a while anyway, but you better use the caller ID and the answering machine to screen calls. Thanks for looking after Andie. She'll be fine in the apartment during the day. See you probably after work Tuesday.

    I love you,
    Melanie

So . . . babysitting a fifteen-year-old nymphet, a runaway stripper, a finalist in the Miss Jailbait pageant. I should just turn around and run like hell. But he didn't. He entered the apartment tentatively, wondering how to approach the situation. He heard a radio playing and wandered toward the sound.

The sight hit him like a bare wire full of juice, bringing him to a stop, instantly alert. The bathroom door was open almost halfway, steam swirling out toward the ceiling. He heard Miranda's high, still-childlike voice singing along with the radio, the words and the song indistinct. He felt rooted to the spot, muscles taut, nostrils flaring, in the instinctive response of humankind's hunter ancestors. All of his attention focused on the bright band of light issuing between door and frame. Her lilting voice, echoing bell-like in the tiled confines of the room, drew him forward, entranced.

The mirrored image, misty but revealing, which panned into his view brought him up short once more. Miranda, naked and shower fresh, stood at ease, her eyes half-closed, lost in the song as she worked at the tangled pile of her hair. Her breasts showed a nearly complete progression into womanhood, with enlarged aureoles and protruding nipples rising out of almost muscular mounds. *They don't look like Melanie's . . .*

they're already bigger than hers and look firmer.

The conflicting and overlapping sensations conjured up by this simple scene rolled over him in disconcerting waves. Miranda was in turn an object of primal carnality, an exquisite gem of luscious eroticism, an ideal of innocent beauty. Powerful currents collided within him, first urging him to leave, then demanding that he stay. The persuasive portion of his mind devoted to gratification did its best to shove aside the numerous and compelling reasons for him abandon his position.

He grimaced and clenched his hands into tight fists, his right hand gripping his keys. *This is not for me! Not to look at, not to think about, nothing!* With a sudden motion he tore himself away, moving off as quietly as he'd approached.

He stopped in the kitchen and stood still, panting. He rearranged his keys so the points were lodged in his palm, then squeezed harder and harder, clenching his teeth as the pain stabbed up his arm. *Make the pain stronger than the desire.* He closed his eyes, his body trembling with pain and effort, his breath shallow through locked teeth. His whole being focused on that point in his palm and he stayed at that singularity for agonizing moments, holding it, forcing out all other thoughts and feelings. Then, with a sudden exhalation, he let his hand relax and his body slacken.

He opened his eyes and breathed deliberately a few times. He looked down and opened his hand. The jumble of keys was awash in blood. He moved to the sink, washed off the keys and set them aside, then let warm water flow over his hand to reveal the jagged, bleeding wound at the center. *Let the blood wash away my sins.*

He shut the water and tore off a couple of paper towels, swabbing his hand dry. He folded part of a towel into a palm-size square and held it there while he fished through drawers, finally pulling out a roll of masking tape and fixing the square tightly to his palm.

As he moved slowly back to the kitchen doorway, Melanie's calendar caught his eye. He paused, glancing at the items she'd crossed off. *"Groceries"* . . . *"laundry"* . . . His eyes stopped. The lone entry for the Wednesday the week prior was "Dr." It had been nearly obliterated by scribbled lines. *"Doctor"? That was the day she took a long lunch . . .*

He shook his head and stepped into the living room, clearing his throat quietly before he spoke. "Hi, I'm home!"

"Oh, hi!" came the echoing reply. He heard the bathroom door close. *Thank God.*

He suddenly felt very hungry and turned back into the kitchen. As he cast about for something to eat, there was a light rapping at the front door. He froze for a moment, coming alert again. *Uh, oh . . .* He crept silently to the door and glanced through the peephole. *Posie!* He unlocked the door slowly, his mind racing again. *I'm sure glad to see her, but not here . . . how did she find me? . . . where's Trish?* He opened the door. "Hi, kiddo . . ."

"Dad!" she exclaimed, lunging at him and hugging him tightly but somehow furtively. "Oh, you feel good. Good ol' huggable Dad."

"Boy, it's good to see you!" he said, hugging her in return. Her ponytail brushed over his arms. "Are you okay?"

"Yeah, I'm okay!" she exclaimed, stepping back. She looked very happy.

"How did you know I was here? How did you get here?" He looked down the hall, somehow expecting to see Tricia standing there, arms folded, scowling.

"I have a question: are you going to invite me in?"

"Oh, sure, sorry sweetie, come on in." *Man, what will she think of Miranda? How much does she know?* He walked her slowly into the living room, thrown off balance by her wholly unexpected arrival and finding it hard to sort out his options.

"Little gloomy in here," she said. "You should open those blinds."

Alright, concentrate on Posie first. I need to find out how she found me, and how much she and Trish know. The couch looked glaringly bedlike with the pillow and afghan. Posie sat in the recliner, fiddling with the footrest handle on the side while he pulled the blinds open. *Playing host to my daughter in my lover's apartment with her sister naked in the bathroom. How much weirder is my life going to get?*

"Would you like something to drink?" he said.

"No, thanks," she replied, finally getting the footrest to release with a wobbly thunk. Wes pushed the bedding aside and sat on the couch.

At that moment, Mimi sauntered out from the bedroom and paused, examining the new arrival. Posie immediately began making little kissing noises with her lips and dropped her hand to the side of the chair, flicking her fingers to encourage a visit. Mimi remained motionless for a moment, then turned and walked toward the kitchen.

"Hey, all animals like me!" called Posie to the retreating figure, a claim she had made many times previously. She sighed and settled back in the chair as Mimi disappeared. "I realize that's unenforceable," she said, to no one in particular. Glancing over, she noticed Wes's taped hand for the first time. "Having trouble using a fork again?"

Wes laughed, partly at this welcome dose of normalcy. "Worse. I cut it while flossing." She giggled. *Boy, it's good to see her!* "So," he said, "tell me what's going on."

"Like, how did I find you? Like, did Mom tell me?"

"Like . . . yes."

"Well, first of all, I don't think Mom really knows where you are, although I think she suspects. Remember, I'm your ace detective." *Yeah, that's a pretty accurate nickname. She's more observant than most adults.* "Anyway, I hear a lot more than you or Mom know. I was awake when she kicked you out . . ." *Ouch! So matter-of-fact.* ". . . and I heard her mention Melanie when she was on the phone with Grandma. I figured Melanie

163

had to be from work, since you don't do anything but work and hang around the house . . ." *Ouch again!* ". . . so I looked in the work phone directory in your desk drawer and there was only one Melanie and I got her address out of the regular phone book and took a cab and there was your car in the parking lot and here I am."

"Wow. You really are some detective." *How old is this girl? Wait . . . uh oh, it's her birthday.* "Oh, gee, it's your birthday today, isn't it?"

"Yep. Had the party yesterday. I missed you."

"I'm sorry, sweetie. I don't even have a present for you. I've been a little preoccupied."

"I bet."

At that moment, Miranda, wrapped in a towel, peered into the living room. "I thought I heard a new voice." The wound in Wes's palm throbbed. *Darn! I should have forewarned Posie!* He could feel himself turning red. Posie was looking at Miranda with a stunned expression.

"Ah, yes," said Wes. "This is my daughter, Posie." He looked at Posie, who was now looking at him with the same stunned expression, and gestured toward Miranda. "This is Miranda, Melanie's sister. She's staying with us for a while."

Posie's expression changed to one of mock illumination. "Ahhh . . ."

"Hi, Posie," said Miranda, smiling politely. *I'm sure glad she didn't come out like this while I was alone.*

"Hi . . ." said Posie, turning and waving weakly. Miranda retreated into the bedroom.

Posie leaned toward him with exaggerated seriousness. "Dad, what is going on here? Are you out of your mind?" *Yes.* "Are you . . . you know . . ." She nodded to where Miranda had been.

"No, no, of course not. She's just . . . staying with us for a few days. Melanie's . . . not here right now."

"So, what's the deal with her? You going to get divorced

from Mom and marry her? Or just live together?" *Where does she get this stuff?*

"Well, I'm not . . . hey, what *about* Mom? What did you tell her when you left?"

"She's over at Mrs. Myerson's, getting a haircut. I knew my friend Kylie was going to be gone this weekend with her family, so I left a note for Mom that Kylie called about going out shopping with *her* mom and I hoped Mom wouldn't mind." *This girl is too clever for her own good.*

The sound of a blow dryer came from the direction of the bathroom.

"So," said Wes "how are you doing with all this? You seem awfully calm about the whole thing."

Posie paused, looking down. "I cried a lot Friday morning. I didn't let Mom see it, and I didn't let on that I knew anything when she told me you were away on business." She looked back up at him. "I don't want to not see you anymore. I miss you already." She nodded her head at the apartment. "I guess if you're happier here than with Mom, you should stay. But I hope I can still see you a lot." She got out of the chair and joined Wes on the couch, hugging him again.

Wes put his arms around her, stroking the back of her head. She snuggled into him. "I love you, kiddo," he said wistfully. "I won't let you out of my life. I'm sorry I've made things so complicated for everyone. I hope I can get it figured out soon so you won't be worried. But I'll always be your dad, that'll never change."

Posie snuffled a bit. Tears trickled down her cheek. "You're a good dad," she said wetly. They sat for a few moments without speaking. *Well, I'm a loving dad . . . above all this, I do know without a doubt that I love her. But I've been pretty inattentive lately, and I sure didn't think much about how this relationship with Melanie could affect her.* Posie's tears dribbled to a stop without escalating into full-blown crying.

The dryer shut off, and Wes glanced up to see Miranda wander out and into the kitchen, smiling at them as she went. She was barefoot, dressed in worn, glued-to-the-skin jeans shorts, and a sleeveless crop-top under which it was very apparent that she was braless. Her fingernails and toenails were painted bright, orange-red, and her subtly reddish-blond hair was poufed out to maximum volume. He could tell that Posie was also observing. She sat back in astonishment and made a little choking sound in her throat. She tilted her head toward him and whispered, "What's *her* summer job?"

"Stop that!" he whispered back. "Just don't you ever dress like that!"

"Will you pay me not to?"

"You little mercenary!"

"A girl's got to get paid," she responded, waggling her eyebrows.

All Wes could do was look at her with bemused exasperation.

"Dad, it's starting to feel kind of weird being here. Can we go somewhere else?"

"Sure, of course. Let's go." He walked over and stuck his head in the kitchen. "I'm . . . going to take her home now. Will you be okay?" *Feel a little silly asking her that . . .*

Miranda was picking through a can of mixed nuts. "Oh, yeah," she said, waving him away. "I'll just hang out here in Excitingsville. Bring back a couple of tacos, though, okay? My sister must live on cat food and dust bunnies."

"Sure. The fridge *has* gotten a little bare lately."

Wes and Posie departed, ending up at a burger place when she, too expressed an interest in food. The conversation stayed on lighter subjects. *See, why couldn't I think to do something like this more often? It's nice to give her attention for no particular reason, to talk about whatever's on her mind. It's easy to let a kid go on autopilot at this age. I let her become just another thing to schedule, someone to chauffeur around, to say, "Good morning," and, "Good night," to.*

As they finished eating, Posie switched to a tone of mock maturity. "Well, Dad, it's been fun. We really must do this again soon."

"I agree. You're wonderful company, my dear."

"Yes, yes, I know. Thank you so very much. Now go away, you bother me." *She's a very strong girl. I sure wasn't this self-assured at her age.*

"I suppose we'd better be getting you home."

"Yeah, Mom will need someone to complain to about her hair."

As they approached their street in the neighborhood, Wes slowed, doubting the wisdom of having Tricia see him drop Posie off. This apparently entered Posie's mind simultaneously.

"You better drop me off at the corner. I'll say that Kylie and her mom were in a real hurry, that there was a horrible shopping accident or something."

Wes pulled over and stopped. They hugged, then she kissed him quickly on the cheek and stepped out. "Thanks, Dad," she said through the open door. "I hope you figure it out soon. Don't worry about me. I'll call next time."

"I love you, sweetie."

"I love you too." She closed the door and trotted off toward the house. She waved and smiled at him as she turned into the driveway, but as he waved back, he saw her hide her face with her hand and run toward the house. He lost her behind a tree and drove off slowly, with a heavy heart. *She doesn't deserve this pain. What a wonderful kid . . . I'm so lucky to have her.* He breathed deeply and tried to shake off the darkness. *Well, back to the Teen Temptress.*

*   *   *

Wes shuffled into the apartment with two bags of groceries, a case of beer, and a fast-food bag containing four tacos, which Miranda grabbed before he could set them down.

"About time, guy! It's not like I have a lot of body fat to fall back on!" *Hmm . . . hadn't noticed.*

"Sorry. She ended up needing to talk some more."

Mimi entered, demanding dinner. "Oh, yeah, the cat," said Miranda, fetching the bag from a lower cabinet and hastily overfilling the bowl. She poured herself a glass of soda and chomped into a taco. "Anyway, Melanie called. I said you were out with your daughter. I think she was a little mad that I was stuck here alone, but I said, 'No, he's just taking her home, but he's been gone for a while.'" *Gee, thanks, I really didn't have quite enough trouble in my life . . .* "Anyway, she says she's feeling . . . doing fine and she misses you." *"Feeling?" Was she feeling sick again? It seemed like she was doing better.*

Miranda gobbled away at her tacos while Wes put away the groceries. *I hope Melanie doesn't mind beer in the fridge . . . shoot! I should have gotten some better wine.* The nearly empty bottle on the counter reminded him of bad things. He slid the case of bottles in and shut the door.

* * *

Later that night, Wes changed into his nightwear and lay on the couch, numbing his brain with a beer and an old issue of a celebrity gossip magazine while Miranda got ready for bed. *What are my chances of a goodnight hug, a goodnight kiss? I would go to sleep happy if I could get either, and very happy if I could get both . . .*

"G'night," she said, already in the bedroom before he could see what she was wearing.

"Good night," he said toward the bedroom. He put the magazine down and turned off the light. *How can I even think that way about the underage sister of my very young mistress? I don't want to be that person anymore . . .*

CHAPTER 21

Monday dragged on and on. *Seems like I've gone from way behind to hopelessly behind. Torching the place and starting over is about the only way I'll ever get caught up. Odd that Ben hasn't chewed on my ass lately. The few times I've seen him, he's looked as distracted as I feel. It's possible that he really is as bad at his job as I am at mine. No comments from anyone yet about me and Melanie. Maybe it doesn't qualify as exciting news . . . but no, in the world of idle gossip, no tidbit is too small to pass on. When Ben hears about it . . . when Mark hears about it . . .* He tapped a finger slowly on his desktop. *Screw it. Nothing I can do about it.*

He got up and wandered to a window, peeking out through the partly closed blinds at his hectic domain. *I really should stay late, but I wouldn't mind spending more time in Miranda's proximity . . . which, really, I should not do . . . but I should get dinner for her. I got the groceries, but she doesn't strike me as someone who takes initiative in the kitchen.*

He picked up pizza on the way to the apartment, consuming almost two slices before arriving. *They call me the host with the least . . .*

When he entered the apartment, he was surprised not to find Miranda hypnotized in front of the TV. He peeked in the bedroom and saw her lying on her stomach on the bed, reading a book that was propped up on a pillow. She was also listening, through headphones, to something on Melanie's boombox. She was dressed in an oversized sweatshirt, out of which protruded her long, bare, legs. Her hair was still sleep-mussed. Her feet were high in the air, crossed at the ankles, twitching along to the music. Mimi was observing Wes from her nest in the cast-off clothing on the chair near the bed.

"Hi," he said, loudly. "What are you reading?"

Without looking at him, she held up the book so he could see the cover, which was immediately recognizable as one of Melanie's romance novels. Wes shuddered.

"It's Melanie's," she said, also loudly, laying it back on the pillow. "Pretty hot stuff." *Maybe TV would have been better. Speaking of which, I think I will indulge in some tonight, with a beer chaser.*

"I brought pizza."

Miranda threw the headphones off and leapt out of bed. She brushed by Wes in a rush for the kitchen, followed loudly by Mimi.

A couple of hours later, Wes's brain was floating rather nicely as he sat in the recliner, staring at the television. *It's working tonight. The world will feel okay for a while.* He heard Miranda stir, and water running in the bathroom, followed by the blow dryer. *What, is she going out? Little late to be getting ready for the day.* He saw a flash of motion as she moved from the bathroom to the bedroom, then heard more preparatory sounds. *I think she really is getting ready to go out. What'll I do if some guy shows up for her? Would Melanie want me to stop her? How could I?* He sighed and turned what was left of his concentration back to the TV. *Fuck it. She can do what she wants.*

From inside the bedroom came Miranda's voice: "Hey, could you shut the TV for a minute?"

Huh? "Sure . . ." He pressed the power button, leaving the room lit by a single table lamp. He stared blearily toward the bedroom. After a slight pause, the bedroom light went off. A moment later, he was startled by the pounding, driving beginning of a rock song that had become a strip club standard. A moment after that, he was catapulted from surprise to hyper-alertness as Miranda made a dynamite entrance into the living room, strutting like a frisky foal. She was wearing one of his dress shirts, buttoned up, sleeves rolled up to mid-forearm, and glittering, strappy high-high heels. What she had on underneath was the age-old question of the profession.

My shirt . . . those legs . . . holy shit . . . He sat bolt upright, feeling as though he was about to levitate. *I shouldn't be watching this. She shouldn't be doing this. But how can I stop her? She's been rejected, abused . . . I can't shut her down just like that. I've got to be careful.* That was good enough for his impaired conscience. He settled back down and gave her a dazed smile of encouragement.

She was good, a natural dancer. She could hit the rhythm, slide through it, move against it. *Strong and sexy . . . man, is she good! And in that makeup, she could easily pass for eighteen.* She smiled a good, professional dancer's smile. *You can start to believe that they really like you. And this one just might. Or at least need me. Jeez, she makes Melanie look middle-aged . . . calves like steel cables.*

Miranda strutted, unattainable; she flirted and winked, wetting her lips with her tongue; she curled and swayed, lost in her own body. *I've seen quite a few dancers . . . she's better than any of them.*

Her hips swiveled and snapped as she turned to face away from him in the middle of the room. Her thin, muscular legs were twin rails slanting up to connect at a destination of delight that was curtained by his shirttail. She raised her hands to comb through her wild, golden-red mane.

Wes was riveted, heart thumping, starting to sweat. *Things are really stirring belowdecks . . . man, she's good!* He quickly shot a hand down into his pants and redirected his erection. *Steady . . . careful . . .*

Still facing away from him, twitching to the beat, Miranda unbuttoned the shirt and slowly opened it. *Curtain parts . . . beginning, second act.* She opened it wide, then glanced over her left shoulder with a look that shot right into the center of him. *"Yes, I can take you there . . ."* An inaudible moan rose in his throat.

In one glorious, flowing motion, she whirled about and flung the shirt off into the shadows. She froze for a fraction of a moment, legs apart, arms fully outstretched, lips parted, chin up, looking down into his eyes. She wore the barest string-bikini outfit he'd ever seen, in a shade of orange reminiscent of road-crew safety vests. Her body seemed to be rodlike sinew from head to toe, including her memorably firm breasts. Wes glanced down. *She shaves, probably all of it.*

She jumped back into the beat, doing a little Egyptian bit, then shook her head, laughing, her eyes twinkling at him. *Man, those eyes can talk! "Hey, we're having a party! Isn't this fun? Enjoy me!" Oh yeah, I'm enjoying you!* She stepped closer to him, chin down now, looking at him through lowered lids. *Oh boy, here it comes . . .* She stopped short, shot him a sly smile, and turned her back once more. Her smooth, tight buttocks were twin echoes of her breasts. The flaming-orange bikini string disappeared tantalizingly between them, like a line on a treasure map.

Her top was tied in two bows: one behind her neck and one just below her shoulder blades. She turned her head to look at him out of the corner of her eye as one hand reached up and over and the other reached around back to grasp the bowstrings in long-nailed fingertips. She shimmied her skinny shoulders, and the corner of her mouth curled up deliciously. She slowly pulled the knots loose, then flicked the top away. *Oh boy, oh boy . . .*

She spun around, clapping her hands to her breasts just before he could see them. He felt again as though his body was about to climb out of the chair and grab her on its own. *Easy, boy! Down, boy!* She bent a little at the waist as she moved slowly closer, massaging her breasts, her eyes lidded and fluttering, her mouth enticingly pursed. *She's got Melanie's lips, like two little pillows . . .*

There was a sharp knocking on the door. The mood changed in a snap. Miranda was gone in a flash of flesh, snatching up the discarded apparel, shutting off the boom box in the bedroom, and slamming the door shut. Wes was on his feet, walking awkwardly toward the door, wishing his erection would soften a little faster. *"Please disregard that bulge behind the curtain!"*

"Who is it?" he called as he neared the door. *Could it be Ron?*

"It's me," came the irritated voice of Melanie. *Fuck!*

He took an extra beat to try to compose himself before opening the door. Melanie gave him a dark glance as she brushed past him toward the living room. "Forgot my key. You guys having a party in here? I could hear the music all the way outside."

"Yeah, I guess she really likes that song . . ." he replied, lamely. *Jeez, she's looking bad! Pale and thin . . .* She glanced disapprovingly at what looked to Wes like about four hundred beer bottles by the recliner. *"Need something done wrong? Call Wes. Disappointment guaranteed."* She continued into the kitchen and put her purse on the counter, shadowed closely by Mimi, who was demanding attention. Wes followed a few steps behind. *Don't try to explain things right now. You're too stupid with beer. Change the subject.*

"How was your visit? You're back early."

Melanie scowled even more, sitting on one of the dinette chairs and inviting Mimi into her lap. "Lousy. That's the last time I visit her."

He heard the bedroom door open, followed by the bathroom door closing. *Getting rid of the evidence. Miranda's probably as nervous as I am. That's not something you do to your sister.*

Melanie stroked Mimi halfheartedly for a few moments, then said, "I need to go to bed." She rose listlessly and made her way to the bedroom, preceded by Mimi and followed by

Wes. Sitting on the bed, she bent to remove her shoes. She got both shoes off and reached down to get the socks when something broke inside her. She slumped sideways onto the bed, sobbing. "Oh, Wes . . ."

He sat next to her and put a hand on her back, which was shaking with sobs. *Is she mad at me? . . . I don't think so . . .* "What's the matter?"

She shook her head. "Just hug me . . ."

He lay down behind her, on his side, and pulled her toward him so that they were curved into each other, her back to his front, his arms around her. *Wish I hadn't had so much to drink. I can't think what to say.* It didn't seem to matter to Melanie. She snuggled tight into him and cried on and on. Mimi got into loaf pose a short distance away, watching Melanie silently.

Wes saw Miranda stop short at the bedroom door, back in her sweatshirt, now with the addition of some gym shorts. "I'll . . . sleep out here tonight," she said quietly. Melanie was too lost in her tears to even look up. Miranda paused for a moment, looking with concern at her sister. Then, apparently deciding there was nothing she could do, she gave Wes a sympathetic shrug and an encouraging smile and disappeared. The living room lights went out.

Melanie's crying slowly subsided, and they lay quietly on the bed. Eventually, without saying anything, she disengaged and got up. As she rose, Wes saw, in the crook of her elbow, the telltale sign of an IV insertion. *Oh no . . .* He got up as well and they worked around each other in the bathroom getting ready. *I have to ask . . .* "Melanie," he said, as compassionately as he could. She looked at him with tired eyes. He pointed at her wound.

She jerked her arm close to her body, protectively. "No!" she said, with a ferocity that startled him. It seemed to be directed as much at herself as at him. She looked away, jaw clenched, breathing with exertion. Her eyes darted about, as though she was replaying a scene, or perhaps trying to see into the future. "No," she said again, quietly, with a note of sorrow.

"I'm sorry," said Wes, with full sincerity.

Her eyes darted to his, then away, and she shook her head gently. She turned to him and put her palms on his chest, tapping firmly as if to make something happen. She lowered her head and rested it just above her hands. He put his arms around her in a light embrace. She sighed and said, "It'll be okay, really." She looked up, forcing a smile. "Sorry."

"It's okay. Don't worry." *I don't even know what I'm talking about.*

They finished getting ready and got in bed. "Goodnight," she said, with a small wistful smile. "I love you."

"I love you too. Sleep well."

Melanie was asleep almost instantly. Wes was slower to drift off.

*   *   *

Having already arranged to have the day off, Melanie stayed home when Wes left for work the next morning. When he returned that evening, Miranda was gone. "Dad's not going to make bail, and of course Andie couldn't stay away from Jeremy for long. If Dad gets out, I guess Jeremy's family has a place she can stay where he couldn't find her. She took the train this time." She shrugged and sighed.

Yeah, it's for the best.

Melanie spotted the unbandaged wound in his palm and took up his hand. "Oh, baby, what happened? She touched it gingerly.

Time for the all-purpose excuse . . . "Just work. A box knife slipped." She winced.

"Do you want anything on it? It looks pretty raw still . . ."

"No, that's okay. It'll heal faster if it gets some air."

"Okay," she said, letting his hand down. "Just be more careful." She looked at him suggestively. "You do such wonderful things with your hands . . ." *I really don't feel like sex tonight. How can I get out of it?* He noticed that she had done herself up, apparently an attempt to feel better by looking better. *Restaurant time!*

"Hey, you look great. Why don't we go out?"

Her eyes lit up. "Oh, good idea!" She bustled off to get ready.

Melanie chose a popular chain restaurant of the sort that feature suspiciously lengthy menus. As they were being escorted to what seemed like the table most distant from the door, Wes felt like he was running a gauntlet of stares. *Yep, we're having an affair all right! Jealous men! Disapproving women! Please, make us feel as uncomfortable as possible!* Melanie was happily oblivious and chatted away through the long meal. Wes had a hard time thinking of things to say and ate until he was uncomfortably full.

CHAPTER 22

Tuesday passed in what seemed like it might become a new normal. Melanie did not make an afternoon appearance.

Wednesday, the gossip hit the fan. Midmorning, Mark fell into step next to Wes as he was walking from the warehouse onto the shipping floor.

"Are you really porking Melanie? Wes, you've got to stop taking me so seriously!" *Well, there it is. But I really don't care much anymore. How much worse can things get?*

"No, you heard wrong. I'm actually sleeping with her brother," Wes responded. He stopped and turned to Mark. "We can still be friends though, right?"

Mark gave him a walleyed look, backing away. "Sure, Wes, whatever you say. I'm just going to slip away for a moment and put on my latex bodysuit. And staple my asshole shut." He quickly slunk away as Wes chuckled to himself. *It's the new, don't-give-a-shit Wes!*

That attitude lasted until late into the workday, when he next encountered Mark, who was working with unaccustomed vigor.

"This isn't the Mark I know and loathe . . ." Wes began. He glanced at what Mark was working on and his heart went to his throat. *A Milland order! Late!* "These were due out two days ago!" he gasped. "What happened?"

"Those last two temps you hired didn't show up today. No call, nothing. Turns out they didn't do much of anything Monday or yesterday, just piled all this stuff behind some pallets. When are you going to find us some *real* help?"

What'll I do? They could call here any second. "Ben-hole

won't give me enough money for real help. Unless you can persuade everyone to take a pay cut . . ."

"Well, if I tied them up and took locking pliers to their nuts . . ."

I just don't have enough time to catch up. I can't concentrate here anymore. "Bring your car around. I'll get this stuff ready to go and you take it over."

Mark choked. "Are you crazy? Remember the last time we did that? They said we didn't have insurance . . ."

"That's because we *told* them. Now, if we lose these guys because of a screw-up, we'll both be out on our asses." Wes was already digging in. "Go! Hurry up, and keep your mouth shut!" Mark trotted off reluctantly. *It seems like I can usually trust him to at least save his own skin, but sometimes he's too big a jerk even for that.*

"Wes!" came a shout. Wes jumped inside. *Man, scared by own name!* Danny was holding the work floor phone. *It's not a good call. I can tell by his face.* He beckoned to Danny, who spoke into the phone briefly, set it down and trotted over. "It's someone from Milland . . ." he said.

"I know," said Wes tensely. "There's been a screw-up. This is the order." Danny looked dismayed. *He's losing what little respect he has for me.* "Keep going on this. I'll be right back." He walked to the phone, thinking fast. *Standard stuff. . . had to wait for a couple of items, it went out yesterday, we'll check on it . . .* "Hi, this is Wes . . ."

"This is John, at Milland. I need to know where our last order is." *Moderate-to-heavy anger. Fairly controlled at this point.* "We have a firm go-live date and we're in real danger of missing it." *I've done this one.*

"Yes, I'm very sorry, I should have called you. We were out of a couple of items . . . the rest of the order was supposed to ship two days ago, but mistakenly got put on hold until it was complete. The whole thing's on its way right now . . . by special courier. You should have it any minute." He glanced over at Danny, who was doing his best. *Where's Mark? That asshole better not just wait out in his car . . .*

"Alright, I'll pass that along, but I'm not at all happy about it. I may have to take this farther up." *Oh, shit . . . I hope you don't. I'd better work on a story for Ben, just in case.* "Okay, I'm very sorry. We'll make sure it doesn't happen again." He hung up and hurried back over to the work table, glancing aside just in time to see Ben looking his way. *Uh, oh . . . act cool . . . better hurry up with that story.* He began working at the table, anxious to get it done but trying not to move unusually fast. Danny had also spotted Ben, who was now walking toward them with his usual air of critical suspicion. Danny gave Wes a worried look, then buried himself in the task at hand. Wes felt shaky inside and started to sweat. *No time, have to make it up as we go.* Ben arrived and smiled a sour, mouth-only smile.

"Hello, Wes. How are we doing today?"

"Hey, Ben. Doing okay, just wrapping up a few things."

"Mm. I haven't looked at the numbers for the past couple of days. What sort of improvement are we showing?" *I haven't looked, either. What'll I say?*

"Good, good, I think we're getting over the hump." *Please, don't ask for specifics.* Ben looked even more suspicious. Danny looked very nervous. Wes felt close to breaking down. Mark came in from the loading dock . . . *no, not now! . . .* but veered off as soon as he spotted Ben.

Ben directed his attention to the order they were working on. "Who's this for . . ." He looked at the paperwork, " . . . hmm, Milland." *Don't ask when it was due out.* Wes glanced at Ben and noticed for the first time that he looked distant and distracted, that the sourness and suspicion were likely just reflexive. "Well, I'd better let you get to it. I need to run along." *Thank God!*

Mark finally departed, at high speed, with the precious cargo. *That guy can get places in a hurry. I don't know anyone who's ridden with him more than once.* Wes wandered into his office, closed the door, and slumped in his chair, putting his arms on the desk and briefly resting his head on them. *I'm getting farther and farther behind, telling more lies all the time. Ben is probably looking up those numbers right now. Then what'll I tell him? "Yes, declining numbers are actually a good thing; once we get to zero, anything will look like an improvement."* He tried to laugh, but it came out as a grunt.

*   *   *

Thursday, Wes found out that Ben would be gone until Monday to attend a trade show. *Thank you, God! I needed a break. Maybe that's why he didn't nail me yesterday: he was preoccupied with the trip.* Wes had his first really productive day in a long time, working late with Melanie's blessing. *I could make this work. I could succeed at this if I really put some effort into it.*

CHAPTER 23

Supper that night was another Melanie Special: small "pizzas" consisting of soft tortillas topped with spaghetti sauce, honey ham and low-fat cheese slices. *Maybe Trish would let me back in just for meals . . .*

While Wes rinsed the dishes and loaded the dishwasher, Melanie pulled jars and sandwich bags full of dried plant material out of the cupboard and drawers and started heating water on the stove.

"Do you ever drink tea?" she asked.

"Not often. Once in a while when I have a sore throat I have some with honey and lemon. So tea reminds me of having a cold. *Well, that was pleasant. What a wonderful conversationalist I am. Should I discuss diarrhea remedies next?*

"Well, this will be different. You'll like it. I make it myself."

Sound curious, not worried. "So, what is all that stuff?"

"My aunt had a book on herbal teas when I lived on the farm. I used to go out and pick things and dry them. I still do, when I get the chance."

"So, it's not like crushed grasshopper thorax or anything?"

The joke fell flat. "No," she replied. *Pick up the conversation, don't let it just hang there.*

"It's interesting that you use a teakettle. Anyone I've seen make tea lately just puts a cup of water in the microwave."

"I don't like it, all that radiation zapping through it. I don't mind microwaves for food, but for tea I think natural heating works better. *Like a coiled electric heating element is natural.*

As the kettle began to resonate with heating sounds, Melanie poured leaves and fragments from the various containers into a ceramic bowl to create an aromatic, textured mound. She ground it into flakes with an old wooden pestle and filled two well-worn metal tea balls with the flakes. "This will be a good one for snuggling and sleeping. It helps to settle your stomach." *It'll take more than one cup of tea after that meal . . .*

Wes was wiping down the counter when the kettle whistled. He hung the dishrag over the sink spout and watched Melanie pour the steaming water over the tea balls, which rested in large, mismatched mugs.

"Let's drink it out there," she said, indicating the living room with her head. Wes obliged, carrying the mugs out. He heard the sound of a match being struck back in the kitchen. As he set the tea down on the coffee table, the lights went out, replaced by the glow of two candles floating out in Melanie's hands. Wes felt a twinge of discomfort. *Kind of reminds me of that Saturday . . .* She set one on each of the end tables and the two of them settled into the couch. The mugs were becoming quite fragrant.

Melanie looked into his eyes. "You make this feel like a home, Wesley," she said warmly.

A little wave of sadness washed through him. He sighed imperceptibly. "Thanks . . . you make me feel at home. You're good to me." *She does try . . .*

"And you're very good *for* me. I needed someone like you, someone who knows about life, about what's important." *Well, that's not me. Apparently I haven't learned anything about life, or what's important.*

He sighed again and smiled weakly at her, unable to come up with more lies.

"You're the most beautiful man I've ever met," she said, smiling warmly. *Open your eyes, little girl . . .*

She pulled the tea balls out of the mugs, placing them in an empty candy dish on the table. "Here," she said, handing him a mug. She picked hers up and held it under her nose, smiling approvingly. "Mmm." She took a sip.

Wes lifted the mug to his lips and inhaled the rising vapor. *Strong stuff. It actually smells pretty good.* "Yes . . . nice aroma." It was still quite hot, so he took a small sip. *Whoa! Bitter!* "My! Rather strong!"

"Give it a minute. It'll change. Try another taste."

The bitterness was fading fast as he took another, bigger sip. The bitterness came back, but with more flavor behind it this time. *This really is different. More interesting than other teas I've had* . . . "Yeah . . . it's growing on me."

"It really helps open you up."

He let his last sip run its course, the bitterness disappearing entirely into a richness he hadn't encountered in a tea before. "In a way, it's almost like a . . . like a good liquor." Melanie looked pleased. *I don't think that reference has meaning to her.*

He took three sips in a row, as big as he could without burning his tongue, and was interested to see how the established flavor in his mouth smoothed out the bitterness and made it a welcome sensation. He closed his eyes and enjoyed as one subtle, delicate flavor after another floated across his palate. *This is the first time in quite a while that I've been simultaneously sober and free of anxiety, without being naked.* Warmth began to spread through his body. *Yes, like brandy* . . . "Well, you brew a very good cup of tea," he said, then shook his head once, gently. *My voice sounds odd . . . a little removed.*

"I want our lives to move closer together," replied Melanie. "Drink up, baby." As Wes did so, letting a long, warm swallow flow down his throat, Melanie put down her own mug and snuggled closer to him. Her hand on his arm was warm even on top of the warmth that now permeated his body, like a little iron pressing through his shirt. He felt very good. *This is what drinking should feel like. It's like I'm being al-*

lowed to feel good instead of being tricked into it. Melanie began nuzzling his ear, licking and sucking. *Whoa! Sounds like she's right inside my head!* He took another drink. *I feel like I'm watching myself drink instead of just drinking. Interesting . . . high on tea . . .* He began to hum "Tea for Two," but realized that the melody was mostly in his mind. His throat was making little sounds intermittently, like a bad drive-through speaker.

He took one more drink, then watched his arm move away and set the mug down on the rather distant coffee table. His arm returned to his side and he settled back into the couch. *Life is good.* He felt Melanie get up. He didn't feel like moving his eyeballs, so she just appeared in his field of view, far off behind the table. She picked up the mugs and moved out of sight.

Some time passed. The coffee table slid away. This was a little distressing. Wes had lost track of his body; his mind watched, entranced.

Melanie reappeared, nude, her skin radiant in the candlelight. This caused a little more distress. Wes knew that he should be feeling something and probably doing something at this point, but he was only able to observe. He stared as she stood in front of him, running her fingers over her body, around her face, through her hair. Her hands dropped to her breasts and appeared to knead them so forcefully that he became certain that she was going to rearrange her flesh, like clay. This was fascinating. She ran one hand down between her legs and tucked the fingers in tightly, massaging vigorously. Again he felt anxious at his nonparticipation. She withdrew her hand and reached out toward him. It looked huge and distorted, like a reflection in an old brass doorknob. His felt his lips and nose being massaged wetly, and his nostrils suddenly felt like twin storm drains flooded with scent. The smell of her arousal barreled into him like a hit of distilled sex; erotic, stimulating, and gloriously fulfilling. He could feel himself sucking breath after breath through his nose, drinking in the almost physical odor. As the sensation began to fade, his consciousness began to refocus on the input from his eyes.

A mountainous breast loomed into view, filling his field of vision. The nipple at the center jutted up like an aerial view of a skyscraper, surrounded by a range of hill-like hair follicles. He heard his heart thudding, like it was beating between his ears. The fingertips returned and played with the nipple, flicking it about, flipping it up and down, pulling it so that it stretched out and subtly changed the shape of the breast.

Then the fingers dropped out of view and parted his lips. The breast disappeared as well; he felt the nipple enter his mouth. There was pressure on the back of his head as the breast pressed against his lips, and his mouth began to suckle.

It was another hugely sensual experience. It felt as though he was actually swallowing the breast, sucking it into his belly, satiating an enormous appetite. He felt that he could go on forever, blissfully ingesting this succulent breast-flesh, but at some point the suction broke, and the breast moved back to rejoin Melanie, off in the distance. He wanted more, much more, but he was unable to communicate this to her, and unable to make his arms and legs act to bring her back. She left. More time passed.

Suddenly, her face appeared, planet-like, in front of him, her huge eyes gazing into his. Then she withdrew a bit and her giant hand moved off to the side of his head, where he felt large, pillowy fingers brushing his skin and hair. When her hand returned to his field of vision, he found it astonishing. *Why, that's not a hand at all . . . it's a paw . . . no wonder it was so soft.* He focused again on Melanie's face. She was smiling, but now with two rows of sharp, white fangs; her pupils were long, vertical slits. Wes knew that he should feel distressed at these developments, but in an odd way felt concerned that he wasn't distressed. The cat-woman moved out of sight and the light of one candle disappeared. There was a flash of motion across his view and then the other light vanished.

A long time seemed to pass. With no more light, he was unable to tell if he was falling asleep, or sleeping, or awake. Eventually he settled on one thing: it was too dark. It was so dark that it was hurting him, pressing into his head. The pressing made his head hot and sweaty. There was definitely something wrong. It gradually came to him that it was so dark because he was *in* something, something that was pressing into his head. Finally, all at once, the horrifying truth made itself clear: as he sat helplessly, a monstrously huge and malevolent Mimi had his head in her mouth and was chewing on it, her harpoon-size fangs digging into his temples and puncturing his skin. It wasn't sweat, it was her hot saliva, mixed with his blood, that he was simmering in as his head was ground into meat and bone. He became furiously angry and terribly fearful. He desperately wanted to yank his head free and go for the throat of this hellish feline. He struggled to begin struggling, pushing and flexing against some elusive, paralyzing force. Finally, he felt the force weakening and he lurched into action, lunging at the huge mass of black fur.

It was amazingly easy to get his hands around her throat and he gripped it as though crushing it in a vise. There was light again; he was out of the mouth and free to destroy his attacker. There was someone shouting. He stared fiercely at his tenaciously gripping hands, but the black fur was gone. The light was now uncomfortably bright.

"Wes!" cried a voice. *Melanie?* His vision cleared and he saw that he was strangling a lamp, the light from its bare bulb glaring into his eyes. He relaxed his grip. He was on his stomach on the couch, still dressed, arms hanging over the edge, holding his prey. The afghan lay jumbled on the floor.

"You okay, baby?" came Melanie's voice, sounding concerned but a little odd, and when he tried to respond, he found that he couldn't speak. *Still weak . . .* The lamp was lifted out of his hands. With great effort, he rolled himself heavily onto his side, dragging his arms back up. As his eyes closed, he felt the afghan settle over him.

"G'night, baby," said Melanie.

He grunted in reply and was gone again.

*   *   *

Wes was looking at something. *It's back!* Giant Mimi was sitting there, staring at him. *Can I move? If I can move, I'll kill it.* He twitched some muscles. They responded weakly. *Shit! What'll I do?* Then he noticed that Mimi was no longer black and was not quite as big as before. And she was talking to him. *This seems familiar . . . maybe I can understand . . .* As the moments passed, the cat seemed less and less threatening. *Maybe I won't kill it. It's kind of nice, really.*

He sucked a lungful of air, moved his head from side to side to stretch his neck, and blinked a couple of times. The cat turned out to be Melanie, looking over at him as she drove. She smiled. *Human teeth. I'm in a car. Her car. We're on the way to work.*

"Wes, are you okay? You don't seem to be paying attention this morning." *Have we been talking? What have I been saying? How did I get here?*

"I . . . uh . . . I guess I don't quite feel awake yet." *I feel like I'm forgetting everything as it happens.*

"You had some rough spots last night, some nightmares. You almost felt feverish at times. I was wondering if you had a little flu or something. Hopefully it'll be an easy day."

Wes collapsed back into the car seat. "I *still* feel wiped out. I haven't felt this weak since . . . well, since I had the flu as a kid." *What the hell is happening to me? I don't remember getting ready at all.*

"Here, I brought a can of soda," she said, gesturing to the cup holder.

"Thanks," said Wes. He straightened up and, with some effort, picked up the can and opened it. *I can't believe this . . .*

I have so much to get done . . . the place is already a shithouse, I'm so understaffed . . . what happened last night? Was it just another nightmare? He felt the side of his head. *No wounds.*

As weak as he was physically, Wes felt a surge of anger rise inside him. *Would you mind if I asked you what the fuck was in that tea? And would you care if I had Mimi X-rayed to check for demons? Just idle curiosity. And would you take offense if I asked you if you were a goddamn fucking witch?* He was overtaken by a sudden compulsion to fire the can out the window and demand that she let him out. *No, no, calm down, calm down . . . man, get a grip . . .* He took a gulp of his drink and closed his eyes, breathing deliberately.

Melanie was fidgeting a little as she drove, glancing over at him frequently. He took a better look at her and was taken aback. *She looks like I feel.* His anger went through a partial transition into concern. "You look a little worn out yourself. How are you feeling?"

"Oh, okay. I didn't sleep all that well last night, so I'm really glad it's Friday. *Hardly makes a difference anymore. Every day should be a work day for me.*

It was, of course, not the "easy day" that Melanie had wished for him. Although Wes gradually regained more and more mental function over its course, even the normal challenges of the day threatened to overwhelm him, and he made none of the progress that he'd hoped for.

Melanie went to bed not long after dinner that evening. Wes cleaned up, then settled in on the recliner for on an excursion to TV-land. He fell asleep almost immediately.

CHAPTER 24

It didn't take much to keep him in the apartment all weekend. He woke up much later than planned Saturday morning, still feeling muddle-headed. When he went into the bedroom to check on Melanie, she looked even worse than the night before, tucked into a fetal position, wearing her worn-out bathrobe over her T-shirt, with Mimi curled up next to her.

"Please don't leave me," she whispered, without opening her eyes. And that was that.

Sunday was much the same.

By Monday, Melanie had improved enough to go to work. Wes, feeling mostly recovered himself, cleared out of the apartment as early as possible, leaving her to get ready at a more leisurely pace.

Late afternoon found Wes was at his desk, drowning in anxiety. He was in way over his head now and he couldn't surface. His chest and throat felt tight no matter how often he loosened his tie and collar. The top of his desk looked far away, like he was watching it on TV, and beyond the desk, beyond the walls of his office, he could sense his department spinning out of control. The relative optimism he'd felt on Thursday was completely gone.

His phone rang. He'd always disliked it when the phone rang; even when things were going well the phone always brought bad news or complaints or more work. Now, when things were going very badly, he hated and feared the phone.

He answered it, trying to disguise the edge of panic in his voice. "Shipping. Wes."

"Wesley, this is Ben. Could you please come over to my

office?" *Oh no oh no oh no oh no oh no . . .*

"Sure. Be right there." He hung up the phone. He felt as though he'd just stepped out of an airplane without a parachute.

He rose like a marionette and walked out of his office, staring straight ahead, not wanting to walk but knowing he had to. Time expanded and contracted around him. He was afraid to get to Ben's office but desperately wanted whatever it was to be over. The door to the shipping area closed behind him, shutting out the noise. He entered the executive area, the carpeted quiet making his fear feel even more acute.

Judy was not at her desk. *Poodle-lady is always here . . . maybe she had to go to the vet . . . or maybe she's hiding behind the door in Ben's office, ready to gnaw on my ankles . . .*

The office door was partly open. Wes rapped on it. "Hi, Wes. Come on in," came the voice of Ben. *He almost sounds like a normal human. What's going on?* Wes entered, nearly shaking with dread. "Why don't you close the door?" said Ben. When Wes had done so, Ben motioned to the chair in front of the desk. "Please have a seat." Wes complied, and Ben smiled as friendly a smile as his unpracticed facial muscles would allow. *What the hell . . .? I give up. I can't figure out anything anymore.* Ben paused a moment, glancing down at his desk and tapping his pen a number of times, even though it looked like he already knew exactly what he was going to say. He looked up.

"Wes, we both know that things haven't been going well in your department for a while, and I can tell – and I've heard this from some other people as well – that you seem to be under a lot of pressure, that things . . . aren't quite right."

Wes opened his mouth to speak, without really knowing what he was going to say, but all he could do was nod his head slightly.

Ben tapped his pen again, nervously. "I try not to pay attention to rumors, but it seems that . . . . uh, that you and a staff member are having a relationship, and that, of course, while you're not her supervisor . . ." He trailed off, apparently losing enthusiasm for the topic. "Anyway, you've been here a long time and you . . . you've done some good work for us. I know you have a lot of potential . . ." He sighed, casting about. *I think I'm getting fired. Where's Kim, our one-woman HR department?* "Wes, everyone goes through rough patches at some point. Good lord, I think I wrote the book on rough patches." He tried smiling again, then gave up, as some apparently unpleasant memories ran through his mind. "Anyway, you and I both know that things can't go on this way."

Wes felt lightheaded and tried to focus on his breathing. "Yeah, things could be better," he said, shaking his head a little. *He's firing me, which I deserve, but nicely, which I did not expect. He's not very comfortable with this.*

"It's just that . . . we really need to get our product out the door in a timely manner and you . . . well, it seems clear that you need to take some time and get things settled in your life. I'm sorry it had to end this way, but we're going to have to let you go."

Well, there it is. "Yeah, I know it hasn't worked out. I'm very sorry . . ."

"Well, things happen," said Ben, rising from his desk. "We'll get a check to you . . . sick pay, vacation, whatever." *Shouldn't I be signing something? This is so strange . . .*

Wes rose as well, shaky but relieved, feeling oddly grateful to this man whom he'd reviled for so long. He held out his hand. "Thanks, Ben. I appreciate it. I really am sorry."

Ben shook his hand firmly. "We'll get by, don't worry about it." He paused and sighed a little, glancing down. *Okay, what now . . .* "Of course," Ben continued "this means I may have to talk to Mark for a few days." This time, his laugh sounded more natural.

As Wes opened the door, Ben said, "You can get what you need from your office. Just leave your keys and your card at the front desk."

"Okay, thanks again," said Wes.

"Take care," said Ben.

Wes closed the door and walked toward his former department. *In the past few firings, they've had security guys escort the person out. Maybe I'm not perceived as a threat. Or maybe Ben just doesn't know what he's doing.*

Back in his office, Wes stood and stared, trying to absorb what had just happened. *Well, I'm done, and I can't say I didn't have it coming. Time to get out of here and see what I can salvage of my life.*

With some effort, he focused on the office, trying to decide what he wanted to take with him. *I feel like lighting a match and having done with it.* Instead, he emptied out a small cardboard box and set about filling it with his personal effects. *Picture of Posie . . . picture by Posie . . . coffee mug, with layers of residue in the bottom . . .* He pulled open the middle drawer. . . . *good pen . . . picture of Trish . . . Swiss Army knife . . .* He opened one of the side drawers and stopped cold, staring. Inside, lying on a mass of papers, was a male fashion doll, wearing a shirt, tie, jacket, and shoes. *No pants. Is that how she sees me? And how the hell is she doing this?*

The next thing he knew he was walking through the work area, the box of belongings tucked under one arm. He was holding the doll in his other hand, still staring at it.

Mark hurried to intercept him as he neared the door. "Uh, Wes . . . Wes, can you hear me?" Wes stopped, then swung his head to look at Mark. He had no idea what to say. "Excuse me if I'm wrong," continued Mark "but it kind of looks to me like you're leaving . . . uh, leaving in a big way." Wes remained silent. "Okay, the *box* makes you look like you're leaving. The *doll* . . . well . . ."

Wes looked back at the doll, then shoved it into Mark's hands. "Here. Enjoy." He strode off toward the door. As he passed through it, he heard Mark's voice:

Little Witch

"Hey, where's his dick . . . ?"

CHAPTER 25

Wes took off his coat and tie, tossed them haphazardly in the back seat, and sat in his car in the parking lot. He felt strange; it took him a few moments to realize why. *I feel free.* He sat for a while longer, absorbing the feeling. *When getting fired feels this good, this soothing, it's time for a change. I feel like I can keep going, cut things off with Melanie and figure out how to get back with Tricia.* The thought of Melanie made him shiver a little. *Should I go back in and find her? No, not at work.* He suddenly felt the parking lot exit beckoning to him. *Time to get out of here.*

He left the lot and drove around, pondering his next move. *It's tempting to go to her apartment now, while she's still at work, get my things and go home . . . but I'd have to face her sooner or later and I just don't want to operate that way anymore. I'll drive over and wait for her and end this thing right. What can she do to me? Work is no longer an issue. Tricia can't get much angrier than she already is. I just can't cave in to her sickliness this time. I feel sorry for her, but that's not something to base a relationship on.*

He parked in a spot at the apartment complex where he could observe Melanie's arrival discreetly. *I don't want to wait in her apartment. Too creepy now.* The early evening sun beamed into his car. He tipped his head back against the headrest and fell into a now-familiar trance-like state, observing himself experience the passage of time.

When he finally surfaced, the sun was peeking through a developing line of clouds. Melanie's car had appeared. *Time flies. Well, time to do it.*

He stepped out of his car, stood and stretched mightily, and entered the building. He paused for a moment at her door, trepidation tempering his resolve, then tried the knob. The door swung open and he entered quietly. The apartment was dark except for the reflected flicker of a candle in the living room. *Enough spooky shit.*

As he flipped the light switch, Melanie leaped off the couch. "Wes?!" she cried, in a tear-filled voice, then a relieved, "*Wes!!*" as she rushed toward him. She embraced him passionately; he put his arms around her halfheartedly. *Stay distant. Keep away from her claws.* "Oh, baby," she sobbed. "I've been so worried. They told me you left, that you were fired, and when you didn't come see me, when you didn't call . . ." She looked up at him, tears streaming down her face, and stroked his face passionately. "Oh, I just thought the worst! I thought I'd never see you again!" *Don't do it! Don't let her get to you!* When he didn't respond, her look became questioning. "Baby, talk to me. Are you okay? What's going on?"

He continued to look at her, feeling a mixture of pity and apprehension. He pulled back a little but she gripped his forearms tightly. "I wish I could say that this was working," he said. "I do care for you, I really do, and I want the best for you, but I don't think I'm the man for you."

A chasm of sorrow opened in her face. "Oh, baby . . ." she whispered. "Oh, no . . ."

"I'm sorry if I misled you . . . I don't want you to be alone."

"No no no, Wes, you're the perfect man for me. I . . . I can be whatever you need me to be. I know you can be happy here."

"I just . . . you're a wonderful woman, but I just don't know if I really love you. I'm sorry, I have to leave." He moved toward the bedroom, more assertively this time.

She let go, tears streaming out of her eyes, and gestured, "Stay, stay," with her hands. She turned and rushed into the bathroom, breaking into sobs as he walked into the bedroom and turned on the light. He heard Melanie alternately bawling and blowing her nose as he set about gathering up his things. *Okay, I got it started. I just have to keep moving, not give in.*

He was briefly startled by the clatter of something falling in the living room. His eyes flicked to the door in time to see Mimi racing toward the kitchen. *Even she's on edge.* He knelt to look under the bed for his sneakers, which he found among an assortment of shoe and boot boxes. *Ah, the stocking collection.* He heard water running. *Washing her face. I wonder what other treats she has under here.* He slid the nearest box out, a large boot box, and lifted the lid. *Dolls.* He picked up the top one, with a bushel of blond hair and a skimpy, lacy outfit. *I'm pretty sure I've seen the Wes doll. This must be Melanie.* He picked through the pile of plastic and cloth. *Sure has a lot of clothing options.*

In one corner of the box he saw another doll that had been wrapped in paper towels, the bare feet sticking out. He unwrapped it. A bolt of horror shot through him. The doll's head, with its crudely cut brown hair, clownlike face, and deep teeth marks, had been reattached to the body. The paper bag that passed for an outfit had been ripped to shreds. *Tricia. My God.* He felt nauseated. *I have to confront her with this.*

Something was wrong. *Burning smell.* His head jerked to the doorway. Small tendrils of black smoke were creeping under the top of the door frame. *Fire!* He slammed the box back under the bed. "Melanie!" he barked, racing into the living room. The couch, a pre-fire-code pile of tinder, was partially ablaze and losing ground quickly. The candlestick on the coffee table lay on its side, pointing toward the couch. On a cushion, the green, melting remains of the candle were rapidly disappearing into the flames. *Mimi! She knocked it over!*

Melanie appeared, stifling a scream. "No!"

His mind was flying. *Fire extinguisher! Hallway!*

Melanie darted into the kitchen as Wes raced to the door

and flung it open, spotting a familiar red cylinder on the wall two doors down. Shutting the door behind him to limit air flow, he ran to the extinguisher, snatched it off its bracket, and raced back down the hall. He bolted back into the apartment, whipping the door shut behind him. *Don't alarm the neighbors unless we have to!*

Melanie rushed by him carrying a metal pot and hurled water onto the flames, resulting in a hiss, a cloud of steam, and a momentary diminishment of the flames directly underneath. *Why haven't the apartment smoke detectors gone off?*

Wes yanked retaining pin out of the handle and popped the hose off its clip, pointing it at the couch cushions. *Aim at the fuel, not the fire.* He squeezed the lever and a cloud of powder jetted out of the nozzle, sounding a bit like a giant can of whipped cream. The flames began to abate almost immediately. *Thank Christ. We might get out of this without the fire department.* He swept from side to side, knocking out the flames, hitting the cushions from all angles, then spraying behind the couch and underneath.

When the extinguisher was exhausted, he stepped back, joining Melanie in surveying the damage. The couch and the area around it were shrouded in ghostly white. The picture on the wall above had blackened and shriveled inside the glass; the bottom of the frame was soot-covered and scorched. There was a dark spot on the ceiling above the couch and a swirling haze of smoke drifting over the rest.

Melanie turned, wordlessly, and went about opening the windows and the sliding glass door. Wes put down the extinguisher and walked over to the smoke alarm high on a wall opposite the couch. He reached up and twisted off the cover. *No battery, of course.* "The chirping bothered me," said Melanie, walking through. "I kept meaning to tell the manager."

She stopped and looked about, apparently trying to comprehend the situation. She clutched her hands nervously. *Ironically, this is a situation where we should be able to sit on the couch and collect our thoughts.*

"We can't stay here," she said, numbly. "Just the smell . . ."

"Yes," replied Wes. *Looks like I'm stuck with her, yet again, for a while longer. I thought I'd found a way out. Do we go to a hotel? I can't afford much.*

"Will you take me to the farm?" *Oddly enough, that sounds like the thing to do.*

"Sure," he said. *Well, I get to visit the farm after all. I'm sure as hell not in a party mood.*

They packed in silence, working around each other, avoiding eye contact. Wes collected all of his belongings. *That box . . . that doll. I really have to question her at some point. Or maybe it's better that she doesn't know I've seen it. This relationship is a minefield . . .*

Melanie deposited a large duffel bag by the front door. She closed the sliding door and the blinds, then closed the windows halfway, shutting the lights as she went. As she came out of the bedroom with Mimi, Wes was putting their bags in the hallway. Melanie picked up her purse from the kitchen counter, fishing out her keys as she exited the apartment and locking the door behind her. Wes shouldered her bag and picked up his two and they padded toward the stairs.

As they left the building, Melanie said, "We'll take my car, the sheriff knows it." She popped the trunk as they approached and Wes stored the luggage. Melanie handed him her keys as he got in and they got underway.

Wes slowed as they approached the exit. "Which way?"

"Turn left," she replied. A few blocks later, she said, "Here," and they got on the interstate loop and headed north in silence. Wes glanced over at Melanie, who was staring straight ahead, mindlessly stroking Mimi. *Well, I doused the pyre. I helped the enchantress and her familiar escape . . .* Mimi was almost totally obscured by shadow, but her eyes shone as she stared back at him. *I don't hate cats, but this one gives me the creeps.*

Melanie gave the necessary directions but otherwise remained silent as they switched onto darker and narrower roads
and left the city behind them. A shadowy fear that had been
drifting around inside him finally surfaced. *I'm going to have
to live my nightmare to get out of this.* A feeling of resolve
followed on the tail of this revelation. *All right, bring it on.
No running and hiding.*

CHAPTER 26

They pulled into the dirt driveway from the gravel-covered road and drove the remaining fifty yards to the house. Wes killed the headlights and switched off the engine. He exited the car at a deliberate pace, in no hurry to proceed. *A bigger place than I anticipated. They must have been prosperous, maybe a large family. I don't want to go in.*

Melanie stood for a moment, regarding the house. *A lot of memories for her. What kind of memories will we carry out this time?* Mimi was already on her way up the porch steps. Wes looked back the way they'd come. The city lights were a faint orange glow in the distance. The only other illumination was provided by the moon, which was struggling to shine through a thickening parade of clouds. *Storms soon.* Crickets chirped off in the darkness. Wes pulled the bags out of the trunk as Melanie started toward the house. Mimi was pawing at the front door, meowing to get in.

Wes was still feeling the effects of the adrenaline rush from the fire. *Takes a while for that stuff to cycle out of your system.* He carried the bags to the house, his feet making distinctive sounds as he walked through the shadows. *Dirt . . . gravel . . . patch of grass . . . more dirt . . .* then up the steps and onto the lightly groaning boards of the porch.

Melanie unlocked the front door and held the screen door for him as he passed through. Mimi scampered off into the shadows. Wes's footsteps on the wood floor echoed through the house. *Why do houses sound so different when there's no one home? . . . so hollow?* Melanie flipped a switch, turning on a frosted glass wall fixture in the entry area that illuminated a stairway leading to the second floor, a hallway receding toward the back of the house, and a large living room. Wes put the bags down next to the door.

Melanie stood motionless in the vintage light. *She's lost . . .* Wes turned to face her, looking into eyes that stared straight ahead. *Opaque.*

"How're you doing?" he said. She glanced up at him briefly and shrugged, silent. "I, uh . . . where's the bathroom?"

She tilted her head. "Down the hall."

He walked into the gloom, finding an open doorway that looked like a good bet. He reached inside and flicked a light switch. An ancient round fluorescent ceiling fixture blinked to life, casting a synthetic luminance over the small, dingy bathroom. He stepped in and closed the door, letting his eyes adjust to the light. Squinting, he looked in the mirror. *Jeez, I look I'm morphing into a mule . . . a particularly unattractive mule. I'm just going to stop looking in mirrors.* He sighed as he stepped to the toilet, unzipping and relieving himself. *What am I going to do? Things keep shifting . . . I can't get traction . . . it's like running in a dream. But I'm going to end this somehow.* He turned on the water, letting it run for a moment to clear out the pipes, then washed his hands and splashed his face. He dabbed himself dry with the worn towel that had been hanging forlornly from the ancient rack over the toilet.

He turned off the light as he exited the bathroom and was immediately struck by the change in illumination from the front of the house. The wall fixture had been turned off, and there was a dim glow coming from the direction of the living room. *Candlelight! How could she, after the fire? What's she thinking . . .?* He proceeded cautiously.

He found Melanie sitting cross-legged on a large rug in the center of the room, her hands on her knees. She was staring at the small burning wick of a can of chafing fuel on the floor in front of her. A few feet behind Melanie, in her shadow, sat Mimi. *Oh, shit. I don't like this at all . . . I should . . . no, no,*

I'm going to see this through.

As he approached her, he became aware that she was gently rocking back and forth. He opened his mouth to speak, then thought better of it. Moving closer, he saw that her lips were moving, just barely, but making no sound. He stood, watching, uncertain. *It feels like there are a lot of wrong buttons I could push here. I have to be careful . . .* He bent slightly, seeing if she would look at him. "Melanie . . .?" he whispered. There was no sign of a response.

Melanie rocked and stared and mouthed something over and over. *What's she saying? Can't make it out . . .* He slowly knelt to the floor in front of her, then sat, mirroring her pose, keeping his eyes on her. Her gaze went through the flame and far beyond. *Should I touch her? It seems like there's a force field surrounding her . . . wait, her voice . . .*

The softest of whispers floated through the air between them. He focused on her mouth, matching the sound with the motion. *There's an "s" . . . and a hard consonant, a "k" . . . this is like a game show from hell. I can almost pick it out, it's getting louder . . . He looked back at her eyes, with their limitless gaze.*

". . . comes . . ." whispered Melanie. *"Comes" . . . what? What comes?* ". . . it comes it comes it comes it comes it comes . . ." she chanted, rocking with the words. *What comes? I really don't like this . . .* Slowly, the volume increased. ". . . comes it comes it comes it comes . . ." She rocked and stared. Her face began to take on a look of great concentration. *I don't like this at all. What should I do? I have no idea.*

"Melanie," he said again, his voice much quieter than he intended. He couldn't stop looking at her eyes.

". . . it comes it comes it comes . . ." Louder and louder. Her movements were becoming more vigorous, her eyes wider. Wes felt himself being drawn into the mantra and rooted to the spot. *She's got me again.* ". . . COMES IT

COMES . . ." *Can't break free. Whatever's coming is on its way . . . I can feel it. Her eyes . . .* With that thought, the focus of Melanie's eyes lasered in from the distance, into the center of the flame. The chanting stopped. The rocking stopped. Melanie's unblinking eyes burned as brightly as the fire.

Then Wes saw her lips move again, soundlessly as before, but this time the volume rose much faster. ". . . now now now now . . ." Her voice filled his head; there was no room for thought. ". . . Now Now Now Now . . ." Her eyes closed as she arched back, tilting her head toward the ceiling. ". . . NOW NOW NOW NOW NOW . . ." It looked as though her spine was about to bend back on itself but the words ended abruptly, and after the briefest moment she snapped forward and blew out the flame.

Wes sat motionless, eyes darting, ears on alert, casting about for a glimmer of light or an identifiable sound. *Back in the darkness with my enchantress. Where will she appear this time?* A gust of wind passed. It rattled a loose pane and whistled briefly through a small gap in a frame. *Storm front coming through.* He began to feel unmoored. *Should I move? I'll have to, eventually. Where is she?* He heard thunder, getting nearer. *Lightning soon, then I'll see.*

Just then there was a distant flash that briefly, dimly illuminated the room. It left him feeling even more disoriented. *What did I just see? This isn't the living room . . .* He reached down to steady himself on the floor and was shocked to realize that he was sitting on a mattress.

There was another flash, a little brighter. *I'm in bed, in a bedroom. I think Melanie is next to me.* He reached over cautiously and felt the shape under the covers. He rested his hand there long enough to feel gentle breathing. *Feels like we're still in the farmhouse. We must be upstairs . . . how did I get here?* He touched a hand to his chest, then his abdomen. *Only wearing my briefs. Where are the rest of my clothes?* He heard the sound of raindrops peppering the roof and walls. More gusts of wind puffed about, stronger, occasionally prompting the house to groan in response. He remained motionless for a time, searching for some inner island to stand on.

The image of the doll head – of Tricia – materialized into his consciousness. *I've let things slide . . . so many things, for so long . . . neglected my responsibilities, abandoned my family . . . weakness begets weakness. Whatever I might owe Melanie, or whatever she thinks I owe her, I can't leave Tricia unprotected. I don't know if I've somehow put her in danger, but I can't take any chances. I have to get up. I have to get out of here. I have to go to her.*

The rain increased from drops to a downpour, driven by the rising wind. Thunder boomed, setting up deep vibrations in the structure. Lightning strikes increased in frequency and brightness, helping him get a sense of his surroundings. *Bed is in a corner, just enough room on Melanie's side for a small night table. Night table beside me, under the single window. Must be in the middle of the house. Dresser on the wall opposite the bed. Door to the foot of the bed, wooden chair next to it, looks like my clothes might be hanging on it.*

Melanie had not moved. *Seems pretty asleep. Time to go.*

He slowly uncrossed his legs and swung them off the edge of the bed, dropping his feet quietly to the floor. He paused. *Nothing.* There was a lull in the lightning. He crept toward the door, stepping gingerly to avoid any sudden creaking from the old floor, his hands outstretched to avoid a collision. *Back where I started, floundering in the dark . . .*

His hand jerked as it touched something. *Good, the door frame.* He groped over and down until he felt the back of the chair. *My shirt and T-shirt, draped over the back.* He picked them up and resumed his search. *Pants folded on the seat. Wallet and keys still in the pockets.* He paused. *I can't take her car, I'll leave the key. I'll get dressed, maybe wait on the porch until the storm lets up. Stop at the first farmhouse I come to.* He knelt and felt under the chair with his free hand.

Yep, shoes, with the socks inside like I always do. He rose and bundled everything under one arm, leaving the other free to help him find his way.

He put his hand on the door frame and stepped into the hallway, still enveloped by darkness. *Where are the stairs? I need a lightning flash, just one . . .* He took a cautious step to his right.

The sound froze him like a statue. "Wesley," whispered a faint voice. From in front of him. *In front of me!* he screamed inside. *She was in bed! No one passed me!*

Again came the voice: "Wesley, don't go." *Her voice . . . it sounds so strange . . .*

Barely containing his panic, he began to edge back into the bedroom. He dropped his bundle of clothing in the direction of the chair, readying himself for a confrontation. He felt Melanie's presence here and there and back again, now to the front, now behind him, closing in on him. He patted the wall frantically and found a light switch, but it clicked up and down inertly. He backed in further, feeling his way past the chair, putting his back against the wall next to the dresser.

He listened as intently as he could but could hear nothing above the rain and the wind. In a brief flash of lightning he saw a familiar shape near his feet, next to the dresser: an ancient lantern flashlight, basically a car headlight with a handle, fastened to the top of a large, bricklike battery. He reached down, curled his fingers around the metal handle and lifted the unit silently off the floor. He pointed the light in the direction of the bed. *Please work!* Five heartbeats went by, then he depressed the plunger switch with his thumb.

Although the yellowish beam was a bit feeble, it was like a floodlight in the pitch black, illuminating most of the room. The bed appeared just as he'd left it, with Melanie bundled up on one side and his side rumpled and bare. He glanced to all corners of the room, each time returning his stare to her unmoving form. He saw nothing in the doorway, no voice followed.

He breathed a degree deeper, his panic subsiding a notch. He swallowed dryly.

"Melanie?" he breathed, so softly that it was hardly more than a thought. Something in the corner of his eye . . . his head jerked toward the door as he redirected the beam of the flashlight . . . *Mimi!* She sat motionless in the middle of the doorway, regarding him coldly. *She was in the hall!* His skin prickled so hard it hurt. *That can't be . . . oh my God . . . what a nightmare . . .* His eyes darted back and forth, woman to cat to woman . . . *I just want this to be over.*

"Melanie," he said, pushing his voice out toward her. Still nothing. He took a step toward her, then another, shining the light on her half-buried face, searching for some small motion. The beam appeared to be taking on a slight bluish hue, but his attention was too concentrated on Melanie to take much note.

He tried again. "Mel . . ."

The covers snapped back with a strobe-like jerk. Her eyes were wide and fixed on his, her face a frozen mask. She was wearing a plain white bra and panties. He lurched back, into the dresser, the flashlight flying from his hand into a corner. In the shadowed angle of the beam he saw a flash of movement as she leapt toward him with feral speed. The force of her attack slammed him over the dresser, shattering the mirror with his back and knocking his skull against the frame. Streamers of light and bolts of pain shot through his head. Her arms locked around his neck and her legs around his waist as he bent forward to escape the falling shards of glass. She clawed into his back and clamped her teeth into the side of his neck, biting deep. With a grunting cry, he clapped his hands to her sides and flung her away in one spasmodic motion. She flew across the room, almost to the opposite corner, and landed with a sprawling, sliding thud. Wes's momentary certainty that she was injured disappeared as she sprung up and lunged back at him in a fury.

He was ready this time but found it hard to focus his efforts through the throbbing pain in his head. Melanie was now wild-eyed, screeching like an animal, teeth bared, flailing away wildly with her nails. He bent and tried to fend off her attack, grabbing for her wrists. He caught hold of one, but she wrenched away and whirled toward a nightstand. She grabbed a table lamp and flung it toward him with superhuman strength and accuracy. His dodge was too late; the lamp shattered on his shoulder, sending another shock wave of pain through him and switching his fear to rage.

"Bitch!" he yelled as he rushed at her.

"Motherfucker!" she shrieked, meeting him head-on. She went for his throat, with fingers curved in rigid claws, but this time he caught both of her wrists in iron grips, and the two of them struggled against each other, standing their ground. Their eyes met and held, and as he watched, her face disfigured into a hideous, reptilian expression. A loud hiss rose out of her throat, and a surge of strength brought her clawing nails close enough to graze the skin of his throat.

This is it! There's no waking up!

Just as he felt that he might overpower her, there was an impact near the top of his back, and a shock of pain knifed through him as Mimi sank her fangs and claws into his flesh. He gave a strangled cry as Melanie broke through his grasp and dug into his throat. He grabbed her at the waist, snatching her from the floor and swinging her to the side. As Mimi leaped off his back, he heaved Melanie high into the air toward the bed. Two brilliant lightning strikes created a vivid, strobe-like effect: in the first image, Melanie had landed, almost comically, bottom first in the center of the mattress, her arms and legs rigidly outstretched. In the next, she had bounded off, as if from a trampoline, and slammed flat against the wall. Then she was gone, hidden from view behind the bed as a blast of thunder shook the house.

His head swam. He stepped carefully away from the scattered glass on the floor, standing for a moment in the middle of the room with his hands on his knees, catching his breath. He kept his eyes focused on the shadowy area behind the bed. There was no movement and no sound. The room began to dim. He thought at first that he might be blacking out, but when he shook his head and took another breath, he realized that the lantern's light was fading. *No! I can't be in here without light! I should grab my clothes and run . . .* He grimaced. *I have to check on her.*

He retrieved the failing light from the corner and began to move warily toward the dark gap. He kept as far away as possible as he circled, crouching, ready for another attack. Melanie's feet came into view, then her legs, and then there she was, sprawled on her side. Her eyes were open, staring off. Her head and limbs were twitching, almost imperceptibly, as though she'd been short-circuited. A thread of blood snaked out of her left nostril. *Omigod, she's badly hurt. What if I've killed her!*

He moved forward and knelt close to her, laying the lantern on its side on the edge of the bed. Tentatively, he reached out and put his hand on her leg. "Melanie . . . Melanie . . . can you hear me?" Her spasmodic motions increased but her fixed stare continued. She appeared to be trying to speak but was succeeding only in making grunting sounds. *What should I do? She could have spinal injuries . . . I should go see if I can find a working phone.* He bent closer and spoke to her as clearly as he could. "I'm going to call an ambulance. I'll be right back."

She turned her head, with some difficulty, to look toward him with eyes that went in and out of focus. She grunted again, ". . . huhh . . . huhh . . . huhh . . ." and reached up with a shaking hand to grip his arm. *I don't like this . . . feels like something's coming again.*

He pulled back a little, removing his hand from her leg and preparing to spring away. Her eyes sparkled a little as they came into focus, and he suddenly realized that the grunting, now coming through weakly smiling lips, was laughter. "Huh huh huh . . ." He jerked free of her hand, grabbed the lantern, and moved back, still crouching. The increasingly blue tint of the fading light perplexed Wes, but not enough to shake his concentration on Melanie.

Her laughter became clearer and louder. "Ahh, ha ha ha ha!" She closed her eyes and clutched her hands to her chest, convulsing in glee. Wes stepped back as he stood up, tensing for another fight. An odd sensation rippled through his stomach, seeming to vibrate with the sound of her laughter. *Butterflies? More adrenaline?* But when he looked down he realized that the surface of his abdomen was actually beginning to writhe and squirm. He touched the area and was horrified by the feeling of bubbling motion there. *Her mark! That's where she marked me!*

Horror exploded through him, and he lurched backward. "No . . . no . . ." he gasped, clutching at the wriggling flesh. His heel caught, and he landed in a sprawl on the floor. He leapt up and raced out of the room, crashing into the wall opposite. He turned and raced down the hallway, the dim yellow lantern beam bouncing from floor to wall, Melanie's laughter following him.

He passed more rooms than he thought possible. *Where are the stairs?* He paused and looked back down what now seemed like a very long hallway. A pale blue light glowed from the thin rectangle of the bedroom doorway. *Is she following?* At that moment a figure emerged, softly radiant in an azure halo, and turned toward him unhurriedly.

"Oh, We-ess . . ." called the sly voice of Melanie, ". . . I wasn't done play-ingg . . ." *Run!*

The hallway took a turn and he stumbled down it. More doors. How big is this house? Where are the stairs?

The hallway ended. *No! She's coming! I can feel it!* Pausing only a moment to overcome a surge of fear, he pulled open the nearest door. *Closet.* He whipped around and tried the door on the other side. *Locked!* He rattled it frantically, pushing and pulling, but it wouldn't budge. *Hurry!* The third door opened into a windowless, empty room. His panic was threatening to overwhelm him and he nearly tore the next door off its hinges. *Stairs!* He glanced down the hall and saw Melanie slowly turning the corner, illuminated by a hazy blue cloud of light.

He plunged down the stairway, nearly falling to the floor when he reached the bottom. *Now where? A door, any door, I just have to get out!* He turned another corner and found himself in a small foyer, with a room to one side and a door to the outside straight ahead. *Side door? Back door? This place is not that big!*

He tried the door. *Locked, or stuck.* He rattled it frantically, and crouched to see if he could unlock it, but found nothing. *Where am I? I can't tell what side of the house I'm on.* Darting into the nearest room, a parlor of some kind, he tried unsuccessfully to push the windows up, then turned in desperation and grabbed the back of a nearby wooden chair. He lifted with all of his strength, expecting to hurl it through the glass, but it hardly budged. *She's getting close again, I can feel it.*

He dashed out of the room's other doorway and found himself in yet another hallway. In the still-fading beam, at the end of the hall, he saw the front door. *Yes!* He sprinted toward it. *Please, please let me . . .*

He stumbled awkwardly and his head slammed into something hard and solid, setting off an explosion of light and pain inside his skull. He reeled, losing all sense of direction, and when he put out a hand to keep from falling, he toppled into space, catching a glimpse of another stairway just before tumbling down it and landing in a heap.

Cement floor . . . basement. He lay still for a few moments, afraid to try to move, afraid that he might be paralyzed. The lantern had shattered in the fall and he was enveloped in darkness once again. He moved the fingers of one hand, then the other. He twitched his feet. *Thank God I can move.*

The feeling of pursuit returned yet again. Stifling groans of pain, he pulled himself to hands and knees and crawled, feeling ahead with one hand. He reached a concrete wall and used it to help himself stand up. He sensed that there was no way out but the stairs. *This is it . . . this had better be it . . . I can't take much more . . .*

The open stairwell began to glow with a now-familiar radiance. Wes stood still, his back to the wall, and saw Melanie slowly descend, drifting down into view without expression. The cloud of blue light enveloping her was brighter now, more intense.

She turned and moved toward him, gliding as much as walking, A trail of dried blood angled across her left cheek. *I've lost my mind . . . I'm dreaming . . . but it feels too real to be a dream.* She stopped a couple of steps away and slowly raised her hand to brush at the dark line on her face.

"Don't worry, big guy," she said, in a voice that seemed to echo from a great distance. "I'll tell 'em I fell in the tub, or maybe down a flight of stairs . . ." *Do something.*

"Melanie, I . . ." he began, rousing himself to step toward her.

"Stop!" she barked. He felt his ability to move vanish. "I'm still in charge here," she said firmly. *I'm weak. My weakness brought me here. She'll do what she wants.*

Melanie moved close to him and stroked her fingers up and down his torso. Her face became a little more animated. "You left before I could show you the *really* neat trick." He glanced down, terrified, as far as his eyes could move.

With one hand, Melanie began stroking in light circles around his abdomen. At first there was only the sensation of her fingertips, but then the disturbing ripples Wes had experienced previously began to reappear. She increased the speed and pressure of her motion, setting up a whirlpool of fleshy waves that churned into the depths of his bowels. "Mmm . . ." she moaned, half with effort and half with pleasure. Wes was convulsed with horror and nausea. With a final frenzied spin she abruptly flung the roiling tsunami down toward his genitals. There was a sharp snapping sound as the mass disappeared beneath the waistband of his briefs, a sound that corresponded with a piercing pain at the base of Wes's penis. He grunted in pain, aghast at what had just occurred.

Melanie pulled her hand back, smiling, resting for a moment from the effort. Wes couldn't speak, couldn't stop staring down. He could feel that something had gone very wrong.

Melanie reached out again, this time pulling out the elastic of his shorts with one hand and grasping his penis with the other. "Maybe you've figured this out," she said. "I left you some clues . . ." He felt a tug, followed by a wet popping sound, and then Melanie was holding his penis, with his testicles dangling from the base, up for him to see. *No! Did she . . .* but he saw no knife, felt no searing pain, saw no blood dripping from his detached member. In fact, he could feel her hands as they held his tender organs. *I can feel her touch! How can this be happening?* Melanie began fondling her toys as she had many times before, stroking his penis into erection. *I have to get them back . . . I have to move, somehow.* But he couldn't find a way of breaking her control.

"Cool, huh? Doesn't this feel neat?" She glanced up from her playthings. "Oh, sorry, I forgot . . . you're stiff all over. Well, I guess I can let you relax." He felt himself slump out of the paralysis. *What's she done to me? How?* Still staring at his detached genitals, he took a step toward her. Her hands tightened uncomfortably around his testicles. He winced and stopped. "I'd say I still had a lot of control, wouldn't you?" she said, smiling maliciously .

She placed the base of his penis on one outstretched hand, and with the other began jerking his member around like a video game joystick. "Vroom! Left! Right! Stop!" Wes shuddered and grimaced at the discomfort arising from her rough treatment. *Keep going.* He took another step.

"Bad boy!" she scolded. She held his penis out so that his testicles hung down like bait on a fishing rod. "Mimi! Kitty kitty!" *Oh no!*

"Stop! Don't" *I should rush her, but she could do a lot of damage in a hurry.* A shot of pain staggered him as Mimi leaped out of the darkness and batted at the dangling lure. "Uhnnh!" he grunted. "Don't! Please!"

Melanie cradled his delicate organs. "That's better. You be good."

"What do you want?"

"Oh! You men and your 'What do you want?'" she scowled. "What do you *think* we want? A good fuck and a box of candy? We want *you*! Y-O-U. All of you. The whole package. But you keep yanking at the leash, wanting to run off and pee on the bushes. You don't realize that all you have to do is quit yanking and we'll take the leash off." She paused, glancing at her toys and then back at him, smiling a little. "Fortunately, you come with a built-in leash, in case ours breaks."

"I'm not going to be your slave."

"You're *meant* to be," she said coldly. "If you're not mine, you'll be somebody else's. So quit jerking around." Her look softened a little. "You *know* that we could have a lot of fun." She lapped seductively at the head of his penis.

Wes's whirling mind suddenly spun to a stop. He looked into Melanie's eyes instead of at his truant body parts, and a great calmness settled over him. *Time to go, Wes.*

"I'm very, very sorry that I hurt you, Melanie. I made a mistake, starting a relationship with you. I can't stay." Melanie's face darkened with anger and fear. Her hands tightened, causing Wes to grimace in pain. "Do what you want," he grunted. "Keep them. I'm leaving." He turned and limped toward the stairs, doubling over as he felt her fingernails digging into his tender flesh.

"Nooooo!" she screeched. "You're *mine!*"

He got up one step, forcing himself through the agony. *Leave the fucking things! You're better off without them.* He made the second step, but an explosion of hideous, tearing pain took all the strength out of his legs, and he felt himself falling backwards as his screams echoed together with Melanie's. Blackness descended.

CHAPTER 27

His mind spun slowly, searching for the locker combination to full consciousness. *I hurt.* One eye crept open. *Daylight.* The other eye joined. He saw rough joists supporting old wooden flooring. *Basement.* He painfully tipped his head back. In his upside-down vision he saw the blocky outline of an old furnace, illuminated by sunlight forcing its way in through a small, grime-coated window high on the wall. *Head aches . . . shoulders ache . . . hip, elbows . . .*

A memory jolted him and his head jerked up, sending a sharp spasm down his neck and pulses of pain through his skull. Cautiously, he touched the crotch of his underwear. *They're back! Pretty sore, but back.* A wave of relief washed through him. He pulled up the elastic for visual confirmation. *Very, very happy about this.* He reached in and tugged to make sure the attachment was secure. "Ow! Ohhh . . ." *Is there such a thing as a dick bandage? But they're on tight.*

Moving gingerly and moaning with the effort, he rolled and pushed up to a sitting position, every joint complaining. *I wonder if she's still here. I wonder if she's alive.* He felt considerably less anxious about her potential presence than the night before. The glow of the sunlight helped.

"Okay, here we go," he muttered, rising slowly and unsteadily to his feet. He straightened up, grimacing.

There was another room in the basement. He peered into the musty gloom. Old wooden benches and shelves, full of canning jars and rusty hardware, huddled in the shadows. He made a halting circuit of the room, checking for any sign of Melanie. *All clear.*

After a slow and agonizing ascent, he reached the first floor. "Melanie!" he shouted. The sound of his voice disappeared into the silence. *Sounds empty again.* The house, as big as it was, seemed substantially smaller than in his disjointed recollections of the night before. *This place is pretty roomy, but it seemed like a labyrinth last night.*

He spotted his bags, still sitting by the front door, as he wandered into the living room and looked out the front window. *Car's gone.* This discovery brought mixed feelings: he was stranded without a ride but it also meant that Melanie had made her exit.

He was overtaken by voracious thirst and hobbled into the kitchen. On the counter was a half-full case of bottled water. *Yes!* He twisted off cap after cap and emptied bottle after bottle, feeling like he had come across the elixir of life. Finally, he'd had his fill. *I wonder if they recycle?* He left the bottles on the counter.

As he was about to leave the kitchen he noticed a phone hanging on the wall. He picked it up and was somewhat surprised to hear a dial tone. *Now what . . . call a cab? Would one even come out here? How freaking expensive would that be? I can't call Tricia . . . I could maybe try Mark if it wasn't a workday . . .* He hung up the phone. *Someone's bound to pick me up on the road.*

He moved gingerly up the stairs to the second floor, stopping outside the door to the bedroom and peering in cautiously. He was shocked to see Mimi staring at him from the rumpled pile of bedclothes. He jerked back, sending sharp jolts to every corner of his body. His breath caught in his throat as his eyes fixed on the dark form. A moment passed with no movement from the bed. He blinked and breathed. The feline shape resolved into a hollow of dark shadows in the twisted blankets.

Jumpy Jumperson.

He found his clothes where he had dropped them, half on

and half off the chair by the door. He got dressed, then sat on the bed and glanced around the room as he slipped on his socks and shoes. *What really happened last night? The mirror's broken, the lamp's broken, I'm beat all to hell . . .* He stood up and walked around to the other side of the bed. He bent to peer at the wall and down to the floor. *Is that blood, those spots? Hard to tell on this old wood . . .* He straightened up and gave the room a quick once-over, finding nothing else that belonged to him.

There was a bathroom just down the hall. He flicked the light switch, to no effect. *Power must have gone out last night.* He stepped in, his eyes adjusting to the available light. He began to make out the features of his reflected image in the mirror over the sink. *Who is that guy? A stranger. I don't even recognize myself. And I look like crap.* He pulled out his comb and, with small dollops of water, made an attempt to return his hectic hairdo to a likeness of normalcy. *I look like a high school dork who just lost a fight. That forehead bruise is going to be colorful. And my neck . . . is there such a thing as a summer turtleneck? Or I could get a padded brace, like I was in a car accident.*

He had just done a final pat-down when a sound brought him up short. *A car engine. Melanie?* He crept out of the bathroom and down the hallway toward the top of the stairs, from which he could see the front door. The car stopped; the engine turned off. He pressed himself into the shadows, leaving only a sliver of the front door window in his sight. A car door opened and closed, followed by the sounds of boots on gravel, then on wooden steps, then on the planking of the porch. *Not Melanie.*

A dark figure loomed at the door. *The sheriff!* A uniformed deputy was peering in, shading his eyes to get a better look. Wes cringed, trying not to panic. *My bags are right there! Can he see them?* The deputy rattled the doorknob and shook the door. *Locked! Melanie must have locked it on the way out. Did something happen to her? Did she report me? I'd have no defense!* The deputy turned and moved out of sight. Wes could hear his clomping footsteps along the front of the house, then a pause. *Checking the living room.* A moment later, he walked back across the porch and down the steps, casting a brief shadow as he passed the front door. *Just checking things out? Maybe that's all. Maybe he saw her car here last night and wanted to make sure it was locked up. And they'd send two officers if they were going to arrest me, right? Or is that just from cop shows?* Hopefulness began to take the place of dread. *I'll wait a few minutes. I hope I don't encounter him on the road.* He caught his breath as he listened to the car drive off, then sat still for a moment, listening to the silence.

When he felt satisfied that it was all clear, he made his way down the stairs and limped to the front door. He unlocked the deadbolt and opened the door, then held the screen door open with his hip while he transferred his bags to the porch. He stepped back in and fiddled a bit to turn the little switch in the doorknob so that the door would lock behind him. The sound of the door latching shut, followed by the thunk of the screen door swinging closed, was very satisfying. He picked up his bags and took in a deep breath of the country air. *Smells like plants and dirt. And freedom.*

He tottered down the porch steps and headed toward the road, pausing to glance back at the house. *I don't know why, but I hope she's okay. And I hope I never see her again.* He turned and resumed his trek. *I have a future to repair. Do I want to stay with Trish? Yes, I do, very much. We're not incompatible; she's disillusioned and I'm directionless. I have a good family, I just need to invest more in it. I'll have to think about a job. Right now, I just need to get home.*

Halfway to the road, Wes felt a sudden dark stirring from deep in his stomach. *Oh no God no . . .*

He tossed his bags aside as a terrifying jet of sickness

bolted up, knocking him to his knees and bowing him over in a rictus of purging. A hard stream of vomit shot out of his mouth onto the ragged, gravelly grass. *All that water?* His abdomen churned like a stormy sea; his throat felt like it was being ripped apart by the force of the expulsion. The first horrible wave was followed by a second one, just as bad. The third one was, if possible, even worse, since his system was now painfully pumping out nothing. The ones that came after that began to diminish in intensity, until he was just panting and drooling, feeling wrung out. *That wasn't the water . . . it was the poison starting to come up. There's more in there, I'm sure.*

Wes rose slowly and unsteadily to his feet. *I should try to get back in, clean up, have a few sips of water, but I really, really don't want to.* He looked down. *I don't think I got any on my clothes.* He walked a few steps to an area of tall, dry grass and ripped up a large clump, using it to clean his mouth and chin as best he could, even running some of it over his tongue. *That should do until I can get to a sink . . . at home? . . . maybe stop at a convenience store first.* He remembered the small container of breath mints in his pocket and popped three of them. *Ahh . . . minty . . . much better. Breakfast of champions.*

He reached the gravel road and headed toward town. *Walk on the left, less likely to get hit. How do I know stuff like this?* Every step was a painful effort; his bags felt like a burden out of mythology. The crunching gravel was the sound of a long, slow journey. *The road to ruin is paved with lies; the road to redemption is scattered with stone.* He pondered that for a moment. *I should write that down.*

Minutes later a truck passed, going the opposite way. It swerved over to give him room but didn't slow. He had a brief image of the driver's eyes glancing in his direction. *I don't belong here. But at least the rain that came through is keeping the dust down.*

Twenty minutes after he began, Wes heard a vehicle coming from behind him. *Please don't let it be the sheriff . . .* It turned out to be another pickup, and it slowed to a stop beside him. A man somewhat older than Wes, wearing a farm-implement cap, rolled down his window.

"Heading to town?"

"Yes," replied Wes, hopefully.

"Where'd you start out?"

He's testing me. He knows. "The Becker's."

"I figured. Hop in."

Relieved, Wes walked around to the passenger side, heaving his bags into the back and stepping up into the cab. *A real working pickup. Dirt, dings, some rust. Everyone I know with a pickup is obsessed with keeping the bed unscratched or the bed liner unscuffed.* Off they went over the rough dirt-and-gravel surface, just a little faster than Wes was comfortable with. *Gravel-road driving is more treacherous than it seems. He obviously knows the limits.*

Wes wasn't sure what to say. He felt weak and ashamed. The driver seemed comfortable just driving. *His hands are so thick and calloused that it almost looks like he's wearing gloves. I'll never work that hard. But I have to do better.* Long moments later, the best that Wes could come up with was, "Uh, you know the Beckers then?"

The driver nodded. "Oh yeah, from way back. Solid people." He paused. "Except the one brother. You probably know who I mean."

"Ron."

"Yep. He wore out his welcome a long time ago." Time passed. Wes felt too tired to come up with more conversation. When asked about his specific destination, Wes gave the location of Melanie's apartment complex, expecting he'd be dropped off at some distance and take a cab the rest of the way. But the driver was generous enough to take him there.

As they entered the complex, the driver turned to Wes and

said, in a kindly but serious way, "I'm sure you already know this, but you seem like someone who should know better."

"Yeah . . ." replied Wes, barely able to make eye contact. "I sure do now." He gestured toward his car. "There."

The one visible window to Melanie's apartment was closed. He didn't see her car. *She's been here and gone.* The truck came to a halt and he opened the door to disembark. "Thanks," he said, as his foot touched the asphalt. "I really appreciate it."

"You're welcome," said the driver. "And you know, there's still time to get yourself right."

"Thanks again," said Wes, nodding. *I hope so.* He closed the door and fished his luggage out of the back. The truck drove off.

CHAPTER 28

Wes drove out of the complex, heading instinctively toward his house, then realizing that he needed a plan. *It's a school day. Posie will get a ride home in a few hours, Trish will arrive around 5:00.* Suddenly realizing that he was ravenously hungry, he got on the freeway and backtracked a little, getting off at the nearest truck stop exit. *A truck stop diner. I can look as rumpled as I want.*

The bright lighting of the restroom did him no favors. He worked a little more on his hair and cleaned off a few spots of dried blood. He tried his shirt collar up and down, settling on down. *Better to look like an accident victim than an old preppy.* He purchased three kinds of pain reliever from a vending machine and took them all.

Upon exiting, he bought a newspaper, sat in a booth, and ordered coffee and the most calorie-laden breakfast option. *Oh, man . . . normal life, real food. What a treat.* He managed to get lost in the news of the day, feeling like he was catching up with the rest of the world.

When he surfaced it still wasn't time. *Wait, should I call first?* He tried playing out the scenarios one way and then the other. *I'm tired of thinking. I'm just going to show up.* He got coffee to go and drove to a park not far from his house to finish the paper while he waited.

At 4:45 he decided to check things out. He drove through the neighborhood, slowing to a crawl as the front of his house came into view. His pulse quickened. *Front door is open. Tricia is home.*

With mounting trepidation, he pulled into the driveway.

He got out in the bright sun with no plan, no opening line prepared. Still, there was one minor decision. *Should I bring my bags with me?* He had a brief image of trudging back to the car carrying the bags, and walked up emptyhanded.

He paused at the glass storm door, peering in. *Posie is likely in her room or in the basement, either way with music on. Tricia will be in the kitchen, or nearby. I really want to talk to her first, before Posie sees me.* He watched for a moment, then saw pale shadows indicating movement in the interior.

Feels strange to be knocking on my own front door. Although I guess it's not really mine right now. He rapped lightly on the glass, trying somehow to direct the sound to the back of the house. In a moment, Tricia's face appeared from the interior. She paused briefly, startled, then walked toward him, emotions flickering over her face as though in a silent movie. She looked irritated, then perplexed, then inquisitive as she approached. She paused for the briefest moment as she arrived, then made her decision. She opened the door. They stood still, examining each other. Tricia suppressed a sudden urge to laugh. Wes looked ridiculously beaten; it was obvious that he had already paid a price for his transgressions. Maybe not enough, but a good down payment.

Wes started to talk, for once not knowing what to say. "I . . ."

She put a finger to her lips, hushing him gently, then turned to the side to beckon him in. "Clean up before Posie sees you," she whispered. "Go upstairs."

They walked together to the foot of the stairs. "Thank you," he said. It felt like the most purely honest thing he'd said in a long time.

"Go," said Tricia, smiling a little. She felt an opportunity opening before her. The clay had been softened; perhaps this time a useful vessel could be fashioned.

They parted ways and Wes followed the wonderfully familiar route to the bathroom. *Well, here we are. What will the*

Mirror of Truth reveal? Yikes . . . I look like I've been living on the streets. Of course, I was literally sleeping on concrete last night. He peeled of his clothes gingerly. His T-shirt was streaked and spotted with blood from his numerous bite and scratch injuries. *I would not want to be one of my T-shirts. Tough job.*

He got in the shower and began to wash away what felt like a lifetime of dirt. *What does it take to wash away what I've done? I guess I'll find out. I'm just glad I have the chance.*

When he was done he used gauze and tape to cover the worst of his wounds, especially the ones most visible on his neck. Then he got dressed in his around-the-house clothing. He was just slipping on his shoes when there was a light rapping at the bedroom door.

"Dad?"

Posie! He was instantly suffused with joy. "Yeah!" he said.

The door swung open. Posie, beaming, slipped in and quietly shut the door behind her, then leaped onto the bed and bounded over to him. "Ooh, Daddy Daddy Daddy!" she said, in a loud whisper. The bouncing sent jolts of pain through his wounded body. He winced and stifled a moan as she landed on his back, hugging and kissing him. "Oh, are you alright?" she said, recoiling a little. "What happened?" She cautiously touched the bandaged area on his neck, then the bruise on his forehead.

"A bit of an accident, I'll be fine," he replied, not wanting to lie but not really knowing what the truth was. "It's great to see you, sweetie."

Posie rolled off to sit next to him on the edge of the bed.

"Mom just got on the phone to Grandma. That should keep her occupied for a while." Wes chuckled, sending another throb of pain through his head and neck. "Are you back for good?" she said.

"Oh, yes. Yes, I sure am. Sorry to put you through all

that." He squeezed her arm. *I never want that kind of distance between us again.*

"It really felt weird not having you here. I kept thinking what it would be like if you never came back."

"Oh, sweetie . . ." he said, reaching up to stroke her hair.

"She really had you hypnotized, didn't she?"

"Hm?"

"Melanie. I could tell in the apartment, even though she wasn't there, she had a spell on you, big-time. You looked like a cartoon character after getting hit with an anvil." *This girl misses nothing. No point denying anything.*

"Yeah, you're right. But really it was my fault . . ."

Posie stared down into the shadows. "Yeah . . . I didn't know real grownups made mistakes like that." *Welcome to adulthood. Sorry it was me who let you down.* "But," she continued, patting him lightly on the arm, "you're back, you're back."

"Yeah. Feels good."

She stood up. "I'd better go. If Mom finds me in here, she'll put a dinner prep spell on me." She paused for a moment, put on a mock-serious expression, and in her "grown-up" voice said, "Well, good luck, Wes. Welcome aboard. We expect great things from you."

"Thanks, kiddo," he said, smiling, as she moved toward the door. "I love you."

"I love you too, Dad."

The door closed. Something gave way inside him, and he cried.

*　　*　　*

Wes awoke in the dark. He felt momentarily disoriented, but pleasantly so for once. He glanced around, reassuring himself that he was in a familiar, comfortable bed, with a familiar, comfortable figure lying next to him. *I'm home. I'm free.* He felt serene for a few moments, then began to ponder his uncertain future. *Okay, not entirely free . . . but at least free to try again.*

He quietly turned the covers back and swung his feet to the floor. *Let's see if Raoul has a fresh bottle of soda. Thinking can wait until morning.*

CHAPTER 29

Ahhh . . . a hot shower before bed. One of life's simple pleasures. One of the magical wonders of life in the twentieth century. Wes stopped washing for a moment and just stood, back to the showerhead, letting the water coat him in warmth. It had been nearly two weeks since he'd returned home, and life was good. Tricia's list of requirements for his reintegration was challenging, but he was fully determined to succeed: he had to go back to school to make himself into an employable teacher again, work part-time to help them get by until he found a position, and make regular, visible progress on updating the house, something he had been attending to on this second Saturday since his return.

Tricia's other condition was more personal. "You need to make an honest decision about how important our relationship is in your life. I don't know who you blame for us drifting apart, but nothing excuses your behavior. I'm obviously willing to give it another go, but I need a serious commitment from you to be the husband you vowed to be." Wes had felt honest with himself and with her in wholeheartedly reaffirming that commitment.

That was as close as she got to mentioning the affair. Nothing about Melanie, nothing about cheating or burdens of guilt. She could have hammered me. I got off light. Man, this water feels good on sore muscles. And it feels good to have sore muscles from finally getting to the projects I put off for so long. It's like penance.

He'd found out that Melanie had stopped showing up for work the day after he got fired and that no one had heard from her. A friend who had gone to her apartment later that week found it empty, with workmen repairing the fire damage. *I really hope that's it. No phone calls, no finger-painting, no sudden appearances out of the dark. Just a gradual, fading memory.*

Wes heard the bedroom door close as he brushed his teeth. When he was done, he shut the light and entered the bedroom, finding it lit by two candles on the dresser. He quickly quelled a short burst of apprehension. Tricia stood by the bed, wearing the long, silky nightgown that she favored when she had sex on her mind. It was filmy enough not to be mistaken for "old lady" nightclothes but chaste enough not to be mortifying in case anyone else saw her in it. *First time since I came back.* She looked beautiful and desirable, and Wes felt a rush of appreciation and arousal as he walked toward her.

"You look wonderful," he said, really meaning it. They smiled warmly as he reached her, and they embraced in a strong, body-to-body way that they hadn't for a long time. They kissed, hard and deep. They had sex, following a pleasing, well-practiced routine from days gone by. It was loving, intimate, and satisfying. *It's the comfort food of sex. It's like good home cooking; it's actually better if the recipe doesn't change much.*

Tricia cleaned up first, returning from the bathroom in her fully sensible nightwear. By the time Wes emerged she was well on her way to dreamland. He pulled back the covers and sat down quietly. As he flipped his pillow over to fluff it up, something underneath caught his eye, unexpected yet somehow familiar. He pushed the pillow to one side and picked up a silky, twisted mound of fabric. *Pantyhose.* He hardly needed to, but he brought it to his nose and inhaled lightly. *Melanie.* The scent shot into the center of his being, setting off a chain of quickly-mutating emotional reactions: Lust. Panic. Rage. He grasped the material in a clenched fist. *I will burn this.* He rose, now trembling with fury. *And I will burn whoever comes for it.*

www.ingramcontent.com/pod-product-compliance
Lightning Source LLC
Chambersburg PA
CBHW070015120726
47909CB00003B/939